THE
DESTRUCTION OF
SEVYN

From Dark Fiction Author

EMBER MICHAELS

THE DESTRUCTION OF SEVYN

Copyright © 2020 by Ember Michaels

Book design by Inkstain Design Studio
Cover design by Laura Hidalgo of Spellbinding Design

THE
DESTRUCTION OF
SEVYN

OTHER BOOKS BY
EMBER MICHAELS

*Cries for justice are often
the bitter laments of the vengeful.*

—WAYNE GERARD TROTMAN

PROLOGUE

LUTHER

Numbness.

It was all I felt since I got the call a few months ago. My mother's hysteric screams and incoherent words still sounded in my head almost every day. I heard that distinct sound as I drove back home from school the day after she'd called me. I heard it every night when I tried to go to sleep. And even though she tried to keep a brave face during the day, I could still hear it echoing in my mind.

The anguish.

The grief.

The loss.

Losing the most important person to you was never easy. How did you say goodbye to your best friend? Your partner in crime?

Your little sister?

I popped the tight rubber band against the skin of my wrist in increments of seven. I needed to feel something, anything to remind me that I was still alive physically, because my mind was too far gone. What fucking life was there if my sister wasn't in it? Time blurred into days, weeks, and months as my family came in and out of the courtroom. I had to watch my mother hold back her sobs of anguish as they displayed the evidence in court...displayed my sister for everyone to see. I listened as Sevyn's lawyer tried to argue that her and the rest of the bitches in her clique were just engaging in "innocent teenage fun" and blamed my sister for not asking for the help she needed. My family and I had to watch Sevyn's smug reactions and fake guilt when her incriminating evidence was display for months during the trial. Now, today was the day the bitch would pay for what she'd done—granted that Daddy didn't buy her a "get out of jail free" card.

And for her sake, she'd better pray to whatever God she believed in that the jury found her guilty today.

I exhaled deeply, my eyes darting to the front of the room as the jurors filed back into the courtroom. Five long months of trials and we were finally at the end. The room was so silent that I could almost hear my racing heart, a mixture of anxiety, hope for justice, and unresolved anger swirling around within me. I pulled at my rubber band, adrenaline rushing through me as I popped it against my skin.

One. *Pop.* Two. *Pop.* Three. *Pop.* Four. *Pop.* Five. *Pop.*

My mom grabbed my wrist before I could pop the rubber band

again. She rubbed her thumb across my reddened skin and gave me what she thought was a comforting squeeze, but it didn't help. Nothing fucking helped if it didn't bring my sister back.

"It's going to be okay," she whispered, tears sliding along her plump cheeks.

I nodded, grinding my teeth as I looked over at Sevyn whispering to her lawyer. Once upon a time, she was my sister's best friend; now she was the bitch responsible for her death. Her family was one of the richest in Miami—the kind of rich that had the right amount of money to make their "problems" disappear. Our family's bullshit lawyer tried to convince us that we had a strong case, that there was too much evidence that would be hard to ignore. In a way, he was right. There was plenty of evidence—text messages, eye witnesses, forum print outs, and a video. In a normal setting with a normal family, he would've been right to say that we would win.

But I wasn't fucking stupid.

I already knew how the trial would end before it even began.

"Has the jury reached a verdict?" Judge Hyland asked, his tone bored as he adjusted his glasses on his old, sagging face.

"Yes, Your Honor," a scrawny man with brown, shaggy hair and pale skin said as he stood up. My fingers twitched to pop my rubber band, my mother's hand still around my wrist as her breath hitched. The judge waved his hand for the juror to announce the verdict and the juror cleared his throat.

Taking a look over at Sevyn, I ground my teeth as I watched her. She stared at the juror with tears in her eyes, her future teetering in the air by a few words on the small sheet of paper the juror held. Even from where I sat, I could see the fear etched into her beautiful, perfect features. Her parents held each other, their heads bowed as they sat behind her on the opposite side of the court room. I ground my teeth and focused back on the verdict.

"We the jury find the defendant, Sevyn Langdon, not guilty," the juror read from a small sheet of paper.

Sevyn Langdon...not guilty.

Not. Fucking. Guilty.

My blood boiled under my skin as I watched her breathe a sigh of relief, suppressing the shriek of excitement that tried to escape her mouth as she hugged her lawyer. Her family cheered on the other side of the courtroom as my mother burst into tears. My breath quickened, my anger rising as I watched Sevyn, her friends, and family celebrate her "innocence." She was found innocent while Logan lay rotting in a cemetery because of this bitch. Sevyn would get to go off to college, have a life, have a husband and children while my sister was robbed of all of that. My family had to watch as the very person who shattered our lives celebrated the fact that she'd get a fresh start, the whole encounter swept under the rug as if it never happened.

As if she wasn't the cause of what ended my sister's life.

My father immediately tried to comfort my mother, his own broken heart showing in the sorrowful expression on his face. It wasn't fair; it just wasn't fucking fair that my sister wouldn't receive justice simply because her tormentor's parents could afford to buy her freedom. I tightened my hand around my keys, the cool metal digging into the flesh of my palm. Sevyn looked up, her smile faltering a bit when her eyes locked with mine. A flash of guilt passed through her gaze but quickly disappeared when her mother hugged her again. *You won't get away with this, you bitch,* I thought bitterly, just as Judge Hyland banged his gavel.

"Order," he stated, his voice firm. The courtroom quieted once again, but Sevyn and her family didn't sit back down. We all turned our attention back to him as he adjusted his glasses once more. "I'm also granting the Langdon's restraining order request against Oliver Evans, Katherine Evans, and Luther Evans."

"Are you fucking kidding me?" I all but shouted, jumping to my feet. "She's the reason my sister is dead and yet *we* have a restraining order against *us*?!"

Judge Hyland hit his gavel again. "Mr. Evans, settle down or you'll be in contempt of this court!" he warned.

"That verdict is bullshit and you know it! The evidence was there! The witnesses were there!"

"Mr. Evans—"

"All they have to do is flash a little money your way for you to turn a blind eye to what that lunatic did to my fucking sister!" I bellowed.

"Luther, please just stop!" my mother pleaded as her eyes glistened with tears. But I couldn't. It wasn't fucking fair that Sevyn got to walk free while we could only return to a house that my sister was no longer in. It pissed me off that Sevyn could go back to her regular life and her family could still see her, love her, and watch her blossom into an adult when my family only had a gravestone to talk

5

to. It wasn't fucking fair. It just wasn't fair.

"Oliver and Katherine, we truly are sorry for your loss," Sevyn's father, Micah said from across the courtroom. "It's unfortunate that your daughter's mental health was on the decline—"

"Fuck off, you pompous dick," I snapped. "It was because of your plastic bitch of a daughter!"

"Mr. Evans!" Judge Hyland shouted, but I ignored him.

"She'll pay for what she's done," I ground out, heat flushing my face as I pinned my gaze on Sevyn. "I promise she'll pay for what she's done."

"Is that a threat, Mr. Evans?" Micah taunted, but the judge hit his gavel once again before I could respond.

"I'm charging you with contempt, Mr. Evans!" Judge Hyland said and looked over to two police officers standing at a door on the left side of the room. "Get him out of here."

"No! Please! He's just upset right now!" my mother exclaimed as the police rushed toward me. But no one listened to her. The two burly men roughly grabbed my arms and pulled me away from my family.

I didn't take my eyes off Sevyn as the police swiftly snapped handcuffs around my wrists. She gave me a small smile, the guilt in her eyes attempting to portray the apology that she couldn't bring her lips to say out loud. Not that it mattered. No apology from her would bring my sister back. It wouldn't heal my parents' broken heart. And it damn sure wouldn't put out the ball of fire that was now my rage.

"Don't worry, son. We'll get you out," my father called out as they pulled me away. I nodded to let him know that I'd heard him, allowing the officers to take me away from the court room. Their grip on my arms tightened as we passed the table that Sevyn and her lawyer sat at. The entire room was silent, everyone waiting to see what I'd do as I walked past her. A hint of fear twinkled in her eyes as she looked at me, but I only winked at her as a promise that this wasn't over. Satisfaction rolled through me as I watched her skin pale before she dropped her gaze to the table, a smirk on my face as I was finally whisked out of the room. This was far from over. She may have beaten the system with her money, but she wouldn't be able to escape me. None of the fuckers responsible would be able to.

I'd make sure of it.

SEVEN YEARS LATER...

"Wakey, wakey, bitch," I snarled, dumping a bucket of ice cold water on the sweaty man stretched out on the table before me. He jolted awake in a panic, his green eyes wide with terror as he looked around.

"What the fu—where am I?" He squinted against the light above him and narrowed his eyes at me. "Who the fuck are you?"

"A blast from the past," I said, my tone flat as I tossed the empty steel bucket to the side.

"I don't fucking know you," he panted. His wild eyes scanned my form, and I couldn't help but to grin.

"But I know you, Hunter York."

I watched as his eyes widened. Hunter fucking York, one of the three rapists who were acquitted despite the video evidence of those fucks raping my sister at a party. It was amazing what being rich could do for you.

"Where the fuck am I?" he asked again, jerking on the chains attached to his wrists. He kicked his legs, jiggling the chains around his ankles. "What the fuck do you want?"

"For you to atone for what you did."

"I didn't do shit."

I tsked. "You and I know that's not true, Yorkie boy," I said and shook my head. "Don't tell me you already forgot about Logan. Seven years wasn't that long ago."

"Logan? I don't know any fucking Logans," he scoffed.

I took a picture out of my pocket and thrust it in front of his face, anger heating my skin. "You definitely know her."

His eyes darted between my gaze and the picture, his chest rapidly rising and falling as his breaths quickened. "I didn't do anything she didn't want me to do! I was acquitted."

"That's not what a video showed me," I ground out.

Fresh anger boiled in my veins. They'd played the video in court, my sister's screams and pleas for them to stop echoing in the silent room. My family and I had to watch as the three teen boys took turns with her, mocking her pain, her tears, her agony. My father kept a tight grip on my wrist to keep me in my seat, as I was seconds from choking the life out of all three of them as they sat at the defendant's table with their bullshit guilty expressions.

His skin paled at the mention of the video and he swallowed hard. "Look, man, I don't know who the fuck you are, but I was found not guilty. I didn't do anything wrong!" he exclaimed. I stared at him long and hard before I chuckled. Hunter's eyes followed me as I took a few steps away from him and pressed the button on the remote I held in my hand.

"This remote controls those chains cuffed to you," I said. "And if I push this button, the chains will retract and pull your limbs." Hunter jerked at the chains again as if it would make a difference.

"You're fucking psychotic!" Hunter bellowed. "This isn't a Saw movie. You're not Jigsaw, you mother fucker!"

I smiled. "Oh, I'm no Jigsaw, as this isn't a game of survival or testing your will to live." I walked over to him and leaned forward until we were nearly nose to nose. "And unlike Jigsaw, I'm not giving you a choice of whether you live or die."

"What the fuck do you want then?" he bellowed, spittle flying from his mouth as he spat his words.

"The truth, you know, the thing that you, your dickhead friends, and Sevyn failed to tell in court all those years ago." I pushed the button and the chains slowly retracted. Hunter's panicked eyes looked around as his arms and legs were slowly stretched. "Well?"

"I didn't do anything that your slut girlfriend didn't want," he ground out. *Slut.* That word was thrown around so loosely at almost every single trial of the people involved. Their lawyers painted pictures with a paint brush drenched in lies of my sister being known to date many guys—and even girls, too—trying to make it seem as

9

if she asked to be drugged. As if she asked to be fucked on camera by three guys when it was clear that she wasn't in her right mind to even comprehend what was happening to her. As if she deserved the bullying, the humiliation, and the shame when the video was posted for the whole student body to see.

But I knew my sister. She wasn't the promiscuous girl they tried to portray her as. It didn't take a rocket scientist to know who helped perpetuate the lie that created that image.

"My girlfriend?" I chuckled and shook my head. "Do you not remember who I am?"

"I told you I don't know you, man. Whatever you're talking about happened years ago. I'm not that teenager I was back then." His voice had an edge of desperation, but I couldn't be fucked to care.

"Yeah, and I'm not the same man I was before my sister died," I replied sarcastically. "I guess we all change, huh?"

"Sister?" He stared at me for a long moment before realization dawned on him. "What the fuck? Luther?"

I waved my hands along my body. "In the flesh."

His mouth opened and closed a few times before he managed to finally find the words to speak. "Th-they said you were dead; that you also—"

"That I also committed suicide by blowing my brains out? I see you idiots believe any rumor you hear, huh?"

Hunter's Adam's apple bobbed in his throat as he stared at me. A storm of emotions swirled in his eyes. Fear. Uncertainty. Panic.

"Seven years ago, you got away with the rape of my sister," I stated as I pressed the buttons to continue retracting the chains. "The justice system failed my family, failed my sister. So since that bullshit judge won't give us the justice we deserve, I'm going to get it myself."

"No, no, no, no!" Hunter exclaimed as his arms and legs were pulled. "Wait, wait, wait. Okay, okay!"

I pressed the button to stop the chains from retracting and frowned at him. "Okay what? Got something you wanna say?" I asked.

Hunter panted, his breaths coming in quick as his eyes glassed over with tears. "You don't have to do this, man. Is it money you want? My dad can give you whatever you want—"

"I don't want your fucking money. I have my own," I scoffed. "But tell me something. What made you and your asshole friends go after my sister in the first place?"

"We were just stupid kids, man," he groaned in despair.

"Even kids know rape is wrong," I replied, my tone flat. He went quiet, so long that I thought he wouldn't speak again. "I guess you're done talking then."

"Okay, okay, okay!" he yelled when I pressed the button again. I stopped the chains once again and waited for him to speak. He licked his lips and exhaled deeply. "She told us that your...sister was into it."

I ground my teeth, already knowing who he was talking about, but wanted to ask anyway. "Who is she?"

"Sevyn," he rushed out. "She said that your sister was that kind of girl—"

"What kind of girl?" I hissed.

Hunter's eyes filled with panic as he swallowed hard. "T-t-the kind that got around," he stammered. "We didn't know she was a virgin until after the fact."

"So let me get this straight," I started as I rubbed my hand over my growing beard. "Because some bitch told you a girl got around, you took that as an invitation to rape her?"

"We were stupid kids back then, man!" he bellowed, his voice echoing in the bare walls of the warehouse. "I can't take back what I've done. I'm sorry about your fucking sister, okay?"

I stared at him long and hard. "Do you have a sister, Yorkie boy?"

"What?"

"Are you fucking deaf? Do. You. Have. A. Fucking. Sister?" I repeated.

"Y-yeah."

"And if a group of assholes took your sister's innocence, taped it, and then posted it for your whole school to see, how would that make you feel?"

The muscle in his jaw twitched when he stared at me. "I'd be angry."

"Then you see my point," I said with a smirk before I started to walk away, pressing the button to start the chains back up. I tuned out his pleas and yelling, as I watched the chain pull him so tightly that his body now hovered off the table.

"Ah! Please, man! I'm sorry!" he begged, wincing against the pull of the chains.

"Your sorry won't bring my sister back from the dead, now will it?"

"Luther, come on, man. Killing me won't bring her back either!"

I nodded. "You're right; it won't. But it'll sure make me feel a lot better to know that one less person responsible for my sister's demise won't be walking the Earth."

"There has to be something I can do! Just spare me, man! Please!"

"There is something you *can* do," I mused.

"Anything, man. Just tell me what you want," he pleaded in desperation, sweat beading along his forehead as he still dangled in the air.

"You can either close your eyes and wait for the inevitable, or you can watch these chains rip your limbs from your body. It's up to you."

"No, please!" he screamed. I walked to the furthest side of the room and slipped on a disposable rain protector and face shield.

"Forecast says it's gonna rain," I said, ignoring his begging and pleading as I walked back over to him. I opened an umbrella. "And I'm a big fan of rain."

"Fuck you, Luther," he cried out. But I only smiled in response as I watched the chains stretch him further and further as he screamed and begged. Just as he and his friends made my sister scream and beg as they ripped her apart that night. And as he screamed his final scream, I put the umbrella over my head just as the chains reached their limit and pulled his arms and legs from his body, the remaining of him falling back onto the long table with a thud.

I chuckled. "Forecast didn't say the rain would be red. What a nice surprise," I mused. Hunter lay on the table, his body jerking as his blood spilled on the floor, his limbs still dangling from the chains. I moved over to him and cocked my head as he gasped for breath, bloody foam coming from his mouth. "Just like the others, you got what you deserve."

His eyes stared at nothing as he bled out, his chest finally ceasing all movement. And as his skin paled, my shoulders sagged in slight relief. Pulling out Logan's picture, I smiled.

"Got the last of the three morons, sis," I said, staring into her smiling face. Now it was time for the main event, one I'd waited seven years for.

When I got my hands on her, she wouldn't know what hit her. And boy, did I have plans for all seven of those bitches.

CHAPTER 1

SEVYN

They said that the number seven meant completeness and perfection.

At least, that was what my parents thought when they named me that. To them, I was their perfect little girl who could do no wrong, but they didn't know what I was capable of. They didn't know the guilt that I carried for seven years. And they definitely didn't know about the cutting sessions I still had when they thought I was "cured" from my depression.

I definitely wasn't the perfect angel they thought of me to be.

There was something about emptiness that was haunting, a spot you couldn't fill no matter what you tried to jam inside of the void. Drugs, self harm, the dicks of many men. Nothing took away the gargantuan amount of guilt that sat inside of it, but yet didn't fill the emptiness. Especially not this moron rutting away on top of me.

"Fuck, Sevyn, you're so tight," he moaned as he pounded into me, but I barely felt a thing. Aside from the emptiness and numbness that I felt most days, the man hardly had a dick to feel in the first place. Women around town didn't call him Micro Marco for no reason, but he was a warm body to occupy my thoughts for the time being. I glanced over at the clock on the nightstand and noted that it was 12:14 in the morning. *Just three more minutes*, I thought to myself. As well as having a micropenis, he didn't last very long either.

He was handsome at least. Muscular build, a head full of soft, dark hair, and the warmest dark eyes I'd seen on a man. He used to supply me pills and marijuana when I used to do them a few years back, but now he was set on keeping me clean because he "loved" me. We weren't exclusive to each other, but he was a good guy whenever I decided to finally settle down. Unfortunately for him, I was incapable of love. The last time I'd loved someone was back in high school, and when he broke my heart in ways that couldn't be overcome, I vowed to never fall for anyone else. Now my life consisted of fucking random men, a shit ton of therapy, and cutting sessions.

I winced when his hand gripped my upper thigh, his fingers pressing along the fresh cut I'd put there moments before he'd arrived. His callused hands probably didn't feel the marred flesh and I purposely kept the room dark so he wouldn't see them. It wasn't a conversation I wanted to have tonight and the sooner he finished, the sooner I could get him out of my bed.

"Fuck...fuck...it's coming," he groaned, his hips stuttering as he quickly pulled out and jerked his tiny cock over my stomach, streams of his cum tainting my skin. I rolled my eyes as he panted above me. "Did you come, babe?"

"I was almost there, but it's okay," I lied, giving him a small smile. I barely felt anything to even get anywhere near the edge, which probably showed on my face with the way he frowned at me. "Really, I'm fine. I'm just a bit distracted right now."

"With what?"

"It's not important."

"Does it have anything to do with why you've started cutting again?" he asked, his voice soft yet accusing.

I sighed deeply. "It's not anything I want to talk about, Marco," I ground out as I tried to sit up. "Maybe you should go."

"I'm not going anywhere until you talk to me. What's going on with you?" he asked, his beautiful brown eyes filled with concern. The streetlights that peppered downtown Miami shined in the window of my condo, illuminating his face in a yellow glow. His eyes searched my face for an answer that I couldn't give him. The last thing I wanted was another lecture on how I was being paranoid and reminders that Luther was dead. It was only rumored that he'd killed himself; no one had any confirmation. My parents hired a private investigator who couldn't find Luther anywhere, but also couldn't find a death certificate, grave site, or any indication that he'd been cremated either. He wasn't dead, contrary to what people said, and the recent murders of old classmates didn't bring me any kind of comfort either.

"I said I don't want to talk," I snapped. "It's getting late. You should go anyway. I have therapy in the morning. I'll talk to him about it."

His thumb lightly brushed over my fresh cut, his brows furrowed. "You know he can't hurt you, right?" he murmured.

"What the hell are you talking about?"

"The guy you're afraid of. He can't hurt you. I won't let him hurt you." He looked back up and met my gaze. "I can have guys posted around your building and—"

"I don't need a babysitter and I'm not afraid of anyone," I retorted, but with the way my voice shook as I spoke, I knew I hadn't convinced him. "I just...two of my old classmates were murdered recently and it's been a bit hard to deal with."

"I'm sorry to hear that," he said. "Were you close to them?"

They were friends of mine back in high school, but I wouldn't say we were close. We just ran in the same group; we were popular rich kids, which was probably the only thing we really had in common. Josh, Tyler, and Hunter were jocks that my friends called "The Three Stooges" because they were idiotic guys who only got girls with their good looks, money, and athletic abilities. They had about as much personality as a wet plank, but were still popular in our school, which made them the guys to want to be friends with.

If they were any other person, their deaths wouldn't have affected me so much. But I couldn't shake that eerie feeling that their deaths were something bigger than just a random murder and too much of a coincidence.

"Sevyn?" Marco called out as he caressed my cheek. "You're always disappearing into that pretty little head of yours out of nowhere."

"Sorry," I mumbled. "No, I wasn't really close to them. It's just sad when someone I know dies."

"What happened to them?"

I shrugged. "Josh was beheaded," I started. Marco squinted at me for a moment before he snapped his fingers.

"Yeah, I heard about that on the news a little while back. And the other dude they think was related to him in some way was shot, right?"

I swallowed hard and nodded, but I knew how the police actually found him. One of my best friends, Rebecca, had a guy she'd dated once who worked in the police department. She used his affection for her to get any information she'd wanted and asked about Tyler's death after she'd slept with him. While he was shot, it wasn't in a normal way. A shotgun barrel had been shoved into his ass and shot through his body. No fingerprints, no evidence, no witnesses, and no leads. Same for Josh's death. The police were no closer to knowing who was going around killing these "stand up men of Miami" and quite frankly, it put me on edge because there was one fact that stood out.

Josh and Tyler were killed seven days apart from each other. And if I were right about my theory of this being connected to me somehow and someone was back to make us all pay, that meant Hunter would be on the news in the coming days.

"Well, like I said, no one is going to hurt you, beautiful. I'll make sure of it. My guys and I will take anyone out that even hints at wanting to cause you harm," he promised, grabbing my hand and kissing the back of it.

I fought the urge to roll my eyes. He irritated me in ways I couldn't explain. His "guys" only consisted of him and three meathead men that were built the same way as him and just as moronic. They couldn't protect a raw egg from hitting the ground, let alone protect a human. Marco always talked of himself as if he was this huge king pin that ruled the streets of Miami, but he was only a petty drug dealer who worked as a bouncer at the club we'd met at in the first place. I doubted he'd be able to protect me from whoever was doing this when the time came, so his words went in one ear and out the other.

"Well, thank you for wanting to keep me safe, but I'm fine," I said, giving him a small smile. "But really. It's getting late and I have therapy in the morning, so we should call it a night."

"You know I can't leave until you get yours, Sevyn," he murmured as he moved down the bed and settled in between my legs. While the man couldn't fuck to save his life, he definitely made up for it with his tongue.

I bit my lip the moment his tongue touched my clit, a mixture of pain and pleasure consuming me as he also squeezed my upper thighs. His dark, hungry eyes watched me as if trying to navigate my expressions like a guide to determine how to please me. I rolled my hips against his tongue and while I saw Marco's face between my legs, I couldn't stop thinking about the one guy that held my heart in a way that no other man ever would. Anytime I was with another man, I still thought about him. It was strange how you could both love someone with your entire being but hate them at the same time for what they did to you. I supposed the latter feeling was mutual because he now hated me, too.

And I couldn't blame him for his reason why.

Marco jerked me out of my thoughts as his rapid tongue assaulted my clit, pleasure gliding along my nerve endings as I rocked my hips quicker. I was so close to the edge yet so far. The build up was always there but I just couldn't reach the top that I needed to. Once I was frustrated enough, I gripped his hair tight and did what I'd always do. I moaned, pulled his hair and bucked against his face to pretend that I'd had an orgasm just so he'd stop and get the hell out. He suckled my clit for a few moments more and I pretended to twitch, purring in hopes he'd think I was satisfied. He peppered my inner thighs with kisses before he finally slid back up my body and planted a firm kiss on my lips.

"Always so wet and sweet," he whispered. I gave him a small smile.

"Now I'm really tired," I murmured, covering my mouth while letting out a pathetic yawn. He chuckled and kissed me on the forehead before getting off the bed.

"Okay, okay, you don't have to keep hinting that you're giving me the boot," he said. I watched his naked form move around in the dark as he gathered his clothes. "When can I see you again?"

I propped myself up on my elbow with a sigh. "I'm not sure. I have a lot of things to do this week and my family is dragging me on vacation. Said I needed to get out more."

"They're not wrong," he said with a smirk, pulling his boxers back on. "I hardly even see you at the club anymore."

"I just haven't been in the mood to go out lately."

"Is it because of the murders that've been happening?"

I shrugged. It was a number of reasons. The murders, my growing paranoia, the fact that Logan's death anniversary was quickly approaching and bringing back my crippling depression along with it. "I just haven't been in the mood," I finally said.

"Fair enough." He pulled on the rest of his clothes and walked over to the side of the bed, still buttoning his shirt. "You know you can call me anytime you need me, right?"

I nodded. "I know, Marco. You tell me that every time I see you as well as in a text message every single day," I mentioned with a sarcastic grin.

"You don't have to be an asshole about it," he said with a chuckle before leaning down to kiss me again. "I'll call you later." I nodded as he started to walk away but he paused and looked over his shoulder at me. "And answer when I do. I'm sick of talking to your voicemail."

"I'll do my best if I'm not too busy," I said. "Promise."

And though he nodded, we both knew I was lying. I only called him or answered his calls if I needed him, otherwise he went straight to voicemail where I'd delete the recording without even listening to it. I got out of bed and followed him through my condo to let him out. He turned and blew me a kiss before winking at me, a chill running down my spine. I quickly closed and locked the door and leaned against it as my breaths came in quick, my anxiety almost crippling me. It was such an innocent gesture that sparked so much fear when that one particular memory came to the forefront of my mind. No matter how hard I tried to block that time out of my life, the devastating guilt and memories of everything always wormed its way into my current thoughts. Sometimes I wondered if it was my spiritual punishment for what I'd done considering that I practically got off without so much as a warning. And honestly, I would've rather served time for my actions instead of dealing with the mental torment that I dealt with now.

I hadn't seen Luther Evans since the trial, but he was always on my mind. Just the thought of him sparked my fear ever since he winked at me in the courtroom, planting that tiny seed of promise and fear before he was pulled away. It was only a wink; he never said a word to me but that sinister grin on his lips and a simple wink was enough to rock my entire world. After being friends with Logan for years, I knew very well what Luther was capable of. Growing up, no one dared to mess with Logan or her friends because everyone knew of her big brother that was nicknamed Lunatic Luther. He'd mellowed out a lot over the years but when Logan died, the lunatic within him returned. And when he winked at me in court seven years ago, I knew deep down in my soul that this wasn't over.

It was far from over.

I padded back through my quiet condo and headed to the master bathroom, turning on the hot water of the shower. As I waited for the water to warm, I studied my reflection in the mirror. It was so easy to pretend you were fine when you really weren't. My light brown eyes appeared to be full of life despite the fact that I felt dead inside. Thanks to spray tanning, my soft, tanned skin gave the illusion that I'd been spending my days on the Miami beaches near my condo instead of my actual reality of being holed up inside my home due to paranoia. My lean, curvy figure hadn't changed despite the multiple times I'd trashed my body with drugs, emotional eating, and self-harming tendencies. People usually thought I had it all just by looking at me, but the only thing I had was the blood of my ex best friend on my hands.

Stepping into the shower, I hissed as the hot water hit my fresh cuts. I wouldn't complain though; pain seemed to be the only thing I could feel these days. I scrubbed my body until my skin was raw and red, pausing when I heard my phone ringing from my bedroom. *Probably Marco already*, I mused, rolling my eyes as I massaged shampoo into my hair. But the phone didn't stop ringing. After one call stopped, another would come in. After the fifth call, I frowned. Considering how late it was, I didn't know who else would be calling other than Marco, but five times back to back was pretty excessive, even for him.

I ground my teeth and rinsed the shampoo from my long, black hair before turning the water off. A sixth call came through as I yanked a towel from the towel rod and wrapped it around me. Strolling out of my bathroom and into my bedroom, I grabbed my phone from my bed to see Rebecca's name on my screen.

"Bec, do you know how late it is?" I muttered as I cradled my phone between my ear and shoulder as I moved around my bedroom to get ready for bed.

"I know, I know, and I'm sorry. But I think you'd want to know this," she said. I paused when I caught the trembling in her voice.

"Is something wrong?"

"So, remember when I told you that I'd asked Donovan to keep me updated on cases that were similar to Josh and Tyler's death?" she started.

"Yeah, and?" I asked. My heart raced in my chest. If she was calling me this late—and back to back at that—then I already had a feeling as to what she was about to tell me.

"They just found Hunter's body," she exclaimed, slight panic and fear lacing her voice.

I nearly dropped my phone at the news. I rushed over to flip on the light switch and moved to look at my calendar. I'd marked their deaths on my calendar when Tyler was killed, mostly to try to convince myself that it wasn't a coincidence and that they were random murders. I looked at the names I'd written in pencil and the dates I'd written them in:

April 1 - Josh C.
April 8 - Tyler F.
April 15 - Hunter Y. ?

I'd told myself after Tyler's death that the fact that Tyler was killed seven days after Josh felt like a sign of some sort. My parents, therapists and friends told me that I was being paranoid as they usually did whenever I expressed my fear about something happening to me. But as I looked at my calendar, I couldn't shake the thought that I'd been right all along, especially after Hunter's death.

Which happened yesterday, on April 15th, just as I'd assumed it would if my theory was right.

"Sevyn?" Rebecca called out, breaking into my thoughts.

"Y-yeah, I'm still here," I stammered, tearing my gaze away from the calendar. "Um, does he know what happened?"

"It's bad. It's so, so bad," she said and sighed. "Donovan said Hunter was literally ripped apart. Like his arms and legs were torn from his body."

"Jesus," I murmured, anxiety creeping over me as I ran my hand through my wet hair.

"Yeah. He said this one was one of the most brutal scenes so far."

"I seriously think it's Luther," I blurted out.

"Sevyn, we've been through this—"

"You guys don't get it," I snapped. "Isn't this a little too coincidental? I mean, hello, last month was the month where I was found not guilty for my part in what led to Logan's suicide seven years ago. And now seven years later, all three guys who raped Logan are now dead and were killed seven days apart. Does that not sound like some kind of warning or sign?"

"You sound like one of those Youtube conspiracy theorists," Rebecca mused, which pissed me off to no end. "No one has seen Luther in years. He's even rumored to be dead. Besides, Josh, Tyler, and Hunter weren't the nicest people and it's probably some asshole that they pissed off that did this."

"Rebecca, as brutal as their murders were, it was definitely personal and done by someone with a shit ton of pent up rage. This isn't something that randomly happens to people to settle a score. I don't even think the mafia does anything like that!"

"I don't know, Sevyn. Even if your theory was to be considered, that would mean whoever killed them is coming for us soon. I don't know about you, but that's not something I want to think about."

But then I remembered Luther's wink back in court. I was unfinished business; we all were. Every single one of us who got off on our charges with a slap on the wrist were unfinished business.

"Bec?" I slowly said.

"Yeah?"

"Do you remember what we used to call Luther when we were kids?"

She was quiet for a moment. "You're really starting to scare me, Sevyn."

"I really think it's him. You need to tell Donovan to at least look into Luther," I said as I sat on the side of my bed.

"No one's seen Luther in years, Sevyn," she said again. "The only person that's worried about him is you."

I sighed deeply and pursed my lips. This wasn't a battle I'd win with anyone. Ever since I had my breakdown years ago, everyone spent so much time trying to tell me that everything I was afraid of was only in my head, as if they weren't legitimate. It was pointless talking to anyone about it because they all said the same thing. *No one's going to hurt you, Sevyn. Your fear is creating scenarios in your mind that aren't true. Are you taking your meds as you're supposed to? The meds should've stopped those delusions.*

"I guess you're right," I finally said, no longer wanting to talk. "I have to go."

"Sevyn—"

"Night, Bec," I said and hung up the phone. I flopped back on the bed with a sigh, staring up at the ceiling. Regardless of what anyone else said, I already knew who was behind it and it was only a matter of time before he got to me.

I unlocked my phone screen and called my mom, continuing to stare at the ceiling until she answered.

"Sevyn?" she said sleepily. "It's very late—"

"Hunter was killed last night," I blurted out.

My mom released a soft sigh, the shuffling on her end of the line signaling that she was sitting up in bed. "I'm sorry. Was this a friend of yours?"

"He was one of the guys that raped Logan," I forced myself to say. "Along with Josh and Tyler, the other guys murdered recently."

"That's terrible." She was quiet for a moment. "Do you need to come here? Or should we come to you? I don't want you to spiral again."

"I think it's best if I come to you. I don't feel safe being alone right now," I murmured, tears burning my eyes.

"No one is going to hurt you. I understand you're scared, but you're safe. Whether or not Luther is alive, there's still a restraining order against him. The private investigator is still searching for his whereabouts as well."

That's what makes him so dangerous, I bitterly thought. The fact that no one knew where he was made this whole situation even more frightening. He could pop up at any moment and at any place and no one would be prepared for him.

"Well, for my peace of mind, I don't feel comfortable being alone tonight," I finally said after a short bout of silence.

"Of course. You know your father and I are here for you whenever you need us."

"Thanks, Mom. I'll be there in a few."

"I'll get a room made up for you. Call me when you're on your way."

"I will. See you in a bit," I said and hung up with a sigh. An unfamiliar ringtone sounded from somewhere under my bed, setting me on edge.

I slowly moved down to the floor practically holding my breath but sighed in relief when I saw that it was just Marco's phone.

"Great. Now I have to see him well before I want to," I muttered, just as a heavy knock sounded on my front door. "Perfect timing."

I quickly pulled on panties and a long purple t-shirt that stopped in the middle of my thighs. Picking up his phone, I padded across the heated wooden floors through my condo and unlocked the door. "I literally just found your—"

My words ceased to exist as I looked up into Luther's angry eyes. He still looked as he did seven years ago. Dangerously handsome, clean shaven, athletically built. His dark brown eyes were hard on me as he took a step forward.

"Long time, no see, Sevyn," he stated, his menacing voice making

29

my skin crawl with fear.

"You're not supposed to be here," I whispered. My brain screamed for me to try to close the door, but I couldn't get my body to follow through.

"And you're not supposed to be a free woman, yet here you are," he taunted. "My sister's in the ground and you're treated to an ocean view condo downtown and living a lavish life. Must be nice."

"I...I...I..."

"You...what?" He took another step forward, now making it impossible to close the door. "You're sorry now?"

"Yes," I whispered. My body involuntarily trembled as his gaze slid along my form, his eyes softening when he met my eyes.

"I've waited seven years to hear you say that," he murmured, the earlier anger dissolving from him. His shoulders sag as he bowed his head. "It was bad enough to see everyone get away with what they'd done; it was even worse that you didn't even appear remorseful about it."

"I was," I said, my voice finally coming back to me. "I didn't want that for her, Luther. I swear to you, I didn't think things were that bad for her."

"You didn't think things were that bad?" he repeated, frowning. "A video of her rape was posted on the school's forum and she was expelled for it while the guys got away with it for being 'exceptional athletes with potential' and you don't think that was bad?"

I swallowed the lump of guilt in my throat. "You're right," I murmured. "I should've stopped it and I didn't."

"Of course you didn't. You only fanned the flames and made it worse," he said, his voice flat. After a few moments, he sighed. "But anger won't bring Logan back. All I can do is forgive you and move on."

My eyes widened at his words. "I...thank you," I stammered. "I know I don't deserve your forgiveness—"

"You don't," he interrupted. "But despite everything you did to her, Logan wrote in her suicide note that she forgave you. You were the reason she felt her life was no longer worth living and yet she forgave you."

Tears burned my eyes as I looked at him. That definitely sounded like something Logan would do. Always gorgeous, always naive. She always saw the good in people, regardless of how they treated her or others, claiming that everyone had a story that made them the way they were. You had to be a special kind of evil to hurt someone as kind, pure, and loving as her. And since I was the one that initiated the entire situation, it made me the worst of all.

"Did you kill the guys?" I forced myself to ask, my heart hammering in my chest. He shook his head.

"No. I only just heard about it when I came back to town yesterday, but I wish I had," he ground out, a dark look passing over his face before it disappeared again. "Anyway, I have to go. Sorry it was so late."

"It's fine," I said, giving him a small smile. "If you ever want to talk, you can stop by or whatever."

He smirked at me. "I'm not even technically supposed to be here, remember?"

"Oh yeah. The restraining order," I murmured. "I suppose I can't hug you either, huh?"

"Why would you want to?"

I shrugged. "You look like you need one, I guess," I said. He stared at me for a long moment, so long that I started to feel uncomfortable. "I'm sorry. Forget I said anything."

"No, you're right," he said and ran a hand down his tired face. It was then that I saw the extent of what Logan's death had done to him. He looked weary, probably from years of anger, grief, and loss—all of which I caused. "Maybe I do need one."

I closed the space between us and slowly wrapped my arms around his neck. He tensed under my touch at first before he stiffly brought one arm around me. His cologne smelled of cedar wood and cinnamon, reminding me of times I'd spent with my first and only love.

"You know what I always admired about you, Sevyn?" Luther murmured as his arm around my waist tightened.

"Hmm?"

"How gullible you are," he whispered just as a sharp pain pierced my side. I gasped in shock and let him go, looking down to see blood seeping through my nightshirt. "Did you think I came here for some kind of fucked up forgiveness pow wow?"

I stumbled backwards, clutching my side. Luther calmly closed and locked the door before stalking toward me. With the condo still dark, I stumbled into furniture as I walked backwards, never taking my eyes off of him.

"Alexa, turn on the lights," I panted. The lights clicked on in the living room, revealing the bloody box cutter he held in his hand.

"Did you think I'd never come for you?" he asked, a sly grin on his lips. "I promised my sister that I'd make everyone responsible pay for what they did to her."

"So, you killed them," I ground out, my side burning like crazy.

He shrugged. "Wasn't it obvious?" he replied and charged toward me. I squeaked and took off running into my bedroom, shutting and locking the door behind me. Luther banged on the door a few times before everything ceased. I pushed my dresser in front of the door, wincing in pain as my side throbbed at the exertion. Once it was in place, I grabbed my phone from the bed and quickly called 911.

"One...two...Luther's coming for you..." he sang outside the door.

"911, what's your emergency?" a bored operator said upon answering.

"Y-yes, I need help," I rushed out, panic strangling my voice.

"Three...four...gonna skin a whore," he continued.

"What's the problem, ma'am?" the operator asked.

"Five...six...you're last on my list..."

"A man I have a restraining order on is in my house. I've been stabbed," I said, tears rolling down my cheek.

"Seven...eight...time to meet your fate...."

"What's your address, ma'am?" the operator said. I quickly gave her my address, listening hard for Luther but no longer heard him singing. "Police and an ambulance are on the way to you, ma'am."

"Thank you," I said, just as my front door slammed shut.

Everything was silent for a long moment. My bedroom lights were still off, the living room lights still on, but I didn't dare move the dresser in case he was actually still in the house. My heart hammered so hard in my chest that I could almost hear it beating in the silence that surrounded me. I forced myself to the bathroom, lifting my shirt to see my bloody wound. I grabbed a box of gauze from under the sink and went to work trying to clean it as best as I could. Sirens sounded in the distance, relief flooding me as I held gauze against my wound to stop the bleeding. I put the peroxide and extra gauze back under the sink and stood upright, a firm hand covering my mouth and a strong arm across my neck.

"Nine, ten, now you'll die my friend," he whispered in my ear. The balcony door. He went through the balcony door of my living room and entered through the door leading to my bedroom. I met his eyes in the mirror, fear paralyzing me as I watched him slit my throat. He let go of me and I fell to the floor with a thud. The last thing I saw was him looking down at me, a satisfied grin on his lips.

"See you in hell, bitch."

I jumped awake with a scream, falling onto the floor. My heart pounded in my chest so hard that it hurt. I felt my neck and checked my body for injuries, only to find that I was still wrapped in my towel from last night. I ran a hand through my tangled, dry hair and rested my head against the bed.

"It was just a dream, Sevyn. Just a fucked up dream," I murmured to myself as I willed my heart rate to go down. I reached back and felt around for my phone, opening my call log. I'd talked to Rebecca, but I never called my mom. I must've fallen asleep staring at the ceiling.

I pulled my knees to my chest. Whether it was a dream or not, I knew one thing.

Luther Evans was coming for me and no one would be able to save me from him.

CHAPTER 2

LUTHER

I sat in my Jeep as I watched Sevyn look both ways before rushing across the street. The sheer panic in her eyes as she looked around brought a grin to my lips. I wouldn't doubt that she sensed I was near. With the way she ran into the mental health clinic, I was sure last night's news sent her running to her therapist.

My phone rang in the cup holder, pulling my eyes away from the building Sevyn entered. My mom's picture showed on the screen, her signature ring tone of chimes filling the space of the car.

"Hi, Mom," I said upon answering.

"Hi, my darling. I just wanted to see if you were stopping by for dinner tonight. I know you've been busy lately but I'd really love to

It wasn't completely the fact that I'd been busy; it'd just been hard to be in the house since Logan died. There was always an eerie feeling anytime I passed her bedroom to go to the bathroom, almost as if I could still feel her presence within the house. I almost felt as if I couldn't be in the house until all of her tormentors paid for what they did, but I knew that wasn't realistic. It still didn't stop me from trying to anyway.

I sighed inwardly. I knew I couldn't avoid my parents forever, as my mother would just keep asking until I finally agreed to come. "Yeah, I'll be there."

"Perfect! I'm even making your favorite just in case you were coming," she said. The excitement in her voice made me smile. Ever since Logan died, my parents weren't the same. They ended up getting a divorce two years after Logan's death and it was hard to hear the sadness in my mother's voice every time I spoke to her. While my father easily moved on, my mother had to deal with the death of her only daughter and the destruction that loss and grief caused for her marriage. So, to hear her excited just at the mention of me having dinner with her was a nice change.

"You didn't have to do all of that, Mom. We can't eat a whole pot roast by ourselves," I said.

"Oh, nonsense, darling." She was silent for a few moments before she sighed. "I, um, I also invited your father. I thought it would be nice to have a dinner as a family again."

"Mom—"

"I know things have been rocky between you and your father

since he and I got divorced, but it's okay. I just want a nice dinner with my family. With the anniversary of Logan's passing coming up..."

I sighed deeply. "I know. And I understand." I ran a hand down my face. "Well, I'll be there. Do you need me to bring anything?"

"No, I think I have everything I need. Dinner will start at 6:30. Please be on time," she mentioned.

I chuckled. "When am I ever late?"

"You've been late to everything you were ever supposed to attend, Luther," she said and giggled.

"Okay, okay. I'll be there at 6:30."

"Perfect. I'll see you soon. I love you, son."

"Love you, too, Mom. See you soon," I said and hung up, putting the phone back in the cup holder and looking back to the building Sevyn disappeared in. After having Paul, my tech best friend from college hack into the phones of Sevyn and her friends, I now could track where everyone was, which was perfect for the plans I had for them all soon.

"Don't worry, I'm coming for you soon," I mumbled to myself as I started my car and sped off into traffic.

I turned the radio up as the warm, salty Miami air wafted through my hair. I pulled my sunglasses from my sun visor and slipped them on as a radio personality read the most recent news.

"So last night, another murder happened on the outskirts of town," the woman said. "Hunter York was found dead late last night in the same brutal fashion as Josh Cannon and Tyler Fox."

"Don't you think it's a coincidence? I think karma came back to get them," her male cohost said.

"What makes you say that?"

"All three of those guys are known rapists. They've been getting away with things for years. I guess someone got tired of them getting off on charges and served their own justice," he said.

I chuckled and adjusted my sunglasses. "You got that right," I mused and continued driving.

While I had no idea about the other rape cases those morons had over the years, they only paid for one. Turned out that they were able to get all of their karma delivered to them in the form of one monster. *Three down, seven more to go.*

"Well, aside from what you think about them deserving it, police are saying that we now have a serial killer on the loose," the woman continued. "They've even gone as far as saying that the killer is a Jigsaw copycat, the fictional main character in the horror Saw movie franchise. Now experts are discussing the harm that gore in horror movies can do."

The man scoffed. "Horror movies have been around since the beginning of time. One psycho taking out the trash doesn't make horror movies the problem," he said. "I watch horror movies all the time and I haven't gone out to kill a single soul."

"But you have to think about all the violence we have in movies and video games. There's been plenty of true crime shows that always start with some kid or teenager having these murder fantasies and when they act on it, their response is usually, 'I just wanted to know what it felt like to kill someone...'"

I rolled my eyes and plugged in my aux cord. Hunter had said the same thing right before I killed him. Jigsaw or any fictional killer was the furthest thing on my mind. The only thing I thought about when planning their murders was how I could make them suffer the most. And after studying to become a civil engineer, I carefully planned all the devices and methods and which I'd kill them. And boy did I have some nice surprises for Sevyn and her bitch friends that I couldn't wait to try.

Traffic slowed to a stop for a red light. As I waited, I put my music on shuffle and put my phone back in the cupholder, drumming my fingers against my steering wheel until the light finally turned green and traffic moved again. I drove across town to my best friend Paul's house, seeing him in his driveway polishing his Corvette. He tossed the towel over his shoulder as I pulled in behind his car.

"Took you long enough," he said when I got out.

"Had stuff to do," I said with a chuckle, playfully punching his shoulder when I approached him.

He looked around and lowered his voice. "I saw the news this morning. That was fucking sick, man! I wish I was there to see it."

I shook my head. "The less you see, the less trouble you'll be in just in case this shit blows up in my face."

"Tell me you at least recorded this one like I asked," he pleaded. I pulled the flash drive from my pocket.

"I mean I brought this thing along, but I didn't know if you'd be into that kind of thing—"

"Count me in, you son of a bitch. Let's go," he interrupted, snatching the flash drive from me. I grinned and followed him into his house. "Plus, the guys are down in the basement. We've been waiting on you to figure out the plan for tonight."

Just the thought of tonight's plans made my skin tingle with excitement. It wasn't one that I could execute on my own, at least gathering up all the girls at once. I didn't want to risk tipping off the other girls and giving them time to run, so I needed them rounded up all at once. Unfortunately for me, I was only one man, but thankfully I had a group a men who were down with my cause and eager to help in any way they could.

Paul and I made our way through his messy house, empty pizza boxes and beer cans littering his living room.

"Another long coding session?" I teased as we headed for the basement.

"You know it, brother. Plus, I had to work overtime creating your alibi like you asked me," he said and winked, opening the door leading down to the basement. The smell of marijuana hit me square in the face as we descended into the smoky basement, Curtis, Ryan, Jake, Tony, and Victor all sitting on the sectional.

"Aye, Luther's here!" Victor said and took a puff from a joint they were all passing around.

"And he brought the video!" Paul said excitedly, holding up the flash drive.

"Well, put that shit on then, brother! Let's see some action!" Curtis cheered. Paul walked over to his projector and turned it on, plugging the flash drive into his computer. Victor held out the joint and blew out a cloud of smoke.

"Want a hit, man?" he asked.

I shook my head. "Nah, I'm good," I said. Marijuana wasn't really my thing, but I didn't mind it. Any other time, I would've taken a puff or two for the hell of it, but I wanted my mind to be completely clear for tonight. I didn't want any mistakes or hiccups. I only had one chance to execute this and I wanted to savor every moment of it sober.

"Hey Luther, did you get all the good parts on the video?" Ryan asked. "I heard the details when my dad was talking to his old partner. He'd said it was one of the worst cases he'd ever heard."

I flopped down on the empty spot of the sectional couch and nodded. "I got every moment of it. I bet your dad is glad he retired now, huh?" I mused.

Ryan shook his head. "He wished he'd have seen it. Said he would've spit on Hunter's body. He sexually assaulted my cousin and got away with it. My dad and uncle were fucking pissed, man."

"Yeah, that fucker got what he deserved," Jake said.

"That dick Justin and Tyler tag teamed a girl I grew up with. People should be kissing your ass and calling you a hero for cleaning up the trash of this shit city since the justice system didn't do anything about it," Tony muttered, taking the joint from Victor and taking a puff.

"Will you dickheads shut up so I can start the video?" Paul said.

"Yeah, yeah, go 'head, man," Tony said, waving his hand at Paul.

"And here we go," Paul said, bouncing around on the balls of his feet and pressed play on his computer.

The room fell quiet as everyone looked at the video. Adrenaline flooded my system as I relived that night playing on the screen, remembering the lingering rage and pain I felt as I forced an explanation out of him. The guys were all silent, my voice from the speakers filling the space around us.

"Good part's coming up," I finally said as they all watched me retract the chain.

"I gotta agree with what the local news are saying about you looking like a Jigsaw copycat," Tony said. "That low key looks like a Jigsaw trap that could possibly be in the movie."

Jake nodded. "There was a trap similar, but it wasn't controlled by anyone. The person had to poke his eyes out or some shit in order to get out of it—"

"Will you shut the fuck up?" I snapped. "I'm not Jigsaw and I'm not trying to be him."

Jake held his hands up. "My bad, brother. I was just saying," he said and took another hit from the joint.

"Shh, shh, shh, the good part's coming," Paul said, his eyes fixated on the projector screen. We all watched as I put on the rain protector and face shield, the guys howling with laughter when I grabbed an umbrella.

"Forget Jigsaw. If they saw this, they'd think you were fucking Mary Poppins," Curtis exclaimed before he howled with laughter.

I chuckled and shook my head, still watching the screen. Paul was damn near salivating over the scene before him, his eyes wide with wonder as we all continued to watch.

"There it is...." Ryan said as he scooted to the edge of his seat. "And....there it is!"

They all cheered when the chains pulled Hunter's limbs from his body. "Holy shit, that was sick! I gotta rewind that," Paul said, going back to his computer and rewinding back to the part where Hunter was still suspended in the air by the chains.

"Did you guys hear what dickhead over here said?" Jake teased, playfully elbowing me in the ribs. "How fucked up is it to talk about the weather to a man that's pretty much already dead?"

I shrugged and smirked. "Maybe he wanted to know the forecast."

"And it didn't even rain that night," Ryan added with a scoff.

"That was the whole point, dumb ass. He was talking about raining blood," Paul said, shaking his head.

"Oh," Ryan said and chuckled. "Fuck, I'm so high, man."

"Isn't it bad luck to open an umbrella inside or some shit?" Curtis asked.

"Probably, but my whole life has been a clusterfuck of bad luck," I said. "One more stroke of bad luck won't hurt if it means that someone dies."

"Right on, man," Victor said, pointing at me.

"I thought he was going to break out into some kind of tune. Imagine the last thing you hear while you're dying is someone singing and tap dancing in your blood? That'd be fucked up to the max," Ryan said.

"I'm not the singing type," I said as I shook my head. "The only thing they'll hear is themselves struggling to breathe."

"Even better," Paul mused.

"So, what's the plan for tonight?" Tony finally asked, settling down in the chair.

"Are you pot heads even going to be able to help me tonight?" I asked the other guys on the couch with a frown.

"This high will have worn off by then," Jake said, waving me off. "Just tell us what you need from us. Do we kill these bitches?"

"Not yet. I'm going to destroy every single one of them myself. I just need you guys to help me transport them where I need them." I looked to Paul. "Can you pull up the info I emailed you?"

"You got it, brother," he said, typing away on his computer with a furrowed brow. The video disappeared from the screen and pictures of Sevyn and her friends appeared. "So here we have Sevyn Langdon on top." He pointed at Sevyn's picture. Her smiling face on the screen pissed me off to no end, but it brought me great pleasure to know that she wouldn't be smiling soon. "And on the second row starting from left to right, you have: Rebecca Colt, Allison Penn, and Crystal Myers."

"That Crystal Myers looks like she can deep throat my cock," Tony said and snorted.

Paul frowned. "Be serious, asshole," he said and turned back to the screen. "And on the last row from left to right, you have: Sarah Andrews, Carrie Tate, and Jamie Scott."

Ryan rolled his eyes. "I know I can't wait for all of this to be over. She's so fucking annoying," he mumbled.

"You mean you're not in love with your little girlfriend?" I teased.

He scoffed and shook his head. "Hell no. I'm only doing this as a favor to you. My dick and I are allergic to commitment. Besides, she's entirely too clingy and I don't do clingy women ever."

"We appreciate your sacrifice for the cause, brother," Victor said, taking a hit off the joint before putting it out.

And what a contribution it was.

I knew I'd need an "in" with the girls and Carrie was the easiest target. It took a bunch of convincing to get Ryan to agree with "dating" her to move forward with our plan, but it worked. Now it was finally time to put this plan into motion.

"Well, the girls made plans to go out to a club. I think we should all go there, get one of the girls, drug her, and bring her out to the cabin. And once they're all there, I can take it from there," I said.

Ryan shook his head. "No way, man. I want to watch."

"I definitely want to witness this," Victor added.

"Well, I didn't expect you guys to leave. You just won't do any killing," I said.

"I can live with that," Paul said with a nod.

"Well, who gets who though?" Curtis asked.

"You guys can decide amongst yourselves who you want, but no one will touch Sevyn but me," I ground out.

"That much was pretty obvious," Paul said with a smirk. "I'll take Rebecca."

"Jamie," Tony said, raising his hand.

"I got Allison," Curtis replied.

"I have no choice but to take Clingy Carrie," Ryan muttered.

"I guess I'll take Crystal," Victor said.

"And I guess that leaves me with Sarah," Jake said with a shrug.

"Cool. The girls claim they're all meeting at Sevyn's at 9:30 and should be leaving for the club by ten. Let's be at the club no later than 10:30," I said. The men all nodded to confirm.

"Should we bring anything?" Paul asked.

"Just bring your masks for when we get to the cabin. You'll have to wear them anytime you're around the girls," I replied as I stood.

"You got it, brother," Jake said. "I'm excited. It's been a while since I've seen bloodshed up close and personal."

"Same. The Brothers of Vengeance are back on the prowl," Curtis said, fist pumping the air. I chuckled.

We spent the next hour handling the finer details of tonight's plan. Excitement ran along my nerve endings the closer we got to the finalized plan. This used to just be a fantasy that I kept safely tucked in the back of my mind, but now it was finally coming to life. I couldn't wait to see the life leave their eyes, to smell their spilled blood, to hear them beg for their life. Justice was long overdue and I couldn't wait to dish out their servings.

"I'll text you guys in a few hours. I have to meet my mom up for dinner. In the meantime, figure out a way into the club's cameras and start creating everyone's alibis," I instructed once we finished. Despite their impaired state, they all immediately jumped into work.

Paul handed the flash drive back to me and clapped my shoulder. "Nice video, man," he said with a grin. "It'll be even better to see this in person."

I returned his grin. "Well, get ready. The grand finale starts tonight." And I couldn't fucking wait.

―――――

"Oh, look at you, you handsome devil!" my mother exclaimed when she opened the door for me an hour later. I'd run to my condo to change clothes and shower, as there was no way I could step foot in my mother's house still smelling like weed. She hugged me tightly, lingering a bit longer than normal and giving me a small smile despite the sad look in her eyes. After a moment, she stepped aside. "Come on in!"

I stepped inside, the delicious smell of her signature pot roast making my stomach growl. "Smells great in here," I said as she closed the door.

"Well, you know I do what I can," she said. "Your father's in the living room."

I sighed inwardly and followed behind her. It was weird that she still wanted to live in this big house by herself even though my parents were divorced and it was just my mom. I couldn't necessarily say that I blamed her. I'd grown up in this house. There were so many memories here that I was sure she wasn't ready to let go of, even more so after Logan died. It was hard to go into the living room to see all of the family pictures on the wall, as if our happiness were frozen in the past and died along with my sister.

My father stood up when I entered the living room, giving me a small smile. "It's nice to see you again, son," he said. After the divorce, I hadn't seen him too often. He'd moved on to another relationship, treating Mom as if she didn't exist. He had another daughter and didn't want to think about Logan too much. I knew that people had different ways of grieving, but I didn't appreciate the way he'd gone about it. I glanced over at my mom, who still couldn't bring herself to look at him, the hurt evident on her face even after all these years.

"Oliver," I stated, my tone flat. I refused to call him my father anymore. I didn't know who this man was that stood before me other than a coward who turned his back on his family when they needed him most.

His smile fell and he nodded in understanding, sitting back down. My mother cleared her throat.

"Well, since everyone's all here, we can have dinner now. I'm sure you're both busy so I don't want to keep you long," she said, sadness lacing her voice.

"I'm in no rush, Mom," I said, taking her hand and giving it a light squeeze. "Not sure if I can speak for Oliver considering he took the first chance he got to bail on you."

"You know that's not fair, Luther," he said as he stood again.

"What's not fair is how you left your grieving wife all because she was drowning in sadness and loss and wasn't interested in sex," I snapped. He swallowed hard but didn't respond. "Exactly what I thought. You have no right to be carrying on about what is and isn't fair."

"Boys, please," my mother said with a sigh. "I just want a normal family dinner. I didn't invite you both for you to fight with one another."

I ground my teeth and nodded. "I apologize," I forced myself to say. There was plenty more I wanted to say to that asshole, but now wasn't the time. I plastered on a fake grin and squeezed my mother's hand again. "Well, let's have dinner. I'm starving."

Most of dinner was awkwardly silent. My mother did her best to try to initiate conversations, but Oliver and I weren't in the mood to talk.

"So, Luther, how's things going at work? I heard your engineering firm was contracted by the city for some new infrastructure," she said as she cut into her slice of pot roast.

"Yeah, we're in the designing phase for a new bridge. It's a pretty massive project and all," I said.

"You were always the smartest in the bunch," Oliver said with a small smile. I fought the urge to roll my eyes as my mother gave me a stern look to behave. Even as a grown man, my mother could still shut me down with "the look."

"Thanks," I ground out.

"Oh, and have you heard about what happened to those boys?" my mother said. "Everyone in town's talking about it. Isn't it horrific?"

"If you ask me, the bastards got what they deserved," Oliver muttered, shoving a spoonful of mashed potatoes into his mouth.

My mother looked at him with wide eyes. "How could you say such a thing? I'm sure their parents are hurting just as we did when we lost Logan—"

"You and Logan are so much alike that it hurts, Katherine,"

Oliver said with a shake of his head. "Those boys raped our little girl—violated and humiliated her—and you feel sorry for them because karma came and bit them in the ass?"

"Not to mention, Logan wasn't the only girl they assaulted over the years," I added. "They've been in a lot more trouble since then and still managed to get off with little to no time."

"Well, that's just ridiculous," my mother said. "It's still hard to lose a child."

"It is, but I'm not going to feel sorry for the parents of criminals," Oliver continued. "In fact, whoever killed them, I hope they go after Sevyn and her little cunt squad."

Don't worry, I'm already on it, I mused, taking a bite of pot roast.

My mother shook her head. "Apparently, this isn't the best topic at the dinner table. Maybe we should talk about something else." She shifted uncomfortably in her seat. "Um...so how's life for you, Oliver? How are Gina and Nicole?"

I ground my teeth, staring hard at him. Gina was his secretary for years until he was caught sticking his dick in her during late night hours at work. Now she was his new wife and they had a four-year-old daughter named Nicole. When he locked gazes with me, he quickly cleared his throat and focused back down on his plate.

"Um, they're good. They actually wanted to come, but I figured it was best if they didn't," he said.

"You figured right," I ground out.

"Luther," my mother warned.

"No, no, he's fine." Oliver sighed. "I know I haven't been the best person lately. And I'm sure you probably feel as if I just abandoned you guys after everything that happened to Logan. I am sorry for how all of that happened. There's no excuse for what I've done."

"Please," my mother interrupted, holding up her hand. "I don't want to hear that anymore. The past is in the past and there's nothing anyone can do about it."

"Katherine—"

"You're happily married now, Oliver. Unless you plan on divorcing her, there's no reason for you to plead your case as if you have something to prove," she said, her voice sharp.

"You're right. I'm sorry," he said softly. The rest of dinner was quiet, no one daring to say anything even after we'd finished eating. I looked down at my watch, seeing it was getting close to 7:30. There were still things I needed to get ready at home to pack my Jeep with and I needed enough time to make sure I didn't forget anything.

"Well, I really enjoyed dinner, Mom. It was delicious," I said as I stood from the table. "I have a long day at work tomorrow, so I think I'm gonna head home to get everything ready for tomorrow."

She gave me a little pout as she also stood. "I feel like you just got here! I wish you didn't have to leave so soon." She moved over to me and hugged me tight. "You should stop by more often."

"I promise I will," I said, hugging her just as tight.

Oliver stood and cleared his throat. "I should probably also leave as well. Thank you for inviting me to dinner, Katherine."

"Of course," she responded, not bothering to look at him. She walked us both to the door, waving us off as we walked down the driveway to our cars.

When we were far enough from the house, he lightly grabbed my elbow to stop me. "Can we talk a second?"

"There's nothing to talk about," I said, snatching away from him and continuing on to my Jeep.

"Did you kill those guys?" he blurted out. I paused but I didn't turn around. "I won't be upset if you did."

"Goodnight, Oliver," I ground out.

I could hear his footsteps rushing toward me before he grabbed my arm again, not letting go this time. "If you did, I hope you get the rest of those bastards for what they did to Logan," he said under his breath. "You make every one of those bastards pay."

I ground my teeth and pinned him with my gaze before snatching out of his grip again. I couldn't even trust this man to stick with his family through one of the toughest moments of our lives and he thought I'd trust him to admit to what I did? I didn't know what kind of delusion he was living in, but he was about to get a rude awakening.

"Don't put your hands on me again," I growled. "And I don't know what the hell you're talking about."

"You don't have to hide from me, Luther. I'm your father," he said, his tone practically pleading with me.

I shook my head. "My father left five years ago. I don't know who you are anymore," I said and walked away, leaving him in the driveway his tears in his eyes as he watched me pull out of the driveway and drive off.

Oliver's words bounced around in my head for the next couple of hours as I went around my house packing up everything I needed in multiple duffle bags. Guns, ammunition, knives, keys. I had so much suffering planned for all of them. I couldn't wait to hear them scream, to see them bleed, to watch them die. I picked up a box of condoms, debating on whether or not to bring them. After a few moments, I shook my head and tossed them aside.

"Pregnancy won't matter when she's dead," I mused. And after what I planned to do with her body when I was done with her, there wouldn't be much DNA left to begin with.

My phone rang in my pocket, displaying Paul's picture when I pulled it out.

"About to leave my place now," I said upon answering.

"Same. We're all leaving from my place. We'll meet you at the club."

"Sounds good. Park on the first level of the parking garage. We're going to need an easy getaway to transport them without looking too suspicious," I ordered.

"You got it, brother. See you there," he said and hung up.

I zipped up the duffle bags and picked them up, rolling my shoulders. Glancing at Logan's picture taped in the corner of my mirror, I sighed deeply.

"This is all for you, sis," I murmured and turned off the light before leaving my home.

A little while later, the guys and I pulled up at the club. Everyone was in their individual cars in the parking garage across the street, watching the girls in line as they waited to get in. My hand tightened on the steering wheel, trying to control my anger upon seeing Sevyn again and knowing how close I was to getting her. She was the one who started all of this shit; the loss of my sister, my family being torn apart, my insatiable thirst for blood. Just knowing that I'd soon get my revenge sent a surge of adrenaline rushing through me. Seven years of waiting, planning, and preparing and now the day had finally come.

It was fucking show time.

CHAPTER 3

SEVYN

"I'm glad you called me, Sevyn," my therapist, William Kennedy, said as he sat down in his leather seat across from me. He was only a few years older than I was, handsome as sin, but unfortunately very professional. His sharp jaw line sported a light five o'clock shadow, his blonde hair styled in a sexy quiff. His navy dress shirt fit him to perfection, his black vest fitting over his broad shoulders and strong chest. If he weren't my therapist, he would've been one of the warm bodies that ended up in my bed. His ocean blue eyes studied me as he waited for me to respond.

"Thanks for being able to see me so quickly." I ran my hands up and down my arms, chills still going through me at the thought o

"Of course. As I've always told you, I'm here for you when you need me." His bright blue eyes focused on me as he crossed his leg over his knee and clicked his pen. "You sounded pretty urgent on the phone. What would you like to talk about?"

I ran my hand through my dark hair and dropped my gaze to my lap. "I learned that Hunter York was killed yesterday," I murmured as I wrung my hands.

"Was he a friend of yours?" William asked, scribbling something down on his notepad.

I shook my head. "Not really."

"So, what about his death triggered you?" he asked. A part of me felt as if it were pointless to even mention the truth. I wasn't in the mood to have people tell me that I was making up my own fears or to get another lecture about my paranoia and asking whether or not I was still on my meds. William looked up at me expectantly. "Sevyn?"

"Even though we weren't really friends, his death just brought some...thoughts to the front of my mind that I've tried to forget."

"What kind of thoughts?"

"Thoughts about...Luther," I admitted.

"I see." He scribbled something down and then looked up at me. "Care to tell me about what kind of thoughts you have about Luther?"

I stood from the leather couch and paced the room for a few moments in silence before I moved over to the window, looking down at the busy, downtown Miami street below. "Josh, Tyler, and Hunter were all guys that I went to high school with," I started.

"I remember you telling me that. I also remember you just saying you weren't friends."

"We weren't," I ground out, never taking my eyes off the window. "But they were very involved in my life during that...year things went to shit."

"I see."

I turned around to face him, leaning against the windowsill. "They were the guys that raped Luther's sister," I stated and dropped my gaze. "And every time one of them was killed, I keep having these nightmares that Luther is coming back to finish me off, too."

William gave me a small smile and put down his pen. "I know that this is probably a scary time for you, especially with this hitting so close to home. Maybe it was a coincidence that—"

I scoffed and shook my head. "I'm getting really sick of people telling me that," I muttered as I looked down at the street. Downtown was busy with life. People walked their dogs, had lunch outside with friends or family, and people rushed up and down the sidewalk to their destinations. I wished my life wasn't so complicated where I could have lunch out in public or casually stroll down the sidewalk without having to wonder if Luther would pop up at any moment to fulfill his promise of avenging his sister.

William sighed. "Trust me when I say that I hear what you're saying, Sevyn," he said.

I turned and narrowed my gaze at him. "You hear me, but like everyone else, you're gonna try to explain to me how my fears are just things I'm making up in my head. Or better yet, you'll tell me that the death of those guys have nothing to do with me."

"I don't believe it has anything to do with you," he said, his voice soft. I rolled my eyes and stomped back over to the couch, pulling my calendar out of my purse.

"When Josh was first killed, I wrote it down," I said, pointing at the date. "And then wrote down when Tyler was killed."

He looked at the calendar and raised an eyebrow. "Why's Hunter's name on here with a question mark?" he asked.

So, you see when Josh and Tyler were killed?" He nodded. "I wrote Hunter's name in case my theory I had about the other deaths were right."

"And what was that theory?"

"Josh and Tyler were killed seven days a part. Hunter was killed last night, which makes it seven days from Tyler's death."

William furrowed his brows and shook his head. "I'm not following."

"These men were killed seven years after they were acquitted for rape in which there was a video proving that they were guilty. And then on top of that, they were killed seven days apart. You're trying to tell me that this isn't something to grab my attention? I mean, hello? My name is Sevyn and I'm the catalyst of the whole fucking thing that started this bullshit!" I all but screamed.

He nodded, his gaze intense as he gazed at me. "Is this what triggered your nightmare?" he asked as he scribbled something down on his notepad.

"Yes," I said and exhaled deeply. "It just felt so…real, you know?"

"Do you want to talk about it?" he asked, his voice soft.

I moved away from him and sat back on the couch, memories of the dream flooding my mind all at once. "It was pretty weird with how it started off," I began, wrapping my arms around myself. "It started with him saying that all he wanted was an apology. We talked a little about that and for some reason, I wanted to hug him."

"I think that plays into the guilt that you feel about everything that happened back then," William said. "It's almost as if his forgiveness is what would make things better for you mentally."

I shrugged. "I guess."

"So, what happens next? Do you hug him?" William asked.

"Yeah..." I trailed, the memories coming in so fast it nearly crushed me. "But it was a trick..."

One...two...Luther's coming for you...

"What kind of trick?"

Three...four...gonna skin a whore...

I ran my hands through my hair, my palms clammy as my heart climbed. "Um...he um..."

Five...six...you're next on my list...

"Sevyn?"

Seven...eight...time to meet your fate...

"He...um...he stabbed me," I mumbled. William scribbled something down on his notepad as my mind spiral out of control. Though he spoke to me, the sound was muffled as if I was underwater. All I could hear was Luther's voice, taunting me with that fucked up song. I could still smell my blood, feel the fear and terror coursing my body as I ran from him. I could—

"Hey, hey, hey," William coaxed, his warm hand covering one of mine. I blinked to bring myself back to my current surroundings. William's warm, concerned eyes looked at me, grounding me back to our session. "Take a couple of deep breaths for me."

I followed his lead, breathing in deeply and slowly exhaling. Breathe in, breathe out.

One...two.....

I closed my eyes and forced myself to focus on breathing.

Three...four....

"Just focus on breathing, Sevyn," William reminded me, but it didn't block Luther's voice from my mind.

Five...six...

"I am...I am..." I say, forcing air into my lungs and pushing it back out.

Seven...eight...

"Are you coming back to me now?"

"Nine...ten..." I mumbled.

"There you go. Just breathe out and open your eyes," he coaxed, his voice soft and comforting.

"Now you'll die, my friend," I whispered.

"Sevyn?" William said. "What did you just say?"

I opened my eyes, tears burning my eyes as I looked into his concerned gaze. "In my dream, Luther was singing this song as he was chasing me through my home," I started, taking a shaky breath. "It's literally all I can hear in my head right now."

"Do you mind telling me the song?" he asked. I repeated the song again. A chill ran down my spine as I said the last line, a fear I couldn't explain nearly strangling me with anxiety. I watched William as he stood from his crouched position and walked back over to his chair. He scribbled a few things down on his notepad before he looked back up with me. "Have you been watching anything scary before bed or anything?"

I rolled my eyes. "And what, you're going to tell me that some horror movie is the reason I had a nightmare?"

"It was just a question, Sevyn. Sometimes all kinds of things can trigger fears and situations in our dream that we don't realize."

I ground my teeth as I stuffed the calendar back into my bag and snatched my purse from the couch. Sometimes I didn't even know why I even bothered trusting people with my inner personal thoughts. No one believed me anyway. A sick part of me almost wished that Luther would just pop up and do whatever he wanted just so all of these fuckers could feel terrible for telling me that everything I was worried about was in my head. I almost started to wonder whether or not my parents paid him to specifically douse out any Luther flames that would cause me to spiral. I wouldn't put it past them; they were so controlling over me even though I was an adult now.

"Where are you going?" William called out.

"Out of here, obviously," I snapped back.

"Just wait a minute, Sevyn," he said. I slowed my walked, but I didn't turn around. "I didn't say I didn't believe you. I just know that dreams manifest things that we tend to suppress. I'm only trying to make sure there are no outside triggers that are influencing your dreams."

"There aren't," I stated.

"Then come have a seat and let's get to the bottom of it," he said. I slowly turned around, half expecting him to have a smirk on his face, but he looked rather neutral. He gestured toward the couch and after a beat, I sighed inwardly and took a seat. "So, you believe that your dreams and the coincidences in your old classmates' deaths mean that Luther is back."

"Yes, as I've said many times in this session already," I said, my tone flat.

"Fair enough." He wrote something down and then cocked his head as he looked at me. "You know, we've been meeting for a long while and one thing you've never talked about is why you did what you did. Do you think the guilt of that is trying to rise to the surface now that your old classmates have been killed?"

I swallowed the forming lump in my throat. It wasn't something I was proud of, nor was it anything I wanted to talk about. Anytime anyone asked, I gave them generic answers that weren't really the truth. The truth? I did it over a guy, but it wasn't the guy that people thought it was.

"The why doesn't matter when it won't change anything," I finally answered. William shook his head.

"It matters when it starts manifesting into other things like nightmares, self harm, and self-destructive behavior," he said. "The mind has a way of making you wake up and listen when you try to shove things to the back of your mind."

"Well, talking about the origin of this would take its entire session by itself," I mumbled, crossing my arms over my chest.

William looked at his watch and then nodded. "Then why don't we go ahead and schedule you a follow up appointment to have this conversation?"

I shrugged. "Whatever."

He stood up and walked over to his desk, looking at an open appointment book. "How about we meet next Thursday at one?"

"If I'm still alive and Luther doesn't get me, sure," I said sarcastically as I stood up, smirking when he frowned at me. "Just kidding. I'll be here."

"That's a better response," he said as he penciled it in. "For now, I have a homework assignment for you."

I rolled my eyes "What's that, Professor Kennedy?"

"Spend some time with your friends or family. Have a night out on the town with the girls or have dinner with your family. I think it'll do you a lot of good to spend some time with other people."

"So...get drunk and party then?"

"That's...not exactly what I said, but you should go out and enjoy yourself," he said and chuckled. "I know it can be hard to enjoy yourself when you feel guilty over your friend's death, but I'm sure she wouldn't want you wasting your life punishing yourself in your condo all alone."

I nodded, unable to deny the truth. Despite everything I ever did to her, Logan would've always forgiven me. That was just who she was. It was why she was my best friend for so long. Always forgiving. Always loving. Always there. I never realized how much I actually missed her friendship until she was gone for good. It was easy to take it for granted when everything was happening because there was always that chance that we would overcome this and it would just be another bump in the road of our friendship. But she took that chance away when she committed suicide, and quite frankly, I couldn't blame her.

I wouldn't have wanted to deal with that torment either, especially not over a stupid boy.

But he wasn't just any boy, I reminded myself bitterly. I turned my attention back to William and forced myself to smile.

"I promise I'll go out," I said.

"Be sure to document it with photos or it didn't happen."

"What if I go to a massive orgy with my friends? Still want photos?"

He smirked at me. "I'd rather you not do that. Stay out of trouble, Sevyn," he said, just as his phone rang.

I left with a parting wave and pulled out my phone when I entered the hall, calling Rebecca.

"Sevyn, darling! I hope you're done freaking out," she said upon answering, which made me roll my eyes. "I almost thought I had to call your parents to tell them you were going to spiral again."

"No, Bec. And why would you call them anyway, for fuck's sake? You're supposed to be my best friend," I protested with a frown.

"Because I love you and only want you to be safe and alive. I don't know what I'd do if something were to happen to you," she said, sadness cloaking her voice.

A part of me was sad. I couldn't imagine how hard it was for my friends to watch me go through the hardest years of my life when Logan first died. There were times where I thought suicide was the best answer for me as well. From the suicide attempts, the drug abuse, and self-destructive behavior phases, my friends were my rock through it all. Even though it irritated the shit out of me sometimes, it made me feel good that they were still in my corner after all these years, long after we'd graduated high school.

I smiled. "I know, Bec, but I'm fine. I was calling because I wanted to know if you guys were free tonight? I wanna get out of the house and I haven't been out in a while."

"Oh my God, this is perfect! The girls and I were already planning to go out tonight—"

"Why didn't anyone call me then?" I asked with a frown.

"I mean anytime we asked you before, you always blew us off. And after our conversation last night, we figured you didn't want to go," she said.

"Well, I want to go out tonight. William thinks it's probably good for me anyway with everything that's been going on," I said as I stepped onto the elevator and pressed the button to the 1st floor.

"William? Is he a new boo thang?" she asked and giggled.

I smirked and rolled my eyes, stepping off the elevator when the doors opened, crashing into a hard chest. "Shit!"

"You all right?" a deep voice asked. I looked up into the eyes of an older man with fair skin and salt and pepper hair, his face clean shaven. He wore a form fitting suit, a suitcase in hand as he looked at me with concern.

I gave him a small smile. "Yeah, sorry. I guess I wasn't paying attention," I said, bowing my head as I walked past him.

"Who was that?" Rebecca asked.

"Some guy that was getting onto the elevator as I was getting off," I said, walking out of the building.

"Oh, good. I thought something happened," she said with a light sigh. "Anyway, about this William character—"

"He's not my boyfriend or any guy of interest if that's where you're leading," I said with a smirk as I walked out of the office building and into the humid air outside. "He's my new therapist."

"Is he hot at least?"

"He's my therapist, Bec. You know, I don't fuck every guy I lay my eyes on," I said, just as I passed a shirtless runner on the street. He grinned at me, looking over his shoulder at me before he continued running. "Well, at least not every guy."

She laughed. "Whatever, you liar. I'll get the details out of you once I get a few drinks into you. So, we haven't decided where we wanted to go. Anywhere in particular?"

"Why not the club down the street from my place? Then we can all get ready at my house like old times."

"Ugh, you always have the best ideas," she gushed and I nearly cringed. Even though we weren't in high school anymore, these women still hung on to my every word. It made me wonder what possessed them to do that, but I'd be stupid to ignore what their potential reasons were.

What anyone's reason was to try to be friends with me.

My family was one of the richest families in the city. Being connected to them would put the world at your fingertips. A call from my oil tycoon father could get you any job you wanted, membership into any private country clubs, and even elected into office. A call from my fashion designer mother could get you on a runway or modeling in magazines, maybe even in commercials. There were so many people who tried to befriend me or date me just to get into my parents' good graces. So many people trying to use me to get internships or climb higher up the ladder of life thanks to my parents. Maybe that was why I was such a bitch. I made people work for my friendship because I was so sick of being used and only seen as a golden ticket. With the number of people that used to try to befriend or date me back in high school, it made me wonder if their parents sent them to school with the main objective of "getting in with Sevyn." But because of who my family was, it resulted in a lot of ass kissing, even from people I called my best friends.

"Well, um, just tell me what the other girls think and call me back, okay?" I finally said.

"Yeah, for sure. Give me a few minutes, though. I have to walk Louie and I'll give the girls a ring!" she exclaimed.

"Okay. Talk soon," I said and slid into my black Corvette. I tossed my purse and phone into the passenger seat with a sigh and started up my car. While I couldn't forget my problems, the least I could do was at least drink until they didn't matter anymore.

———

"Mom? Dad?" I called out when I walked into their house. Their oversized mansion overlooked the ocean, the sounds of the crashing waves filtering through the house. Everything looked the same as it always had, white, sterile, and cold. It was fitting though, as it perfectly explained how my parents were toward me.

When I was little, I didn't spend much time with my parents. I was usually left with the nanny while my parents were out playing politics and making the Langdon name something to be respected in this city. Anytime I did see them, it was over a quiet dinner where no one would talk. They'd left me unsupervised during my teen years, not intervening until I got in trouble or did something that would shame the family name somehow. Maybe it was another reason why all that shit I did to Logan happened. Maybe I just wanted my parents' attention.

Maybe I wanted them to actually love me. For someone to love me.

"Sevyn?"

I turned to see my mother walking toward me with a small smile on her face. I will say that after I was found innocent in Logan's death, it weirdly brought my family together. We had to go through a lot of family therapy sessions, and they'd been trying to be a better support system. Things were still awkward sometimes, but I was glad they were trying, which was a lot better than what I thought they'd do considering their track record.

My mother was beautiful as usual, not looking a day over thirty thanks to all her trips to the plastic surgeon and bi-weekly Botox touch ups. Her long, dark hair cascaded down her back in soft curls, her baby doll face caked on with make-up as it usually was. Even when I was little, I couldn't remember a time my mother didn't wear makeup. The only time I saw her without makeup was in old pictures from when she and my father first started dating, and even then, she was probably still wearing concealer. She looked like the many models that strutted along South Beach, her thin body clad in a bikini and cover up. She pushed her sunglasses up into her hair and stretched her arms out as she got closer to me.

"It's such a surprise to see you! I didn't know you were coming. I would've made something for you," she said, hugging me tight.

"It's fine. I'm not going to be here long anyway," I said and looked around. "Where's Dad?"

"Business trip as usual. He left a couple of days ago," she said, just as a younger, shirtless man with swimming trunks that were low on his hips walked into the house with a bottle of beer tipped up to his lips.

I raised an eyebrow at my mom. "Um...who the hell is that?"

She looked over her shoulder and waved him off. "Michael, honey, I'll be out back in a minute," she said and waved him off. "That's Michael. He's the pool boy."

I frowned and folded my arms across my chest. "You mean your new fuck toy while Dad's gone," I replied, my voice flat.

She let out a light sigh and squeezed my shoulders. "Sevyn, honey, you know that things haven't been well with your father. We're together for the sake of the brand we created together—"

"So, our family is just a brand to you?" I scoffed and shook my head. "You know, I used to try to figure out why I'm so fucked up and all I have to do is come home to remind myself why I am the way I am." I looked around the soulless house, all the white and black furniture that made it feel more like a showroom instead of a home for a family. "Now I know why I hate coming here."

"Sevyn," she called out as I walked away from her.

I stormed back through the door, nearly shattering the glass door when I walked out of it and stomped back to my car. My mother was hot on my heels, her stilettos clicking against the driveway as she rushed behind me.

"Sevyn, would you wait a minute?" she called out.

"For what? Don't want to interrupt your cougar session," I fired back sarcastically.

"Your father and I haven't been in love for years," she admitted. "I told you that a long time ago. We're not getting a divorce, but we're not exclusive to each other either."

"So, you're just pretending then?" I asked.

She gave me a solemn nod. "We've been pretending for a very long time, Sevyn, before you'd even graduated from high school. We'd actually planned on telling you when we decided this, but then everything happened with Logan and you needed us to look like a united front."

"Well, thanks for not pretending anymore. At least I'm no longer in the dark with the rest of the public about the true status of my family unit," I said and got into my car, slamming the door behind me.

She watched me as I pulled out of the driveway and sped down the road. Now I definitely needed a night out. Aside from the Luther drama, I felt like my family and friends were the only constant thing I had in my life. Now that I knew my parents weren't even technically together, it was like half of my foundation was slipping away. After what my mom had said, I didn't even want to believe that my father was out on a business trip. Maybe he was with another woman. Maybe he'd made another family with another woman somewhere in the world. Maybe he had other children that weren't as fucked up as me.

"Sevyn, our perfect creation and the best thing to ever walk this earth," I said out loud. It was what my parents used to tell me whenever they were present in my life. But with everything that'd happened in my life, I wasn't perfect. I seemed to destroy everything and everyone I touched. If anything, I wasn't perfection.

I was destruction, bound to pull everyone down with the flames that consumed my soul. My entire existence was just the result of drunken mistakes, lack of supervision, and an "image" we had to uphold. I wasn't even surprised anymore. Nothing surprised me when it came to that sham of a family I had. If people knew what was underneath the privilege, money, and connections that came with my parents, they wouldn't want it that much.

Money and connections didn't mean shit when you couldn't buy love and affection from the people you wanted it from the most.

"Oh my God, I'm so glad we're going out tonight!" Allison said as she came into my home, lifting bottles of wine in the air. "And I brought pre-game supplies!"

I smiled. It'd been a long while since all of us had hung out all at once. Everyone was either busy with life or I was stuck inside my own head and was in no mood to be bothered. I had to admit that their lively voices and energy brightened up my place. Sarah, Crystal, Carrie, Rebecca, and Jamie all followed in behind her, all of them hugging me as they walked past me. Jamie held me a little longer behind holding me out in front of her.

"You look so good, Sevyn! It's been months since I've seen you. I'm so jealous of this tan you have going on," she gushed.

I gave her a small smile. "Hey, why live in Miami if you don't soak up the sun?" I said, though I hadn't been to a beach in months.

"So true, girl. We're gonna have to go tanning pretty soon then! I'm looking like Casper the ghost these days," she teased before she joined the others in the living room. I sighed inwardly as I closed and locked the door. Even though I did want to do something with my friends, I always hated this part of the meeting. Pretending to be fine was fucking exhausting. It was one of the reasons why I hated being around other people. It was always the same thing.

"How are you feeling?"

"How's therapy?"

"How's life?"

"What've you been up to?"

I couldn't answer truthfully. People never really wanted the truth because they couldn't handle it. If I told them I was depressed or anxious because of the recent deaths, they'd try to explain it away and make me feel as if my concerns weren't valid. If they knew I wasn't going to therapy as much as I should, the conversation would turn into another lecture. They definitely didn't want to hear that I'd hardly left my house lately and that my sun kissed tanned skin was bought at the tanning salon a few streets over. So instead, I smile and lie and pretend that I'm living my life to the fullest.

Like I always had to do.

"So, I kinda have to tell you guys something..." Carrie drawled as she smirked and twirled a strand of hair around her finger. When we all looked at her, she grinned. "So, a guy that I've been dating on and off is back in town. His friend is having a bachelor party, so they're going to be at the club tonight. And they're all fucking hot."

"Carrie, it's a girls' night. We're hanging out with each other, not with your boyfriend and his friends," Allison said and rolled her eyes.

"Seriously, you're gonna want to meet these guys," Carrie said and pulled out her phone. Her finger touched the screen for a few moments before she thrust the phone out for us to see. "That's him and his friends."

"On second thought, when are we meeting them?" Allison said, wiggling her eyebrows.

I looked at the picture. The men were sexy as hell, all of them covered in tattoos.

"Wait a second," I said, taking her phone from her. There was a guy that looked extremely familiar, but I couldn't place where I knew him from. All of his skin that was visible was covered in tattoos, his body muscular and lean. His white t-shirt and jeans he wore fit him to perfection, his beard framing a sexy pair of lips that I wouldn't mind feeling on my body tonight. But there was something about his eyes that both scared me and pulled me to him like a magnet. I knew that I knew those eyes from somewhere and it was frustrating the hell out of me that I couldn't remember who it was.

"Sevyn?" Carrie asked. I looked up to see everyone staring at me.

"Sorry," I said, passing her phone back to her. "I thought I knew one of the guys."

"Which one?" she asked, looking at the phone again. I pointed at the guy and she grinned. "Oh, that's Eric. I think he'd totally be your type since you're into those bad boys."

I gave her a small grin. "I guess."

Sarah clapped her hands. "Well, what are we waiting for? If hot guys are gonna be partying with us, shouldn't we be getting ready?"

Allison poured us all a glass of wine before they all giggled their way to my master bathroom. And while I was excited about tonight, there was an overwhelming sense of dread that something was on the horizon.

"Just relax and enjoy yourself, Sevyn. You'll be out with friends, so you'll be fine," I murmured to myself before joining my friends.

With everything that'd been happening lately, I could only pray that I was right.

CHAPTER 4

LUTHER

I fucking hated clubs but loved the attention I got.

Club Toxic was packed despite it being a weeknight. Techno music pumped through speakers around the room, the base so deep that I could literally feel it in my bones. The air was hazy with smoke, the smell of cigarettes, cigars, marijuana and sweat all clashing together. The smell alone almost made my stomach turn. The club owner was right in calling it Toxic; the air in this place alone was deadly.

The older I got, the more I hated large crowds. It was too loud; and considering that my mind was already loud enough with its own shit going on in there, I didn't need anything else adding to it. It was no surprise when the single women all flocked over to me and my guys, batting their unnaturally long eye lashes at us and biting their bottom lip when they'd say hello. They paraded around us, dressed in skimpy outfits that gave me thoughts about whether or not I wanted to pull one into the bathroom to show them a good time. But unfortunately for them, I wasn't here to mingle or find a one-night stand. I was here for a specific mission and when I looked toward the entrance of Club Toxic, that mission had now just started.

The party goers were a combination of young adults from all walks of life. Many dancing couples either wore all black or a colorful ensemble; there was no in-between. My guys and I scoped the place before actually coming, blending in with our all black attire. My dark denim jeans and black t-shirt was snugly fit over my muscular form, a pair of black Converse on my feet. We all walked through to the back of the club in the VIP area, entering the roped off area for Curtis' "bachelor" party.

"Got everything in order?" Jake asked as he flopped down on the leather couch that practically wrapped around the VIP room.

"Yep," I said as I sat on the far end. "Everybody remember the plan?"

"Yep, but we should probably go through it again for shits and giggles," Paul suggested. I shrugged, so he continued. "Tonight, I'm going by Zach."

"Tonight, I'm Justin," Vincent said. "My mom almost named me Justin, you know."

"Carrie knows me as Mark, so I'm sticking with that," Ryan said as he tapped away on his phone.

Paul looked at him with a raised brow. "Wait, you've been

fucking her for how long and you've been lying about your name the whole time?" he asked.

He shrugged. "What? I'm only dating her to help Luther, so she doesn't need my real name. Besides, I told you the bitch was clingy and clingy women are dangerous. Next thing you'd know, she'd be trying to add me on social media or finding out where I work and shit. So, now she can spend her time searching for Mark Wright on the internet that look like me instead of finding me."

We all chuckled at the admission before getting back on track. Curtis cleared his throat as he sat on the couch.

"Well, I'm going by Phil tonight," he said.

"And I'm Ash," Tony stated proudly.

"Like the Pokémon boy?" Jake snorted.

"Oh, shut up, douchebag," Tony fired back.

"Hey Tony, I dare you to pretend to catch one of the girls in a pokéball," Ryan said and snorted.

I clapped my hands together and frowned. "You guys wanted me to trust you to help me carry this plan out," I reminded them. "Stay focused on what's at hand and be serious. One fuck up and it's over for all of us." They all nodded, all playful tones from a few moments ago now gone. "Anyway, I'm going by Eric tonight. Whenever Carrie texts Ryan to let him know they're here, he'll bring them all here. Everyone know what they're supposed to do?"

"Each of us immediately grab a girl and leave Sevyn no choice but to go to you," Vincent answered.

"Everyone has their pills?" I asked, to which they all nodded.

Ryan's phone screen lit up and he looked up at us. "I guess it's showtime. They're here," he said. My heart raced in my chest as I grabbed a cigar from the table in the middle of the room and moved to the far end of the couch until I was in the dark corner. I needed a few moments to get into my "mask" that most people thought was my true self because of my appearance. When people saw a tall, muscular guy with a beard and covered in tattoos, their first thoughts were that I was either a biker or some kind of bad boy. It definitely made it to where I didn't have to worry about sleeping alone at night; as I always tended to attract all kinds of women into my bed. If people knew the true me, they'd wish the bad boy image was my true persona. In actuality, I was deranged, broken, and really got off on causing people pain.

I was the boogey man the news now warned the citizens of Miami about.

"Hi, fellas!" a female voice said as she entered the VIP area. Ryan wrapped an arm around the woman, signaling to everyone that she was Carrie.

"This is Carrie, everyone," he reiterated. She smiled big and waved at us before looking up at Ryan like a love-sick puppy. I fought the urge to chuckle. I could see what he meant when he said she was clingy.

The other guys moved just as plan to isolate the other girls, leaving Sevyn standing their awkwardly. And even though I hated her and was tingling at the thought of watching her die, I couldn't deny the fact that she was fucking sexy.

She wore a blood red bodycon dress that molded itself to her curvy frame, her makeup looking as if it was done by a professional, her maroon lipstick making my cock stir in my jeans at the thought of seeing that color on my skin later when I rammed my cock down her throat. Six-inch stilettos were on her manicured feet, her long, lean legs on full display. She'd always been beautiful; she knew that, too. She and I had a thing one summer when I was home on break from college and there was no part of her that I hadn't already explored. But it would be pure bliss to cause her pain, to make her scream, to make her beg for her life and the more I thought about it, the harder it was to be still.

I lit the cigar and took a pull from it, watching as Sevyn looked over at me. She slowly walked over and sat a couple of inches away from me despite all the other empty space. Her floral perfume cut through the smell of the cigar, reminding me of old times. Back when things were good. Fun. When Logan was still alive. I ground my teeth and forced myself to stay in character, continuing to ignore her as I smoked. And if Sevyn was the same as I remembered her, she'd only sit there for so long without saying anything, as she hated to be ignored.

"You're Eric, right?" she said over the music. I exhaled, smoke billowing from my nose and mouth as I nodded.

"You got a name?" I asked.

"Sevyn."

I raised an eyebrow in faux confusion. "Sevyn? Like the number?"

She gave me a sheepish smile that was almost cute if I didn't want to already cut her throat where she sat. "Yeah. It means completion and perfection," she explained.

"I don't remember asking what it meant," I said and put the cigar back in my mouth. She narrowed her eyes at me and frowned.

"Are you always an asshole?"

"Do you always think everything is about you?"

"My family runs this town. I'll say that everything is about me."

"Your family?" I blew out the smoke and slightly turned on the couch, draping my arm across the back of it and facing her. "Tell me, Ms. Important Woman, who is this important family of yours?"

"I have an oil tycoon father and a fashion designer mother. The Langdons are important in Miami. You'd know that unless you're not from here," she said, folding her arms across her ample chest. My eyes drifted to the tops of her breasts and the peek of lace that showed from her bra.

"Well, baby doll, I'm not from here, so your family don't mean shit to me," I said and smiled, taking a puff of my cigar and blowing the smoke in her face. When the smoke disperse, I was surprised to see a hint of a smile on her lips as she looked at me.

"Then I guess you're worth my time," she finally mused.

I chuckled and shook my head. "You're awfully cocky to think you're worth mine."

"Am I not?" she said with a smirk.

I shrugged. "I don't know. Depends on what you're into."

"I'm into many things," she said, crossing her legs. It didn't go unnoticed how her dress slid up and exposed the soft skin of her thighs, taunting me.

Two waitresses in leather body suits walked in with a tray of drinks each, one woman passing drinks to the guys and the other woman passing drinks to the women, just as planned. I grabbed a drink from the woman and took a gulp of it. I welcomed the uncomfortable burn as it warmed my body before turning my attention back to Sevyn.

"It's easy to say that until you meet someone who'll push every boundary you have," I said. She took a sip of her spiked drink, something akin to curiosity and budding lust harboring in her eyes. She tossed her long hair over her shoulder before she turned a little on the couch to face me. "You'll learn that I'm not like most women," she said. I looked over to her airhead friends already so infatuated with my guys on the other side of the room. I watched for a few moments as they all flirted with my friends, giving them small kisses, rubbing their arms or legs, and giggling like schoolgirls who'd never gotten attention from a man before. At least, all of them acted like that except one of them. The woman with purple hair, whom I remembered to be Rebecca, didn't seem all that interested in Paul. Though she'd give him a small smile and allowed him to place kisses on her neck, her eyes were trained on Sevyn. There was almost a look of jealousy in her eyes as she saw the two of us together, which made me wonder if she was jealous that Sevyn ended up with me instead of her or if she had a thing for her best friend. I nodded toward them.

"Why are you friends with women like that if you're so 'different?'" I asked, taking another swallow of my drink.

She looked over her shoulder at them and shrugged. "We've been friends for years; a couple of us since elementary school," she said, which I already knew.

"Are you friends with them because they kiss your ass?" I mused.

She smirked. "Is that a crime?"

"I mean it's not a crime to be basic, but if that's what you prefer to be, that's your business," I said and shrugged. Gesturing toward Rebecca, I added, "I think your girlfriend is mad that you're over here talking to me. Might want to go show her some attention."

"Girlfriend?" Sevyn looked over her shoulder and shook her head. "Oh, no. That's Rebecca. She's been my best friend for the longest."

"I think she has a thing for you."

"Oh, shut up. No, she doesn't," she said and looked over her shoulder again. Rebecca gave her a small smile and wave, her eyes lighting up when Sevyn's attention was on her. The moment Sevyn turned away, the light in Rebecca's eyes dimmed again, her face settling back into the uninterested expression she sported.

"You're either in denial, stupid, or both," I said and finished off the rest of my drink, signaling the waitress for another one.

"Why the hell would you think that? You don't even know her."

"I can read people." I glanced back over to Rebecca to see her still watching us. "She's very protective of you, and seems like the type that's okay when you're around other women because she knows you're not into women. But she doesn't like when you're around men because she knows you'll sleep with them, the one thing that she knows will never happen between the two of you."

"I think you're just pulling shit out of your ass," she said and waved me off before taking another small sip of her drink. "Try reading me."

I pretended to regard her for a moment, stroking my beard a bit. "Hmm...even though you like to tell others how important you are, you're really riddled with guilt and depression over something you did either recently or years ago. You prefer to stay alone, have trust issues, and probably live in fear and paranoia for whatever reason," I said and took a puff of my cigar. Her skin paled and her smirk faltered as she looked at me, swallowing hard. "Was I close enough?"

"Not really," she lied, though she already knew that I knew she was lying.

"Sometimes the truth freaks people out," I said and shrugged. "I told you I'm good at reading people."

"Well, if you're not from here, where are you from?" she asked, suddenly changing the subject.

"California."

"Los Angeles?"

"No?"

"Then where?"

"Does it matter? After tonight, you probably won't see me again, so let's not ask irrelevant questions that we won't remember the answers to tomorrow," I said and winked at her. The expression on her face changed in an instant but she quickly recovered and forced a smile.

"Right," she said, sipping her drink and looking around. My

phone buzzed in my pocket. I slipped it out and read the text preview that displayed Paul's message on the screen.

Paul: We gotta start slipping the drug to give it time to kick in. The hack timer on my computer goes out in two hours.

I looked up and met his gaze across the room, giving him a subtle nod before turning my attention back to Sevyn. Rebecca still had her eyes trained on us and it almost made me nervous. I wasn't sure if she recognized me or not but considering that she wasn't hysterical or that she hadn't come over here and attempted to pull Sevyn away, I could assume that she still didn't know. None of these morons knew that they trapped in the web of impending death, the spider of vengeance creeping closer and closer to them as this night when on.

Reaching into my pocket, I pulled out a small tin and popped the top. There was only one actual breath mint in the tin, the rest of them being ecstasy. I could see Sevyn watching me in my peripheral as I slipped the breath mint onto my tongue immediately pushed it to the inside of my cheek to crush between my teeth.

"Taking a trip?" she finally asked.

I raised an eyebrow at her. "Maybe. Wanna be a passenger?"

"What is it?"

"X." I slid my gaze over her. "Ms. Important is into drugs, too? Gotta admit you're surprising me," I said and chuckled.

She shrugged. "I've done a few things here and there. You shouldn't let appearances fool you."

I scoffed. "Trust me, I'm not fooled. I'm surprised you have the balls to admit it," I said. "Still didn't answer my question."

"Which was?"

"Do you wanna be a passenger?" I asked. Her brown eyes were intense as she stared at me, different emotions swirling in her gaze. After a moment, I smiled and shook my head. "It's all good. The ride isn't meant for everyone."

"I never said no," she countered.

"And you never said yes," I reminded her. Though soon, it wouldn't matter what she said. Soon, I'd have her tied up, bloody, and in the ground where she belonged seven years ago. I fought the urge to clench my hands into fists, impatient to get to the next phase of the plan. But I knew I had to be careful. I was sure Sevyn was being cautious and was probably paranoid with the murders of Josh, Tyler, and Hunter.

"Mmm...I'll think about it," she finally said. I shrugged and took another pull from my cigar and blew out a breath, putting the cigar out. My phone vibrated again, another message from Paul.

Paul: We've given the girls the X and most have finished their drinks. What's your progress with Sevyn? Rebecca said that Sevyn doesn't do drugs anymore and has been sober for a few years now.

I ground my teeth. If that was the case, getting Sevyn high enough to convince her to walk out of here with me would be hard. I now had to switch gears in a way that I had no intentions of when I walked into this fucking place. Having any kind of enjoyable sexual contact with this bitch was the last thing I wanted, but if I wanted to convince her to take the drug, I had to put all my cards out on the table.

I ran a finger down the exposed skin of her arm, chuckling when she jumped. "You single?" I asked.

"Does it matter?"

"Not really. I was only making conversation. I'd fuck you whether you had a boyfriend or not," I said and smirked, though I cringed on the inside.

She grinned. "You're awfully cocky. What the hell makes you think you're fucking me at all?"

I had to stop myself from telling her that I'd already fucked her before, and reminding her about how she used to tell me that I ruined her for any other man. How I was the only man she'd come for. How I owned her.

How I planned to destroy her.

Instead, I just shrugged and grinned. "Call it intuition," I said. She gave me a strange look, her eyes searching my face as if she were still trying to place me somewhere in her memory bank. "What?"

"You just look really familiar. I feel like I've seen you somewhere," she said with a slight frown.

I shook my head and leaned back against the couch. "Unless you've been to San Francisco lately, I doubt you've seen me."

The music changed and one of the girls stood to her feet and began dancing around the room, the drug obviously taking effect.

"I feel sooooo good," she said and giggled. Sevyn looked over at her and shook her head.

"This is going to be a long night," she muttered.

"Why long? We're all having fun, right?"

"If I knew we were crashing a bachelor party, doing drugs, and practically having sex on the couch in front of men we don't know, I could've stayed home."

"Are you fresh out of rehab or something?" I asked. She shook her head.

"No. It was a few years ago when I did something. I've been trying to stay away from it."

"Your friends aren't," I said, pointing at them. All of them were almost drooling on themselves from both the liquid ecstasy in their drinks and the pill they'd taken. Sevyn was still nursing her same drink, unlike the other women who'd had at least two at this point. "Anyway, do you dance?"

"A little."

"So, dance for me," I commanded, grabbing the cigar again and relighting it.

She frowned at me. "Do I look like a stripper to you?" she asked, her tone flat.

"I said to dance; not strip. But if you want to get naked for me, I wouldn't mind that either," I said and grinned. "Or are you too scared to dance, too? Never met an important woman who doesn't like to be watched."

From what I remembered about her growing up, she was always competitive. I'd hear her talking to Logan in ways that made it seem as if she was competing with my sister. She'd get snarky if she thought my sister looked better than her in something or would be condescending if someone preferred Logan over her, and other petty shit like that. The one thing she didn't like was backing down from a challenge. And just as I expected, she downed the rest of her laced drink for liquid courage just as a slower, sexy song began to play and stood, taking a few steps until she was in front of me.

I bit my lip as I looked up at her, exhaling smoke into the air. "You're so fucking sexy," I said, and I wasn't lying. The woman was a sight to behold and if things were different....

I ground my teeth. Now wasn't the fucking time to go down memory lane. Things weren't different. Logan was still dead. Sevyn and the rest of the bitches in this room was the reason for that and trapping them was the whole point of being here. I replaced my budding lust with the bubbling anger that dwelled just below the surface, watching her as she slowly moved her hips, her eyes never leaving mine.

"That's a great idea, Sevyn!" one of her friends called out. "We should dance for the guys to thank them for inviting us."

I cocked my head as I exhaled a cloud of smoke. "And you associate yourself with airheads that can't form a single thought on their own?" I asked.

She smirked and shrugged. "They treat me as if I'm their god," she said, making my jaw twitch in irritation.

"Is that what you like? To be treated like a god?" I asked.

"Maybe," was the only thing she said. I chuckled. She'd be treated like a god; it just wouldn't be the god she wanted.

As Sevyn continued to move, her skin became flush. The liquid X was at least starting to work, making her more susceptible to getting the pill to seal the deal. She strutted toward me, sitting on my lap to grind against me. Her perfume and body heat awakened my senses, her movements bound to make me hard.

"For someone convinced that I'm not going to fuck them tonight, your body is telling another story," I murmured in her ear before putting a soft kiss on her neck.

"I don't remember saying you wouldn't; I said what made you think you were?" she said, her head lolling from side to side as her eyes closed.

"Because I always get what I want," I told her. Reaching into my pocket, I pulled the small tin of pills back out and plucked one out, putting it on my tongue. "Turn around."

As soon she turned her face to me, I firmly grabbed the back of her neck and kissed her, transferring the pill into her mouth. She only whimpered in response, her earlier hesitation and worry slipping out the window with every passing second. I kissed her long enough until I was confident that she'd either swallowed the pill or it dissolved a good bit in her mouth. When I finally pulled back, she looked at me in a daze.

"It's been a long time since I've been kissed like that," she murmured.

I grinned. "Don't worry, pretty girl. In a few minutes, the fun will really start," I promised and grabbed my phone to send a text to our group chat.

Luther: Go time in 20. Everyone ready?

I glanced their way, watching as they glanced at their phones and nodded without even looking back up. Even if they hadn't responded, it was obvious that their girls were already too far gone, even Rebecca, her attention solely on Paul instead of on Sevyn and me. I bit back a growl as Sevyn continue to grind on my lap to the beat of the music, my cock growing in my jeans. She pushed herself up to her feet, stumbling a bit before she turned around and leaned over to whisper in my ear.

"Come to the bathroom with me," she said and grabbed my hand as well as her purse from the couch. I stood and wrapped an arm around her waist, the guys looking up at me in confusion when I headed for the door.

"Bathroom," I said and winked, and followed Sevyn out the room. She stumbled as she led me to the bathrooms in the back of the club, giggling when she nearly fell on her face when she pushed the bathroom door open.

"I think you're riding the X train too hard, pretty girl," I taunted.

She looked up at me with hooded lids and smiled. "I'm starting to feel good so that's all that matters." Her hands moved down my chest and settled on my belt. "Now I want something else that feels good. Do you have a rubber?"

I walked her back into a stall and locked the door behind us, letting her undo my belt. I raised her tight dress over her hips, palming her bare ass as she freed my hard cock, stroking it in her soft hand.

"Sluts that get fucked in the bathroom don't have permission to come," I growled as I grabbed a fistful of her hair. "Get down on your knees like a good slut."

She bit her lip and let go of my cock, slowly dropping to her knees in front of me. *An STD or pregnancy is the last thing you should be worried about when I have something so much worse planned for you,* I thought as I tightened one hand in her hair.

"Is your mouth broken?" I asked when she only stared at my erection. "Open wide, my pretty little slut."

She put the head of my cock into her mouth and attempted to work the rest of it in, but I didn't give her the chance. Grabbing her head, I thrust into her mouth, her body tensing up as her gag reflex engaged. But I didn't care. I pumped into her mouth, fucking her throat with long strokes as chills of pleasure ran along my nerve endings. She whimpered around my size, slapping my thighs to probably signal that she needed to breathe, but not yet. She needed to suffer a bit, panic a bit, just as a little warning for the nightmare that was coming next that she wouldn't be able to escape. With each pump, I gave her another inch of cock until her nose practically rested against my pelvis.

"Fuck," I groaned when I hit the soft tissue of her throat. She whimpered again, trying to untangle my hands from her luscious hair, but she was stuck, at my mercy as I used her face like a living fleshlight. Tears spilled from her eyes and drool dripped from her mouth as I continued to torment her. I'd pull back long enough for her to inhale a breath through her nose before I pounded her throat again, tightly pulling on her hair as she helplessly kneeled before me.

"I bet you like being used like a slut, huh?" I murmured, looking down at her. Her answered was muffled around my cock so I pulled out of her mouth. "What was that?"

"Yes," she panted, meeting my gaze with wet eyes.

"Yes, what?"

"I like being used like a slut," she repeated.

I put my cock back into her mouth and fucked her face without abandon. "I'm going to come all over that sexy face of yours," I groaned. She whimpered and looked up at me with teary eyes right before I pulled back out and jerked my cock over her face. Rope after rope of cum covered her gorgeous features, the sight of it pissing me off. Here was Sevyn Langdon, Miami's golden girl being a slut on her knees in the stall of a dirty bathroom. The same kind of slut her lawyer tried to paint my sister out to be. The kind of slut her and her friends tried to paint her out to be. Yet, it was Sevyn with cum on her face, her lips, and in her mouth, still on her knees and looking up at me as if to beg me for more.

I sighed inwardly as my phone vibrated in my pocket, no doubt another text from one of the guys. Stuffing myself back into my jeans, I grabbed Sevyn by the throat and forced her to her feet.

"You're going to come back to my hotel room where I'm gonna fuck you until you can barely walk tomorrow. Understand?" I asked, my voice low.

"Yes," she whispered.

I let go of her and nodded toward the door. "Go clean yourself up. Not ready for the world to know how much of a whore my gorgeous girl is for me," I murmured.

Something strange flashed in her eyes, something probably akin to excitement. It was hard to tell if it was genuine or just the drugs really kicking in, but now wasn't the time to dwell on it. When she walked out of the stall, I buttoned my jeans and fixed my belt, pulling out my phone to see a text in the group text.

Paul: About to head out. Girls are starting to look suspiciously drugged. Gotta get out of here.

Luther: On it. Let's go.

I walked out of the stall to find Sevyn at the sink wiping off all traces of me from her face. Seeing my reflection in the mirror, she tossed the paper towel away and looked back at me.

"Ready to go, pretty girl?" I asked with a grin. She returned it and nodded, stumbling over to me and wrapping her arm into mine.

"I'm definitely ready to be fucked within an inch of my life like you promised," she said, her words coming out a bit slurred. "I don't feel so good though."

"Let's get you out of here then," I said, wrapping an arm around her. Just as we walked out of the bathroom, the guys were leading the girls our way to head toward the back exit. I could see why. A couple of them could barely stand on their own. There was no way we'd be able to get them out of the club through the front entrance without someone stopping us and suggesting to call an ambulance or the police if they realized they'd been drugged. We all led the girls out the back as best as we could to blend into the busy nightlife streets until we reached the parking garage, each of us going to our respective car.

"What hotel are you in?" Sevyn asked as she closed her eyes, her head lolling from side to side.

"You'll see, pretty girl," I said and started the Jeep.

"Well, wake me when we get there," she mumbled before her head rolled off to the side. Grabbing a napkin from my sun visor, I opened her purse and grabbed her phone with the napkin, tossing it out the window before driving out of the parking garage.

Sevyn Langdon was mine now.

CHAPTER 5

SEVYN

Pain.

It was the first thing that registered in my mind when I awoke. The room was still dark, either from blacked out curtains or no windows. *What kind of hotel doesn't have windows?* I mused, closing my eyes as my pounding headache made itself known. Last night was wild. When we arrived at the club, my only mission was to find someone to take back to a nearby hotel to show them a good time and then go back to living my regular life. But then Eric—with his cocky, cool guy attitude—came and blew that plan out of the water.

Despite being in the corner of the room away from the guys, he was the first person I saw when I entered. His dark eyes emerged from the cloud of smoke in front of his face, hinting at the dangers lurking within him. The other men in the room immediately latched onto my friends, and I had to say that it was a bit of a blow to my ego. There was never a time that I was picked second, never mind dead last. Eric never moved though. He only sat and continued looking at me expectantly, as if making it known that my status in this town meant nothing and that I was just a nobody not worth being fetched. And in some kind of fucked up way?

That kind of arrogance turned me on.

So many alarms went off in my mind as I interacted with him, even more so when I saw him pop an ecstasy pill in front of me. I hadn't done drugs in years, even purposely staying away from clubs to avoid them, but there was something about those eyes of his that made me want to trust him even though the entire package of him urged me to run away. He seemed so familiar but yet still a stranger that it frustrated me. I knew those eyes, but I didn't know that body or those tattoos or the rough nature he displayed in the bathroom. Part of my mind rang the "Luther Alert" bells, but it couldn't be him. Luther wasn't covered in tattoos. He wasn't stacked with muscle, and he damn sure never fucked my throat with such aggression the way Eric did last night. I swallowed, wincing a bit as the soreness from last night's event settled in. Either way, had Eric really been Luther, he would've just killed me in the bathroom, not shove his cock down my throat.

My mouth was dry, and my head pounded now that the drugs had worn off. I attempted to sit up and it was only then that I realized

I was restrained.

"What the fuck?" I murmured out loud, jerking my arms and legs. When my mind started to catch up to my growing panic, I used my senses to fill in the rest of the blanks. I tried to move my legs, but my feet were bound together with what felt like thick, heavy rope and secured to the hard object I was lying on. My arms were stretched out in a T, also tied down with the coarse rope. I forced myself to relax. *Maybe things took a wild turn last night,* I thought, trying to rationalize the situation. *Maybe he doesn't know I'm awake yet.*

"Hello?" I called out, my heart racing. My throat felt raw, my voice hoarse as I spoke into what sounded like an empty room. My voice slightly echoed in the room I was in, which set my teeth on edge. "Eric?"

A thin strip of light appeared under the door as heavy footsteps sounded. This definitely wasn't a hotel. Had we even gone to the hotel? Was I taken from there? I tried to forced myself to remember what happened after leaving the club, but the last memory I had was getting into his car. Eric couldn't have gotten me to his house if he wasn't from here.

Because he probably lied, my inner voice said. My hairs stood on end as the footsteps grew closer. What the fuck had I done? I never should've let my friends convince me into hanging with a group of men I didn't know. I shouldn't have let Eric give me that pill no matter what my friends were doing. We didn't know if those guys were killers or sex traffickers and we all blindly followed. Panic hit me square in the chest. *My friends.* I swallowed all the saliva I could muster in my dry mouth and tried to call out again.

"Hello? Please let me out!" I tried again, but my voice was no louder than it was before. Thankfully, the footsteps stopped in front of the door before a heavy lock clicked and the door swung open. I squinted against the light flooding in from the hall, rapidly blinking to try to adjust. My head continued to pound, even when Eric's form stood in the doorway and blocked most of the light from my face.

"You're awake," he said as he leaned against the doorframe. Though he stood close to where I'd assume a light switch was, he didn't bother turning on any lights in the room. "How's your head?"

"It hurts," I said and winced. "I need some water. And I need to get off of whatever this is so I can get my phone and call my friends. I have to make sure they all got home okay."

He shook his head. "No need to call. They're here, too. We were just waiting for you to wake-up."

Despite his words, he still hadn't moved to either turn on a light or untie me. He only leaned against the doorframe, allowing more light to come in. I swallowed hard as my heart rate quickened. "Well? Are you going to untie me or stand there staring at me?" I looked around me now that the hall light lit up the room. Thick brown rope was around my wrists, confining me to what looked like blocks of wood. The room was empty just as I suspected it was, the wall of it made of concrete.

This sounds like the beginning of a horror movie, I thought to myself, just as Eric pushed off the wall and walked over to me. But instead of moving over to the ropes, he came over and stopped at my head, looking down at me. "The rope cutters are in another room, so I'll have to take you there on this cross," he simply said and grunted when he hoisted me off the floor. I gasped at the slight incline as I slid down the cross a bit, the pain in my wrists increasing as gravity worked against me.

"What the fuck? A cross?!" Fear overwhelmed me as he dragged it across the floor. "Why the fuck am I on a cross?" I was angry that my voice was nothing but a dry, pathetic croak. What the fuck did he want with me? Where were my friends really at? "Why are you doing this?"

He chuckled and continued pulling me along, masked men waiting outside the hall. Eric briefly looked down at me. "All I did was fuck your throat last night. I haven't truly done anything to you yet."

"Where are we?" I jerked at the ropes, which only made my wrists burn more. "This isn't a fucking hotel!"

"No shit, Sherlock," he said, frowning as I jerked against the ropes some more. "I wouldn't do that if I were you."

The other six masked men came toward me, each of them picking up a part of the cross and lifting. I was so close to the low ceiling that I could literally feel the heat from the uncovered light bulbs. I wasn't sure if these were the men from last night or a new set of them, but I wasn't liking where this was going at all. All the rationalization in the world wouldn't stop the impending dread that quickly filled me.

"Where are you taking me? Get me off this cross and take me home!" I snapped, my anxiety rising as we continued down the hallway of what looked like a basement. "I hope you know you won't get away with what you're doing. My parents can track me—"

"Through what? Your phone?" He tsked. "Your phone that's now in the parking garage near the club? Doesn't seem like much help to you now."

Terror rolled through me. Now I didn't know what to think or believe. Was it really Luther? I squeezed my eyes shut. Eric's beard made it hard to tell and his tattoos of evil images, flames, and skulls didn't seem to fit the Luther I remembered and dated.

"Your parents—or anyone else for that matter—are the least of my worries right now," he concluded.

This couldn't be happening. This had to be another dream and soon I'd probably wake up on my couch or haphazardly on my bed after finally getting home last night. *This is a dream just like last time*, I chanted to myself as the men continued walking. The incline shifted and the bounces in their movement hinted that we were going up stairs. *It's just a dream. It's just a dream. It's just a dream.*

Only it wasn't.

When another door opened, I could hear multiple people sobbing and pleading. The natural light from the windows we passed sent a pang of searing pain through my head, forcing me to squeeze my eyes closed.

"Sevyn!" someone screamed. *Allison.*

"What the fuck is happening?" Rebecca wailed. I looked over to my right to see my friends all bound in what looked like steel chairs, their wrists and ankles secured to the arms and legs of the chair with steel cuffs welded onto it. They were all still dressed in their clothes from the club. I looked down at myself to see that my dress from last night was replaced with a white strip of cloth tied around me as a makeshift strapless bra and white cloth tied around my hips, almost like a bikini bottom cover-up that still fully exposed my left thigh.

I squeezed my eyes shut. This couldn't be real. *This is just a dream. This is just a dream. I'll wake up soon and all of this with just have been a dream.* But the scene didn't change when I opened my eyes. No matter how many times I opened and closed my eyes, I was still on this cross. My friends were still crying. And I was still fucking terrified.

The men finally came to a stop and put the cross on the ground. Eric hovered over me, tears threatening to fill my eyes as I looked up at him. A slow smile crept across his lips as one of the men passed him what looked like a crown of thorns. He leaned down and put it on my head, pressing down until a couple beads of blood rolled down my face. I cried out in pain, jerking against the ropes. I could barely even hear myself as I cried, my voice going in and out.

"Why are you doing this, Eric?" I asked him as he moved away from me and gestured to the other men.

"You'll see," he said. I cried out in pain when they put the cross in an upright position, gravity pulling me down slightly and causing the ropes to dig into my skin. My head hurt, even more so with this fucking crown on my head. My arms hurt and I could barely feel my feet. My position had me at the head of my friend as they formed a half circle in front of me. They all looked up at me, makeup and tears running down their faces

"Sevyn, what's happening?" Sarah asked as the men left my side,

Eric coming to stand in front of me.

"You remember me from last night, right?" he asked.

I glared at him, a single tear rolling down my cheek. "Of course I remember you, you fucking asshole. What do you think you're doing?!"

"As I said, you'll see." He cocked his head and grinned. "But do you *really* remember me, Sevyn?"

"Didn't I just say I did?" I snapped.

He shook his head and folded his arms across his broad chest. "You said you remembered me last night, not that you really remembered me." He only chuckled when I didn't respond, walking away with the other men and leaving the room.

"What the fuck is going on?" Crystal asked, turning her head from side to side to take in her surroundings. "Where the hell are we?"

"I don't remember anything after leaving the club," Carrie said, her eyes wide with fear.

Rebecca glared at her. "It's your fault we're in this shit in the first place, you bitch!"

"Bec, stop," Jamie whined.

"No, it's true. Her boyfriend or whoever the hell he is drugged us and nowhere we don't know where the hell we are or who these men really are."

"What's the last thing everyone remembers?" I asked, trying to stop their bickering. Now wasn't the time to be against each other. We were all in the same boat and rocking it wasn't productive to anything that would get us out of this situation. "I only remember leaving the club and getting in the car with...."

No sooner than I was about to say Eric, I finally remembered why his eyes were so familiar. I'd once spent an entire summer looking into them, planning a future with them. How could I have been so stupid to not have recognized Luther? He probably counted on the fact that I hadn't seen him in years. The last time I saw him was in court and he'd still looked as he did when he was a senior in high school even though he was a freshman in college. When I was looking out for him anytime I was out in public, I only had that image in my head, never taking into account any changes he could've made over the years.

Allison spoke up. "I don't even remember leaving the club. I just—"

"It's Luther," I breathed. Everyone went silent, Rebecca glaring at me.

"That's not funny, Sevyn," she snapped. "Now isn't a time for one of your psychotic breakdowns."

"Psychotic breakdown?" I shrieked, my voice cracking but at least a little louder than it had been before. "He was literally in front of you and you still think he no longer exists. I swear, I almost hope it's him so you can feel like a fucking idiot for not believing me when I told you he was back in the first place."

"Instead of us fighting with each other, we need to figure out how to get the hell out of here," Jamie said and sniffled. "Whoever it is, whether it's Luther or someone else, I don't think they have us restrained just for fun."

"What if it's whoever went after Josh, Tyler, and Hunter?"

Crystal said.

"You mean Luther?" I asked, my tone flat.

"So, you do remember me, pretty girl," he said as he entered the room again, smiling. He held an electric shaver in his hand, his beard covered in shaving cream. "I almost thought I had to shave off my beard to trigger your memories, but since I already have it prepped, may as well get rid of it. Not really my style to begin with."

I ground my teeth as I watched him shave his face. He kept his eyes trained on me the whole time, and as more and more of the face I remembered revealed itself, I knew that my worst nightmares were coming true. Luther Evans was back, and he was back for the justice he didn't get seven years ago. As I looked at my friends' current predicament as well as my own, I knew there was a 99% chance that none of us were leaving this place alive.

He pulled a towel from his back pocket when he finished, wiping away the excess shaving cream from his face. He'd definitely matured over the years. His beard had hidden the sharpened jawline he'd developed, which was clenched as he stared at me with hard eyes. "It's been a while, hasn't it?" he finally asked.

There was no point in pleading or begging. I already knew what this was about and why we were here. It was what I'd dreaded for seven years, even more so when the deaths of the guys showed up on the news. For years, people told I had nothing to worry about it. But they had no idea that Luther had been planning, plotting, and preparing for this moment for the last seven years. Money may have been able to keep me out of jail, but it didn't protect me from him, especially when I willingly walked into his trap in the first place.

"If your issue is with what I've done, then just deal with me," I said, my voice shaky. "They don't have anything to do with—"

"Wrong!" he interrupted, his booming voice causing me to flinch. "Your friends practically dangle from your clit and will do whatever you ask them to. They blindly followed you and participated in everything you told them to, so they're just as guilty as you are."

He turned to face my friends, his gaze focusing on Rebecca. Her breath hitched as he stalked toward her, recognition settling on her face as she swallowed hard. We all watched as Luther bent down until he was eye level with her. "I heard you didn't think I was real anymore," he murmured and smiled.

Without warning, his hand reached out and grabbed her throat, squeezing hard. Fear and shock robbed me of my voice as my friends screamed and begged him to stop. Rebecca gagged and tried to shake herself out of his grasp, her body jerking in her chair.

"Luther, stop!" I finally screamed. After a few moments, he finally let her go. She gasped for air, sobbing and coughing as she tried to catch her breath.

Luther roughly grabbed her chin and forced her teary eyes to look up at him. "I bet I exist now, huh?" he taunted before he let her go. He then turned his attention to the rest of my friends. "I'm sure it's no surprise for why all you sluts are here right now. You got away with your involvement in my sister's death—"

"She committed suicide on her own, you lunatic!" Carrie exclaimed. "We weren't the ones who killed her."

Luther frowned at her. "I don't think I asked you to say shit," he growled. "Do I need to find a way for you to shut the fuck up?" Carrie looked at his hands, which had balled up into fists and shook her head. "That's what I fucking thought."

"Luther, we're sorry about what happened to Logan," I said. "But we—"

"Sevyn, it's in your best interest to also shut the fuck up," he said and turned around to face me. "You're the catalyst of this whole fucking thing. There isn't shit you can say to me that won't stop me from slitting your throat at the end of this, so I'd advise you to spend your last few days on your best behavior or this is gonna be a long, painful fucking week for you."

I swallowed hard at his threat. He wasn't going to rush this. He was going to make us suffer for as long as he could before he eventually killed us all and there wasn't shit we could do about it. I didn't even know where we were outside of this house we were in. We currently sat in the middle of what looked to be a large living room, the furniture pushed off to one side and covered with plastic. Whatever was going to happen here this week was bound to be bloody if there was plastic involved. The very thought sent a chill of fear down my spine.

"You bitches treated Sevyn like your God," he said, looking at each of my friends before turning around and smirking at me. "Well, let's see if your god can save you from the hell I'm about to unleash."

The other men appeared in the room holding rifles, each of them moving to stand behind one of my friends, pointing the rifle at their heads. Luther gestured to them. "These women have followed you and helped you bully and torment an innocent girl out of your own jealousy and hate," he said. "And because of that, you're going to play God and decide who dies first."

I frantically shook my head. "No, don't make me do that," I pleaded. "Luther, listen. Just punish me. Please don't make me choose!"

"If it makes you feel any better, they'll die regardless if you choose or not. But if you don't choose, I'll punish you until you do," he said with a shrug.

I looked up at the ceiling, tears burning my eyes. My friends all screamed and pleaded for me not to choose, but I felt like I was stuck between a rock and a hard place. *It's your fault why they're all in this situation to begin with*, I reminded myself. I knew that I'd eventually have to pay for my actions and if I had to take their punishment until I no longer could, then I'd rather do that than have someone's death on my conscience.

"Then punish me," I forced myself to say, my entire body trembling.

Luther shrugged again. "I guess you take your position as a god seriously, huh? Sacrificing yourself already. You do know that you can only do that so many times before you eventually can't take anymore punishments, right? Then you'll have no choice but to choose who you want to sacrifice," he said.

"If we all have to die, then why do I have to choose in the first place?" I asked, my body trembling.

He grinned. "What fun would it be to not bring you mental turmoil throughout this?" he said. "I waited for this moment for seven years, Sevyn. I don't plan on making your suffering light." My heart hammered in my chest, the anxiety of not knowing what was about to happen to me sending my fear into overdrive. He walked over to something behind me and after a few moments, one of my arms fell from the cross. When my feet were loose, I fell off the cross, still dangling from one side of it. Pain radiated across my shoulder at the sudden drop and I groaned in pain, collapsing to the floor when he finally untied my wrist.

"Stand up," he ordered, walking back around me. I forced myself to stand on my shaky legs, the room feeling as if it was spinning around me. Two of the guys rolled over a table to where Luther and I stood. The table had cuffs on the four corners of it, probably to restrain me on it. There was also a bottle of what looked like oil on it, which Luther grabbed when the guys clicked the brakes on the wheels of the table.

My body trembled as he untied the makeshift bra, tossing it off to the side. He did the same for the fabric on my hips, leaving me completely naked and exposed to everyone in the room. He said nothing as he rubbed oil all over my body. As each second passed, the oil made my skin tingle, to where it was extremely sensitive to the lightest touch. Luther's hands lingered longer than they needed to as he massaged the oil onto my breasts, ass, and pussy, but the expression on his face was indifferent. Once he was done, he opened the shackles on the table gestured to it.

"Get face down on the table," he said, his voice firm. I forced myself to move and did what he asked. The wooden table was

110

smooth against my legs, the oil causing my entire body to tingle. My friends all sniffled, worried expressions on their faces as they watched in silence. At first, nothing happened. I could only hear Luther's footsteps, but I couldn't see him. Finally, something light ran along my spine that tickled me. It felt as if it was barely there, but the oil he'd put on me seemed to heighten my nerve endings. He ran it up and down my back a few times before holding it in front of my face. A fucking feather.

He tossed the feather to the floor and moved on to something else that I couldn't see. I watched my friends, who seemed to be watching him, their eyes following the directions of his footsteps. I jumped when something pricked my skin. It felt like a million tiny needle tips pricking my skin each time Luther pressed his hand on my skin. He grabbed the back of my thigh, the sharp object on his hand digging into my skin. I bit my lip to suppress a whimper of pain, tears blurring my vision as the pain continued. He kneaded my ass a few times with what he held in his hands, the pain becoming so intense that I couldn't stop myself from crying out. Tears leaked from my eyes as I bit my bottom lip so hard that I could taste the blood in my mouth. But I didn't protest or tell him to stop. To tell him to stop would mean that I'd have to choose. That I'd have to choose which one of my best friends died first. I wasn't ready for that kind of responsibility now or ever, so I'd take the punishments as much as I could.

Luther finally stopped and moved around to show me his hands. He wore gloves that were covered in little spikes that didn't look as sharp as they felt, some of them covered in specks of blood. With the way my skin now burned in some areas, I wasn't surprised that he'd drawn blood. My entire body trembled as I waited for what was next. My friends' eyes widened and before I could even turn my head to get a look at what he could possibly have, I felt the red hot pain of a belt against my oily skin.

I screamed, the sound so loud and strangled that I wasn't even sure if it came from me. The pain radiated well beyond the place it was delivered, the entirety of my body on fire as blow after blow struck down on me. There was nowhere for me to go, no way to run from the belt with my arms and legs secured to the table. No matter how I tried to twist away from the belt's impact, it still licked my skin and set me on fire. Sometimes it hit the sensitive skin of my inner thighs and pussy, sometimes he struck my upper back and the back of my neck. My friends cried silently as the scene before then, the only sounds in the room being my sobs and the belt against my skin.

After what felt like eternity, he finally stopped and walked around to the front of me, showing me the belt as if I didn't already know what he was using. I hiccupped, trying to catch my breath before the next assault happened. My entire body burned and throbbed in pain to where I couldn't even move without pain radiating all over my body.

"Ready to choose someone yet?" he asked me. I sobbed even harder, shaking my head.

"Please don't make me choose," I begged.

"So, you want more punishment then?"

"No! Please," I croaked and coughed. I couldn't imagine what I looked like with my makeup and snot running down my face right now. It was hard to be ashamed when you were in so much pain. Held so much guilt. Every burning part of my body wanted to scream and surrender, but my pride wouldn't let me. Luther was right; despite Carrie's connections getting us into Luther's grasps in the first place, I was the reason we were all here. My actions and my friends following me just because they were loyal to me was the reason we were here. Us getting off in court with just a slap on the wrist was thanks to my parents' money.

I deserved every single thing that happened to me.

"So, make up your mind. Do you want to choose, or do you want more punishment?" he asked. I took deep breaths in an attempt to ease the pain clouding my mind, but it wouldn't go away. I looked into the eyes of my terrified friends and it broke my heart to know that I couldn't save them. Even if he killed me with all of my punishments, it wasn't like it would save them. All this did was prolong the inevitable.

I ground my teeth and squeezed my hands into fists to prepare for what was to come. "More punishment," I said and released a shaky breath.

"More punishment it is," he said with a smirk before he walked away. I couldn't stop my body from trembling. Pain danced along every nerve ending I had and the oil only heightened my sensitivity, making the pain so much worse. "Recite the Lord's prayer."

"What?"

"Are you fucking deaf? The Lord's prayer. Say it," he stated, his voice firm.

"Um…" I wracked my brain for the information. I couldn't even remember the last time I'd been in a church aside from going with a friend's family so many years ago. "I don't know if I remember."

"You better try really fucking hard or else this is going to get really hard on you," he growled.

"Okay, okay," I rushed out, swallowing the ball of fear in my throat. "Um…our…Father who art in Heaven…"

Pain erupted across the back of my legs and I screamed. The lash burned so badly that I'd believed he struck me with something hot. But I didn't smell burnt flesh or anything indicating that he was using something heated.

"Continue," he ordered.

"H-h-hallowed be thy name," I stammered, wailing when he hit me again. "Please stop!"

"Continue!" he bellowed.

"T-t-thy k-k-kingdon come, thy w-w-will be d-d-done—ah!" I screamed as he hit my back. My friends all sobbed and screamed for him to stop, but Luther didn't care.

"You better keep fucking going, Sevyn," he warned.

"On Earth a-a-as it is in h-h-heaven," I continued, squeezing my eyes shut as two more blows came. "G-g-give us th-th-this day our d-d-daily bread—fuck!"

He sprayed cold water on my bruised body from a bottle but with how bad it stung, it might as well have been acid. "Keep going," he stated.

"And forgive us our trespasses," I said in one breath, unable to control my body from shaking. "As we for-forgive those who tres-trespass a-a-gainst us." I clenched my teeth, my vision going in and out as the pain became too much.

"Go!"

"L-lead us not into temptation, but deliver us from e-e-vil," I stammered. Nausea tightened my stomach as Luther delivered blow after blow, not stopping until I mustered up the energy to speak again. "For t-t-thine is the k-k-kingdom, the power and the g-g-glory, forever and e-e-ever." I released a breath, my body going limp on the table. "Amen."

And everything went black.

CHAPTER 6

LUTHER

"Sevyn!" Rebecca screamed, jerking against the cuffs that restrained her. Sevyn lay limp on the table, her body so still that I didn't think she was breathing for a moment. I rolled my shoulders in satisfaction, looking at the mess I made on the backside of her body. She had purplish bruises and welts forming on the back of her legs, her ass, and up and down her back. Some of the welts even bled, drops of blood beading along the bruised flesh.

I grinned at Rebecca. "Are you upset that I bruised your little girlfriend?" I asked. She glared at me without a word, tears glittering in her eyes as her nostrils flared. I took in the expression of terror and shock on the rest of the distraught women. "Looks like your goo

"We didn't do anything wrong! You're acting like we forced your sister to do what she did!" Allison cried, jerking at her restraints. I scoffed and moved over to stand in front of her.

"Oh really?" I pulled a knife from its pouch on my hip and held the sharp tip to her throat. "So if I had one of my guys make a sex tape with you and released it to the public, made you lose your job, harass you online, send messages and texts telling you to kill yourself, you wouldn't succumb to the depression that comes with that shit?" I asked. Her bottom lip trembled as she looked at me, but she didn't verbally respond. "That's what I fucking thought."

"We were stupid teenagers back then!" Rebecca wailed, desperation in her voice. "We fucked up, okay? We're sorry!"

"Sorry doesn't bring Logan back, now does it?" I asked, my tone flat. "But since someone has to die and Sevyn is taking a little nap, I think we should choose the first person to go." I looked around at all of them. "Any volunteers?"

Just as I suspected, no one said a word. They only looked at each other, fear trembling their bodies. I shrugged. "I guess we'll do this the old school way."

"What?" one of them asked, but I didn't look to see who said it. I walked over to end of the line where Sarah sat, putting the blade against her throat.

"No! No! No! Please!" she sobbed.

"Duck," I said with a smirk before moving to Carrie, repeating the same action.

"Please, I'm sorry," she whispered.

"Duck," I said and moved on to Allison. Silent tears fell down her plump cheeks as she looked up at me, but she didn't say a word. "Duck." I moved on to Crystal, who also said nothing as she cried silently. "Duck."

I went along the line, giving everyone else "duck" until I got to the end with Rebecca and smiled. "Goose."

"Luther, please!" she begged. "I swear to you that we were just fucking around—"

"Shut up," I interrupted, pressing the tip of the blade firmly against her throat. A small bead of blood appeared as she whimpered. As much as I wanted to slit her throat, I had bigger plans for her. "You're the lucky one who gets to choose who dies."

"W-what?!" Her eyes widened. "I-I can't do that!" She looked to her friends and then back at me and shook her head. "I can't choose that!"

"Either you choose, or I'll just go ahead and kill you. Makes no difference to me, but someone's dying today," I said with a shrug. Tears welled in her eyes as her gaze drifted up to the high ceiling.

"Carrie," she finally whispered.

"Carrie it is," I exclaimed, excitement rushing through me. Carrie screamed and furiously shook her head.

"What the fuck, Rebecca?!" she screamed. "How could you pick me?"

"It's your fault we're here in the first place," Rebecca countered. I shook my head.

"It's your own fault you're here. I would've gotten you all

regardless," I corrected.

Carrie turned red with anger as she glared over at Rebecca. "Just so you know, you've always been a shit friend! And since we're throwing people under the bus, let me mention that you're the reason Sarah and Jeffrey broke up because you were the whore he was caught getting a blow job from!"

"What?!" Sarah screamed. I put my knife away and folded my arms across my chest. "You literally comforted me when I cried about him and told me he wasn't worth it! You were the redhead bitch people saw with him?!"

"Definitely didn't plan on this becoming Jerry Springer, but I'll allow it," I mused.

"Well, none of it matters anymore because you aren't with him. Maybe if you weren't such a prude, he wouldn't have cheated in the first place," Rebecca snapped. "And you can go to hell, Carrie. I'll enjoy watching you die, you snake!"

I tsked and shook my head. "I can see why you and Sevyn are such good friends, Rebecca. You're both shitty people and will fuck over people you claim are your 'besties,'" I said.

"You don't even know me," she ground out, which only made me chuckle.

"I don't have to know you. What kind of person goes around giving the boyfriend of her 'bestie' a blow job these days?" I looked to my friends. "Is that shit normal to you?"

"Nope," Tony said.

I shook my head. "You bitches are weird," I mumbled and settled my gaze on Carrie. Her earlier anger quickly morphed into fear again as she began babbling and pleading for her life.

"Please, Luther, I'm sorry!" she sobbed. I frowned as she repeated what the others had already said, what the always said right before I killed them.

That they made a mistake.

That they were just stupid kids.

That they weren't the person they used to be.

Pathetic excuses if you asked me.

"I'm gracious enough to accept your apology on behalf of my family," I said. I fought the urge to grin as relief flooded her eyes.

"Oh my God, thank you so—"

"Oh no, don't get me wrong; you're still dying," I interrupted. "But now you can die knowing I forgave you."

"What do you want first?" Ryan asked me, his rifle still trained at the back of Carrie's head. She looked back at him.

"How could you do something like this to me? I thought I meant something to you," she cried. Ryan rolled his eyes.

"You were nothing but a warm body to fuck from time to time," he admitted. "Besides, I was only with your clingy ass as a favor to Luther. My dick and I don't do commitment."

"That was only funny the first time you said it," Paul said, shaking his head.

"How about you shut the hell up? I was telling that to this bimbo anyway, not to you," he fired back.

"Can you both shut up? You're killing the mood of the room and

I quite like all the terror rolling off these bitches," Jake interrupted.

"My bad, brothers. I'll shut up before Luther kicks us all out," Paul said, holding his free hand up in surrender before looking to Ryan. "The floor is yours."

Ryan blew out a breath and rolled his shoulders and narrowed his gaze at me. "As I said, which 'thing' do you want first?"

My hand went up to stroke my beard, but I only felt my freshly shaven skin. Everything I'd planned over the last seven years all boiled down to this moment. I was lucky to have a group of friends like my guys, especially when one of them was willing to "date" one of the girls to build the trust I needed to have an "in" with them. Even after the trial, the rest of them followed Sevyn's lead and got restraining orders and security for the first few years, which only left me with time to think, plan, and prepare. Every single instrument and contraption that would bring them to their death was built by my own hand, and I couldn't wait to see my hard work pay off.

After a moment, I finally grinned. "Get the box," I said. Though the bottom half of his face was still covered by his red tactical skull mask, I could still see the mischief burning in his eyes. Before he moved, Crystal jerked in her chair as if the cuffs restraining her would unlock themselves.

"You're really going to murder us?" Crystal questioned. I looked to my guys, who shook their heads at the stupidity of her question.

"Do you think I brought you guys here to have some extreme, kinky fun?" I questioned.

"Well, I'm microchipped!" Allison blurted. "Someone will know something's wrong and will—"

"There's a couple of things wrong with that," I interrupted, wagging my finger at her. "For starters, microchips aren't GPS systems, dog. No one knows where you are because microchips only work when you use a special scanner. The only time people will be able to find you is when I want them to, and they'll be using that special scanner to identify your body."

The guys all snickered as Allison whimpered in defeat. Looking at her for a long moment, I smirked before I walked off. The house we were in was one that all the guys and I bought together once we'd graduated. We always came out here at least once a year to "blow off steam," doing shit that usually ended up in the news. I couldn't help but chuckle as I walked over to the closet near the front door to get what I needed. I almost couldn't wait to see what they'd say when they started finding body parts of these women all over the city.

I grabbed a collar and a leash from the top shelf usually reserved for Curtis' beast of a pit bull whenever he brought him along, but I had another purpose for it now. When I reentered the living room, the guys looked at me, Curtis furrowing his brows.

"Is that—"

"Yep," I said and walked over to Allison. "Since....what's your name again, dog?" I knew what her name was; I knew all their names. I burned every last one of them into my mind as I sat through session after session of "not guilty" verdicts. But it was all a part of the plan, to fuck with their minds before I destroyed them all.

The muscle in her jaw ticked as she glared at me. I smirked at her. It was rather comical seeing her trying to be a tough girl despite her eyes still welling with tears. Her eyes darted to the collar and leash in my hand before looking back to me.

"He asked you for your name, bitch," Curtis growled, pressing the muzzle of his rifle to the back of her head.

"A-Allison," she stammered.

"Well, Allison, since you brought it to our attention that you're microchipped like someone's pet, let's treat you like one," I said as I lengthened the collar.

"No, please!" she begged, but I ignored her as I moved to stand behind her. Curtis stepped aside as I fastened the nylon collar around her neck.

"You're lucky Beast is a huge dog with a thick neck," I said as I secured it and retightened it a bit. "Otherwise you'd choke to death with a standard collar."

Her body trembled as silent sobs wracked her body. All the tears in the world wouldn't stop what they all had coming to them. Curtis chuckled and shook his head.

"To be honest, I don't remember dogs sitting in chairs like this," he said and shrugged.

I looked at her for a moment and then grinned. "Right you are. Dogs like this belong on the floor," I mused.

"Make her kneel on rice while you're at it," Victor suggested.

I snapped my fingers and pointed at him. "Even fucking better," I said and looked to Curtis. "Mind getting some?"

"With fucking pleasure," he said and left the room.

"Please don't, Luther," she begged. "I swear I won't say another word—"

"I know you won't. Dogs don't talk," I interrupted. "They bark. So, bark...dog."

"What?" she asked, her eyes widening.

I moved to stand in front of her and grabbed her by the throat, grinning when her face turned red. "Bark," I repeated again, my voice firm.

I loosen my grip on her neck as she gasped for air. She panted for a few moments before swallowing hard, her cheeks flushed with embarrassment.

"Arf," she said, so quiet I barely even heard her.

"What was that?" I asked, cupping my hand to my ear. Her eyes darted around to her friends, who all looked at her with wet eyes. She trembled under my touch, refusing to look at me.

"Arf," she said a little louder. I smirked at her.

"I know you can be a little louder than that," I said. "You were loud when you announced you were chipped in the first place. So, let's hear that voice, dog."

"Please," she whispered as she shook her head, fat tears rolling down her cheeks.

"Bark," I ground out. "And you better be loud enough, or I'll go ahead and crush your trachea and end you."

"Arf! Arf! Arf! Arf! Arf!" she barked, her eyes glassy with tears. I chuckled and let her go.

"Fucking idiot," I mumbled and nodded to Curtis, who'd just

returned from the kitchen. "Put her on the floor."

Allison sobbed as Curtis spread white rice on the floor before releasing her restraints and pulling her from the chair. With a rough grip on her shoulder, he forced her onto her knees. She wailed as the white granules dug into her skin. Tony pulled the chair out of the way as Curtis tightened his hand around the leash that was now connected to Allison's collar.

"Good dog," he mused, the rest of the men chuckling.

I looked to Carrie, who had this look of devastation on her face as she kept her eyes trained on her lap. I couldn't blame her; I'd probably look that way too if I knew I was about to die.

"Are we doing this now or are you going to wait on her?" Victor asked, nodding toward Sevyn.

"I'm about to wake her up. I want her to see each of these bitches die one by one before I deal with her," I said. "Get the box, Ryan."

He nodded and propped his rifle up against the wall away from the women and disappeared from the room.

"What you're doing is bullshit, Luther," Rebecca suddenly snapped. "You're not all that innocent either."

"Oh?" I turned to face her, folding my arms across my chest. "I don't remember being the one sending my sister texts, or uploading her sex tape, or telling her to kill herself. But I remember seeing your name. In fact, I saw her name..." I pointed at Crystal, "And her name..." I pointed at Allison, "Her name..." I pointed at Jamie, "Her name..." I pointed at Sarah, "And last but not least, her name," I concluded, finally pointing at Carrie.

Rebecca glared at me. "Killing us won't bring your sister back. You'll just end up in jail."

"Only idiots who get caught end up in jail," I said with a shrug. "I mean let's look at this logically. The police don't have a single lead on all the three murders I've already committed, and it's been three weeks. And when they find your bodies, my guys and I will get away with it again and we'll go back to our regular tech lives as if none of this even happened."

"Great, we're going to be murdered by a bunch of fucking nerds," Sarah mumbled under her breath.

"But nerds are the scariest type," I mentioned. "We can hack shit, build shit, and cover up shit. You whores don't stand a chance."

All conversation ceased when Ryan returned back to the living room, rolling a glass box on a hand truck. Sarah had no idea how right she was when she called us a bunch of nerds; she'd soon learn how much of a nerd I was when she saw all the deadly contraptions for every single one of their demises except Sevyn. No, I wanted to end her with my bare hands.

"What the fuck is that?" Carrie asked, panic in her voice.

"Unless you're blind, it's a glass box," Ryan stated, his tone flat as he unloaded the box in the middle of the semi-circle the women sat in. In retrospect, the box wasn't very scary. It simply looked like a glass box with a small hole in the top, perfectly sized for the hose that would be attached to it.

"We're not using this box just yet though," I said. "Sevyn isn't awake yet and considering the truth bomb that you just dropped, I'm kind of curious as to what other secrets you all are keeping." No one said anything. "Oh? Cat got everyone's tongue?"

"I don't even know why we're all here. This was all Sevyn and Rebecca's idea," Allison said from the floor.

"I swear you all are just backstabbing bitches," Rebecca mumbled under her breath, shaking her head.

"Like you have room to talk," Paul scoffed.

"Shut up, asshole," she snapped.

"It's not like he's wrong," Sarah growled. "Or did you already forget about the time you gave my boyfriend a blow job?"

"Oh, fuck you, Sarah. You act like you're so righteous and good when you were the one who convinced Hunter to upload the video in the first place," Rebecca stated and looked to me. "You wanna know secrets? Sarah was the one who uploaded the video that got Logan expelled."

"No, I fucking didn't!" Sarah exclaimed.

"I mean...you did kind of push him to do it," Jamie said sheepishly.

"Well, this is interesting," I mused, leaning against the heavy glass box. "Why would you even do something like that? Had your parents not gotten you off, you would be in jail for child pornography."

"I didn't fucking upload it!" she screamed. "I didn't have control over Hunter; he could've always said no. You're acting like I held a gun to his head and made him do it."

"Doesn't matter in the end, does it? Hunter's dead now, so it's not like I can ask him about it," I said and shrugged. "Anyone else wanna say anything?"

"If I'm going to die, I really want to lay into Rebeca before I do," Carrie ground out.

Rebecca giggled. "You're so weak. You cry when someone yells at you," she said and rolled her eyes.

Carrie turned red as she leaned forward in her chair and glared at her. "No one even likes you. We only put up with you because you were friends with Sevyn."

"Oh, boo hoo. I'm going to cry because you don't like me," Rebecca drawled sarcastically. "All of you can kiss my ass quite frankly."

"So, you'd hit her if given the chance?" I asked with a grin. Girl fights weren't a part of the plan, but what the hell; why not? After all, I was a slightly merciful man to grant the unfortunate their final wish and final meal.

"Yes. I've wanted to do it for years," she answered.

Rebecca scoffed. "Then why haven't you done it?"

"Let her loose," I said, nodding to Ryan. He raised an eyebrow at me but unlocked the restraints on her wrists and ankles, quickly training his rifle on her. Carrie wasted no time moving to the end of the line of women and pummeling Rebecca's head with punches. They were weak at best; if anything, it looked as if it amused Rebecca instead of hurt her.

"Knock it off, you crazy bitch," Rebecca finally said after a while. With her hands still cuffed to the chair, she couldn't block Carrie's attack. Carrie cocked her arm back and swung as hard as she could, hitting Rebecca square in the mouth. Rebecca gasped, her bottom lip dripping blood as she shook her hair from her face.

"It serves you right, asshole," Carrie panted, drawing back again and hitting Rebecca in the stomach.

Amusement coursed through my veins as I watched them, a smirk on my lips. It was always interesting to see how potential danger could change the dynamics of friendships. Maybe they weren't as close as they were back in high school, but I never thought it was *this* bad. In all honesty, it was probably Sevyn and the secrets they all kept that glued them together. Considering the way Carrie pummeled into Rebecca and the other women never encouraged her to stop?

That glue holding them together was probably completely dissolved now.

"Fucking get her away from me!" Rebecca screamed.

I shrugged. "Oh, I don't know. You did choose for her to die first."

"Because it's her fucking fault we're here!" she snapped. "Had we not agreed to meet you fucks—"

"You must be really hard of hearing, because we've discussed this situation already," I said with a sigh. "What part of 'you're here for your own actions and I would've gotten you all eventually' didn't you hear the first time I said it? Not to mention, we already knew where you were headed, so we would've been there whether she invited us or not."

Rebecca spit blood on the floor in response, resulting in Paul hitting her in the back of the head with the butt of his rifle.

"Fucking disgusting," he mumbled as Rebecca's unconscious

body slumped down in her seat.

"You can sit down now, Carrie," I ordered. She licked her lips, her eyes gazing beyond my guys and toward the foyer teasing her behind them. I shook my head as I saw the gears turning in her mind. "Trust me, you won't make it. You're more than welcome to try, but I promise you'll be shot dead before you even pass my guys."

Her shoulders sagged in defeat after a moment of hesitation. A single tear rolled down her cheek as she sulked back to her chair and sat back down, flinching when Ryan roughly clamped the restraints back down on her wrists.

"Next order of business," I announced once she was settled. "What would you like your last meal to be, Carrie?"

She furrowed her brow at me, confusion coloring her face. "Wha-what?"

"Your last meal," I repeated. She still had that idiotic look on her face as if she had no idea what I was talking about. I ran a hand down my face in frustration. She was living, breathing proof of the "dumb blonde" stereotype. "Last meal, Carrie, the last thing you want to eat before you die. You know, like they do for death row inmates before they're executed."

"But we aren't inmates!" she protested.

I frowned. "You should've been," I growled. "Either choose something or die hungry. Makes no fucking difference to me."

She looked down the line of women with tears in her eyes. The others looked apologetic and sad, a hint of fear in their gazes as they realized that they'd soon be in the same position.

"Um," she started, licking her lips again. "I don't know what to choose since I don't know where we are or what's available."

"It doesn't matter where we are. Just choose something."

"Um...Chipotle or something?"

I rolled my eyes. "Fuck, you're aggravating the shit out of me," I grumbled. "And what do you want from there, Carrie?"

"I'll have a rice bowl with both chicken and steak. Oh, and I also want cilantro lime rice, pinto beans, tomato green-chili, cheese, and guac. And a side of queso and chips."

"Got that down?" I asked Ryan.

He scoffed. "You expected me to actually pay attention to this air head while she spoke?" he asked with a raised eyebrow.

Carrie turned slightly in her chair to face him as best as she could and frowned back at him. "You don't have to be an asshole, Mark. It's bad enough that you're even doing this to."

He rolled his eyes. "The name is Ryan, actually. And I don't give a shit about how you feel about anything. You're practically a dead woman walking."

I chuckled at his bluntness. It was a good thing that he and his dick were allergic to commitment. With the way he talked to women, it was surprising most times that he even convinced them to sleep with him.

"Just get her order and run into town and get it, man," I mused.

"Or I'm going to have this shit delivered at the gas station nearby," he said as he pulled his phone from his pocket.

I frowned. "Just go to the damn place and pick it up," I stated. "I don't want to run the risk of anyone getting too close to this place."

He looked at me for a long moment before he finally released a deep sigh. "Fuck. You're right," he finally said. Narrowing his gaze at the back of Carrie's head, he said, "Repeat your pretentious ass order again."

He typed it into his phone as she repeated it again, putting his phone in his pocket when she finished.

"Thank you," she murmured and bowed her head.

Victor raised his hand. "Since you're going out, I want to place an order, too," he said. Ryan glared at him.

"Do I look like a fucking Doordash driver to you?" he snapped.

"I mean you're already getting food. It's not like it's an inconvenience," Jake said and shrugged.

"I'm not getting you fuckers food. It's not even lunch time for us anyway," Ryan countered back.

"He's right about that," I said. "Just get Carrie's order and hurry back."

A groan sounded behind me just as Ryan was about to say something. I looked over my shoulder to see Sevyn slowly wiggling around on the table. Five of her friends sat up straighter in their seats, probably hoping that Sevyn being awake could save Carrie's life if Sevyn took another punishment for her. Too bad for them that it didn't work that way. One of these bitches would die every day for the next seven days and Sevyn would witness every single one of them meet their end.

I moved over to her and firmly slapped her cheek. She cried out, her gorgeous features contorting in pain before her eyes fluttered open.

"Welcome back, sunshine," I said as her gaze finally settled on me.

"Wha…" She lifted her head and peered around at her bound friends, one of them still unconscious. "No…this…this isn't happening…"

"It's definitely happening," I said with a chuckle. "Now let's get you back on your cross. You carry the burden of this whole situation after all, right?"

But she didn't respond to me. She kept murmuring how this wasn't real and this couldn't be happening.

"This is just a dream…this is just a dream," she kept chanting as I unlocked the cuffs that held her wrists and ankles. She screamed in pain when I yanked her off the table, falling into me as I tightened my firm grip around her arm.

"Does that pain feel like a dream? You're in a living nightmare right now and there's no waking up from that," I said with a dark grin. I looked down at her trembling, naked body. "And I think I'll just keep you naked. I always loved seeing you naked."

"I hate you," she whispered as a single tear rolled down her cheek.

"The feeling's mutual, baby," I said and dragged her back over to the cross. Victor, Tony, and Paul moved away from their girls and put their rifles on the table. We each grabbed one of Sevyn's limbs as she kicked and screamed.

"No!" she screamed, but her movements were weak. Tony and Paul held her legs against the wood and tied them down as Victor and I tightly secured the rope around her wrists.

"I'll be back!" Ryan called over his shoulder. "Don't do anything fun without me."

"Fuck, this hurts!" Sevyn screamed, trying to arch her back so that it wouldn't touch the wood. It wasn't like that would help; the whole backside of her body was badly bruised.

I slowly nodded. "Yeah…that's kind of the point," I said, the guys and I sharing a "duh" look.

"I have to go to the bathroom," Allison said from the floor.

"Guess that's my cue to take the dog out," Curtis said.

"Out? Out where?" Allison retorted.

"Outside. Where'd you think you were going? To the bathroom?"

"Dogs don't use toilets," Tony taunted, and Paul snickered.

"But—" Allison started, but was stopped when Curtis yanked the leash attached to her collar. Allison squeaked in surprise, falling back on her ass. Curtis didn't bother waiting for her to get her bearings; he dragged her along the hardwood floor, practically choking her as he did so.

"Now this I gotta see," I mused and looked back to Sevyn. "Don't go anywhere." I winked at her, grinning when her face grew red with anger. I couldn't help but to chuckle. She made it far too easy to fuck with her.

When Curtis reached the front door, Allison gasped for breath as she pulled at the collar.

"Are you ready to walk or do I have to drag you outside, too?" he asked her.

"I'll walk," she panted and moved to stand on her feet.

Just as she moved to stand, I tsked. "No, no, no. Hands and knees, dog," I said. She ground her teeth and moved to get onto her hands and knees, slowly following Curtis out the door as he yanked the leash along.

Watching her try to navigate the stairs on her hands and knees was rather comical. She was more worried about her dress, which rode up her thighs with each step she moved down. Curtis rolled his eyes and roughly yanked the leash, sending her tumbling down the rest of the stairs with a grunt.

"What the fuck?!" she protested as she fell in the mulch next to the stairs.

He shrugged. "Shouldn't have taken so long." He gestured over to the grass. "If you have to piss, then go."

"In the grass?!"

"I mean that's where dogs usually go, right?" I taunted.

"You can't be serious," she said with a frown.

"We wouldn't be outside if we weren't," I said. When she didn't move, I grinned. "Oh, I'm sorry. Are you the type of dog that can't go while people are looking? We'll turn around."

Curtis looked at me with a raised brow and I nodded before turning my back to her. He sighed inwardly and also turned around, shaking his head. After a few seconds, she muttered curses under her breath before the unmistakable sound of her peeing in the grass sounded.

I snorted and looked at her over my shoulder. "Good girl. Look at you going to the bathroom outside like the dog you are," I teased.

"Fuck you, asshole," she snapped. Her hand was under her dress, probably holding her panties to the side to go to the bathroom considering that she didn't pull them down.

"What's the plan for the girls in the meantime?" Curtis asked me.

I put my hands in my pockets. "They'll eat, I'll kill Carrie, and then they can be put back into their rooms until tomorrow. You can do whatever you want with the girl you have except kill them."

"Anything?"

"Anything that won't kill them," I repeated with a frown. His eyes glistened with anticipation and I knew what that look meant. Allison would definitely be screaming later, and it wouldn't be because of me.

"I'm done," she said suddenly.

"Let's go then, dog," Curtis grumbled under his breath and pulled her along. I stood outside for a few minutes and took a deep breath. A sinister grin crept across my lips as I watched Allison walk on all fours up the stairs. As soon as Ryan returned, the real fun would start.

And I couldn't fucking wait.

CHAPTER 7

SEVYN

I'd had many nightmares over the years of what I thought Luther would do to me if he were to ever get his hands on me. In every dream, it was usually a quick death, one where he'd taunt me a bit before he either stabbed me, shot me, or strangled me.

But not even in my worst nightmares did I ever imagine something like this.

Carrie silently cried in her seat and my heart broke for her. I was the reason all of my friends were in this situation. Realistically, I knew there were only so many punishments I could take, and Luther wouldn't allow me to die, not yet, anyway. I looked to Rebecca, who was limp in her chair, her mouth bloody and a slight bruise growing

"What happened to her?" I asked, a ball of guilt settling deep in my stomach.

"I happened to her," Carrie said bitterly. Before I could question her, Sarah answered my unasked question.

"Because you weren't awake to choose who'll die first, Luther made Rebecca choose and she chose Carrie," she said, glaring over at Rebecca.

"What?!" I exclaimed. A large, tall glass box was positioned a couple of feet away from me. I had no idea what it was for, but I didn't want to think about it either. Whatever it was for, I was sure we'd all know about it very soon.

"Yeah," Carrie said. "So, I'm waiting for my last meal to be given to me before he kills me. This isn't fucking fair."

"I'm sorry," I said. I wasn't sure what I was thinking when I figured that Luther would just torture all of us before he eventually killed me. But he was seriously going to kill my friends and in reality, there was nothing I could do to save them. There was nothing that could save me, just like there was nothing that could've saved Justin, Tyler, and Hunter.

"Well, as Luther said, sorry won't get us out of this, so I guess it's pointless for any of us to apologize now," Sarah said bitterly. "I wish it was actually Rebecca dying first."

"Don't say that," I said, wincing in pain. Even talking made pain radiate across the back of my neck and my upper back. "She's your friend. Now isn't the time to turn on each other."

"Apparently she was a shady bitch long before we got here,"

Sarah fired back at me. "Did you know about what she did to me?"

I furrowed a brow in confusion. Rebecca never told me anything she'd done to Sarah that I could remember. I shook my head. "No?"

"Yeah, well, she gave Jeffrey a blow job and was the reason we actually broke up," Sarah snapped. "She was the slut that everyone said they caught him with."

I shook my head. "Who in the hell said that? I don't think—"

"I had another friend who was there. She was the one who sent the picture to me. It was definitely matching everything Rebecca had on that night from the picture she sent to us in our group chat for a party she was going to that night," Carrie interrupted. "You're really blind if you can't see the snake you're so close to. Just like with us, she'll bite you soon enough."

"She won't bite anyone she's in love with," one of the masked men said with a chuckle.

"She's not in love with me, you weird fuck," I said through my teeth. I'd known Rebecca for years; she'd never been with girls as far as I knew, and she didn't act in any way that would make me think she was in love with me.

"The bitch will get what's coming to her, that's for sure," Sarah muttered, just as a door slammed shut. All conversation ceased as Luther and another masked guy made their way back into the room. It was surprising to see Allison with a dog collar and leash on her. Humiliation colored her features as she crawled back to her spot. She stopped briefly when she got to the little grains of rice scattered on the floor.

"Please don't make me kneel in this," she begged. "I won't say anything else; I promise!"

She looked up at Luther, her hands clasped as she pleaded. He studied her for a few moments and shrugged. "She's been a good dog. Put her back in the chair," he finally said.

Relief shined bright in her eyes. "Thank you so much," she breathed. Curtis put her chair back with the others and Allison quickly sat in it. Curtis reattached her cuff restraints and took the leash off of her, leaving the collar. Luther focused his attention on me and smiled. It'd been so long since I'd seen him genuinely smile. Even when we were on good terms, he didn't do it very often. He was one of those guys who was one of few words, but he always seemed to transform when we were alone together. Those times alone were the times I saw him at his most vulnerable, and it was one of the most beautiful things I'd ever seen. His smile always filled my stomach with butterflies whenever he'd grace me with it. It made me feel special to see when he smiled since it was a rare thing. He only did it when he was genuinely happy about something and seeing that he was smiling at me now sent terror through me.

His smile was no longer in adoration. It was now in thirst of blood.

"Now that you've joined us, it's time for the real party to begin," he said to me and then glanced over to the guy standing behind Rebecca. "Wake her up."

The guy reached into his pocket and pulled out a little white pack and popping it. He held it under Rebecca's nose, and she jumped up in seconds, her wild, unfocused eyes darting around before she finally settled her gaze on me.

"Sevyn! Thank god," she exasperated, her shoulders slumped in what seemed like relief.

"Yeah, your girlfriend is fine," Luther said sarcastically, rolling his eyes. "While we wait on Ryan to get back, I feel like we should talk a little about what happened."

"You already know what happened," I ground out.

"No, I want to know what happened behind the scenes," he growled, moving closer to me. "I want to know everyone's part and I want to know why you did what you did. You don't go from being best friends with someone to telling them to kill themselves."

"You keep talking about us but you're not innocent either, Luther. You doing this is no better than what we did."

"The difference between you and I, Sevyn, is that I'm finishing what *you* started. All of this—" he waved his hand around the room. "—is because of you. Everyone is here because of you. You can try to say whatever you want about how I'm reacting to what *you* did, but the fact of the matter is that it started with you."

I ground my teeth, the truth sitting on the edge of my tongue, but I forced myself not to say it. It didn't matter what I said. Whether I told him the real reason or not, it wouldn't make a difference. He'd still kill my friends. He'd still kill me. If anything, I'd wait until they were my dying words before I told him a damn thing and then he could live with his own guilt just as I have.

He scoffed. "Yeah, I bet you don't have anything smart to say after that," he muttered and walked off. Looking to the men, he said, "The kitchen."

All the men filed out, leaving me alone with the girls. Rebecca's eyes were glued to my body, which was still naked. I had to admit that it was a bit humiliating being naked in front of everyone, but with the pain I was in, I didn't really care too much. And with the way Rebecca's eyes scanned my naked form, I couldn't help but to wonder if what the others said had been right.

"Did you really suck off Jeff?" I asked her. The odd lustful gaze that'd once been there was quickly replaced with shock as she blinked and brought her eyes to meet mine.

"What?"

"Sarah's boyfriend. Did you do what they said you did?" I asked. I definitely remembered the way we all comforted Sarah after she'd told us that someone had caught him cheating. Rebecca was the main one allowing her to cry with her head in her lap, stroking her hair and trying to comfort Sarah by telling her men were a waste of time because all they did was break your heart. To know that she was actually the woman he cheated with was as appalling as learning he'd cheated in the first place.

Rebecca rolled her eyes, as if she was tired of the conversation already. "It happened years ago. I literally don't see why everyone wants to keep talking about it."

"That's really shady, Bec," I said with a frown. The smug look on her face melted when she saw the disappointed expression on mine. She began babbling all kinds of excuses to defend herself, anything to make her remain a "good friend" in my eyes.

"He came onto me, you know? He said he and Sarah were on a break—"

"But you know if they actually were, Sarah would've said something about it. Anytime shit like that happens with any of us, we always go out as a group to help that friend forget about him for a little while," I interrupted.

"Exactly," Jamie said. "Rebecca was just going around whoring just because she literally doesn't give a fuck about anyone but Sevyn."

"She was literally just saying that I should've taken better care of him and he wouldn't have cheated," Sarah added. "All the other bullshit she's spewing is a complete lie. I don't even want to talk about this anymore because it's doing nothing but pissing me off." She shook her head. "Can't even believe I've been friends with the likes of her for so long."

I sighed. I could understand her frustration. It was betrayal at its highest point. "Sarah—"

"This whole group and friendship is toxic as fuck. You know what? Maybe we all deserve this. We were stupid enough to follow you. I knew it was wrong but because I was more worried about being popular, I did something I knew I shouldn't have done. Logan didn't deserve any of that and I allowed you to control me like a puppet."

I narrowed my gaze at her. "You all had a choice. I didn't force any of you to do anything," I reminded her.

Crystal shook her head. "You kinda did, Sevyn. I mean you were always giving us ultimatums back then. You had it in your head that you had to make Logan 'pay' and if we didn't help you, then we weren't your real friends."

"No offense, but you were a real self-centered bitch back then," Jamie added. "And to be honest, I told my parents about it but because they needed my friendship with you to help my dad, you didn't give me much of a choice either."

"Wow. Sounds like you were a super shitty friend there, Sevyn," one of the guys said as they returned to the room carrying trays.

Anger boiled under my skin, but I couldn't even say they were wrong. So what if I were selfish or self-centered. For me, it'd always been a defense mechanism to weed out the people who were only using me for the connections my family had. Sure, it was no excuse for me to act the way I did toward people, but it pissed me off even more that these women only sucked up to me because of what me and my family could do for them. Hearing them admit this now pissed me off to no end. They were just as guilty as I was, but yet they were putting all the blame solely on me. If they truly thought it was wrong, they wouldn't have done it. The only person who really protested against the idea was Jamie. Everyone else seemed just as excited as I was as soon as I spoke the idea into existence and to now try to flip this on me was shady as fuck.

"Sevyn's a shitty friend and you bimbos are fucking idiotic," Luther said, shaking his head as he put the tray he held on a table. The other guys walked over to the girls they were guarding and unlocked one of the cuffs on their wrists before placing a tray holding a peanut butter and jelly sandwich and bottled water onto their laps.

"Um, I'm allergic to peanut butter," Rebecca stated, wrinkling her nose. I frowned at her. She wasn't allergic; she just didn't like peanut butter because she claimed she didn't like it getting stuck to the roof of her mouth.

Luther only shrugged in response. "Well, if you're allergic, then I guess you won't be eating until it's your day to die," he said.

"There's nothing else here?"

"Nope. I mean you can ask Carrie if she'd share her last meal with you," he taunted, folding his arms across his broad chest.

"The answer would be no, you slimy whore," Carrie immediately fired back.

Luther chuckled. "I guess that idea is out then. Looks like you'll be starving today."

"This is fucking bullshit," Rebecca mumbled.

"Just eat the sandwich, Bec," I said. "You're not allergic. You always use that bullshit excuse when you don't want to eat what someone is serving."

She glared at me. "Well, thanks for throwing me under the bus, *friend*," she sneered.

Allison snorted. "As if you know how to actually be a friend, Rebecca," she mumbled and bit into her sandwich half. When Luther raised an eyebrow at her, she dropped her eyes to her tray. "I'm sorry. I won't say anything else."

"You better not or you're going back on the floor," he said, his voice flat. He turned his attention to Carrie, who didn't have a tray nor a guy standing behind her anymore. "Since you're going to be leaving us first, I'll start with you. If you had to choose who was the most responsible, who would you say?"

Carrie furrowed her brow in thought. After a few moments, cut her eyes to Rebecca and then looked back to Luther. "I'd say Rebecca," she stated confidently.

"Bull-fucking-shit," Rebecca fired back. "You're just upset that I chose you to die."

"Even though Sevyn initiated the whole plan, Rebecca was the one dishing out majority of the ideas," she said, ignoring Rebecca's outburst.

"Are you seriously going to let her spew lies, Sevyn?" Rebecca exclaimed. I bit the inside of my jaw, unable to even meet her gaze. There was nothing I could say in her defense because Carrie wasn't lying. I'd admit that I wanted Logan to hurt as much as I did. My original plan was a lot weaker than what happened because I really wanted her to suffer. In my eyes, Logan destroyed so much in my life that I still hadn't fully healed from to this day. To admit this would be admitting the real reason I'd done what I did, which I wasn't completely ready to do. My friends didn't even know the full truth and with the way they were turning on each other right now, I was so glad they didn't.

"The main thing that was Rebecca's idea was Logan's rape," Carrie continued, which made Luther frown.

"Oh, was it?" he asked.

"Uh oh," one of the guys said under his breath.

"Yes," Carrie responded confidently. "When Sevyn gave the

green light on any idea we could think of to destroy Logan, Rebecca recommended putting a bug in the ears of the Pussy Bandits, who were known for raping girls who've been drugged or were drunk out of their minds."

"I'm assuming this is Josh, Tyler, and Hunter," Luther mused. Carrie nodded.

"Sevyn did wonder if it was a bit extreme, but the rest of us co-signed the idea. I mean it doesn't make us any better either because we all still went along with it. It was really fucked up and we were all stupid then and had no idea the true consequences of our actions then."

Even though his back was to me, I could see his skin turning red. It crept up his neck, even visible under his tattoos. I knew he was beyond angry now. A part of me wanted Carrie to shut the hell up. The minute details of everything only seemed to be pissing him off even more than the things he'd learned about in court. I was worried about how this would affect us later, as I was sure the day was just getting started.

"Interesting," was the only thing he'd said, just as a door opened and closed in the distance. Another masked guy came in with a Chipotle bag, no doubt Carrie's last meal. How she ate from that place as often as she did was beyond me, but it was heartbreaking to know that after she ate, he'd kill her.

And it was all because of me.

The guy plopped the food in her lap and unlocked both of her hands, unlike the other girls. "Make it quick," he growled.

Luther turned to face me, his face a lot redder than I assumed just by looking at the back of him. "On second thought, you won't eat today," he growled. He picked up the sandwich and pulled the halves of it a part, smearing the peanut butter and jelly all over my face. "Eat on that, bitch."

My entire face was sticky and felt gross. It felt as if it was on my eyes, in parts of my hair that hung in my face. I was nearly afraid of opening my eyes in fear that some of it would get in them. I tried to wipe my face as best as I could by rubbing my face against my shoulders until it no longer felt as if I had a bunch of sticky jelly and peanut butter on my eyelids. It seemed to make it worse, but it was enough to where I didn't feel as if I'd get any in my eyes.

He stomped over to Rebecca and punched her in the face before snatching her tray away as well. "I'll make sure you're the last to die because I'm going to take great pleasure in breaking you until I eventually kill you," he growled and hit her again. "Get her the fuck out of here."

"So…if she's done for the day, can I…you know?" the guy behind her asked.

"Do whatever you want to her except kill her." He paused for a moment and shook his head. "Actually, no. Not yet. Matter of fact, she'll stay here until everyone is in their room and then I want three of you to recreate what happened to my sister with her. Since she can easily come up with ideas like that, how about we bring that to life for her, too."

"Luther you don't have to do all of—"

"Shut the fuck up!" he bellowed, spittle flying from his mouth.

"You're the last fucking person to tell me what I should and shouldn't be doing. If you want to keep running your fucking mouth, I can arrange for three of us to do the same fucking thing to you, too. Is that what you want?!"

His voice was so loud that it made me flinch back. I'd never witnessed him this angry before, not even in the court room. I mean he was angry, but he was more so angry at the jury and the judge. All of it wasn't even geared toward me in that moment, but witnessing it now was terrifying.

I shook my head, fear making it hard for me to verbally speak. His eyes blazed with rage and untamed fury. Anything I said probably would've set him off and prepared me for another punishment that I didn't think I could handle right now. After a few moments, he turned his attention to Carrie.

"You have fifteen fucking minutes to eat. Whether you're done or not, you're going in the box," he snapped and then left the room again. Carrie sobbed at the news and my heart broke for her all over again. The guilt I'd carried all these years was nothing in comparison to the guilt I felt knowing that I had to witness all of my friends' deaths. I'd been so, so stupid back then, thinking my family's status and money could get me out of any trouble I'd gotten myself into. While they helped keep me out of legal trouble, they couldn't get me out of trouble with Luther. I wasn't even sure if they'd realized I was missing yet. It wasn't like I checked in with them every day and after the last conversation with my mother after seeing her very young boy toy, she probably wasn't even expecting to hear from me for a while. I bowed my head.

I was so fucked.

The room was completely silent aside from Carrie sobbing. She'd barely touched her food, her time quickly ticking away. Not that I could blame her. There was no way I'd have an appetite knowing I was going to die soon after either. A timer finally went off from somewhere and Luther finally reappeared in the room.

"Time's up," he said, his voice low and deep.

"Luther, please don't do this," I said when I finally got my voice. Carrie sobbed even harder to the point to where she was hiccupping. "Look, I'll take another punishment if I have to. Please don't—"

"That's not how this works, Sevyn," he tsked. "You only take a punishment so that you don't have to choose who dies next. It won't actually save them from not dying." He nodded toward the guy standing behind Carrie. "Get rid of the food and put her in the box."

"No, please!" Carrie begged. "I swear I didn't mean anything I did! I'm sorry!"

"It's a little too late for sorry," the man said as he took away all the untouched food on Carrie's lap. She begged and pleaded with him as he unlocked her ankle cuffs, roughly pulling her out of the chair. It fell on deaf ears though, as Luther walked over to the glass box and opened the door. The man pulled Carrie over to the box and my heart sunk as I watched. Tears burned my eyes when the door was slammed closed. One of my best friends would die soon and she was spending her last minutes terrified. I didn't want that for her; I didn't want that for any of them. For the first time in a long time, I wasn't in control of a situation, and that alone terrified me also.

Once Carrie was secured in the box, Luther put a much smaller, identical box on the table I was on earlier. "I'm sure you guys are familiar with vacuum sealing things," Luther announced. "Carrie is the self-proclaimed minimizing queen according to her Instagram profile. She vacuum seals things all the time to make room for all the shit she buys to 'minimize space.' So, I'm sure you know what happens when you vacuum seal things. But in case you don't, let me demonstrate."

The guy who guarded Carrie walked over with a tray of unwrapped Twinkies and handed it to Luther. Luther stacked the cakes inside the glass box and then closed it, attaching a small hose to the corner of it. We all watched as he flipped the switch to a black pump next to the box and at first, nothing happened. But then the cakes started to grow abnormally large the longer the pump went on. Carrie screamed inside the glass box and I damn sure didn't blame her. Was I going to watch her explode?!

After the filling in the Twinkies fell out of the puffed out cakes, Luther finally turned the pump off. "As you know, a vacuum seal takes the air out of things. Let's see what happens to a human in a vacuum seal."

"No!" Carrie screamed as she beat on the glass. I couldn't stop the tears from pouring from my eyes as I watched one of the guys help Luther drag a pump into the room and attach a big hose at the top of the box.

"Please don't do this!" my friends all shouted, excluding Rebecca.

She only stared at Carrie with an indifferent look on her face, as if she didn't care whether she lived or died. But I couldn't even focus on her. My full attention was now on my friend of almost twelve years trapped in a glass box. I tried to commit her to my memory. Her short blonde hair, her flawless tanned skin that I used to be jealous about when we were younger, her soft, round face, button nose, blue eyes, and pouty lips that she'd had injected over the years. But now, her pretty features were covered in tears, running mascara, and fear of what was about to happen to her.

I sobbed as she slid to the floor of the box in defeat, her head against the glass as she sobbed and begged whatever God that would listen to her for forgiveness. As she begged Logan for forgiveness. Her parents that she was leaving behind for forgiveness. Luther's family for forgiveness. My friends all bowed their heads and sobbed as well. There was nothing any of us could do to help her; all we could do was face the music of our actions and get what Luther felt we deserved.

He said nothing as he turned on the large pump. Within seconds, Carrie seemed to swell a little and turn red. She screamed in pain, but her scream was short. While she didn't explode like the Twinkies, her death was just as disgusting. Her eyes turned blood red from popped blood vessels, blood coming out of her eyes, mouth, and nose the longer the machine went on. She writhed and twitched in pain until she finally went limp, her open eyes staring at nothing as she finally died. Luther turned the machine off and took the hose from the box, releasing the seal.

The swelling in Carrie's body slowly went down, more blood oozing from every place it could. Her eyes, mouth, nose, ears. I sobbed in grief, knowing that all of this shit was my fault. The bubbly personality that always had positive words was now gone because I led her down a path she was never meant to be on. Seeing how my bad decisions were now affecting my friends made me feel even more like shit than I'd already felt.

"God, I'm so fucking sorry, Carrie," I sobbed. "She didn't deserve this at all."

Luther stalked over to me and lifted my head to meet his hard gaze. "And neither did Logan," he said, his voice low before he let me go. "But we're nowhere near even. You'll get yours, Sevyn Langdon. I promised you that seven years ago and I'm a man of my word."

Then he winked again, reminding me of the promise he'd made the last time I'd seen him. That same sinister action that promised pain, revenge, and spilled blood. My eyes drifted back to Carrie's body when one of the guys popped the glass box open. He grabbed her by her hair, as if she was a trash bag and plopped her onto a sheet of plastic. Three more guys helped him by grabbing a corner of the plastic and carrying her out of the room. A part of me wanted to keep convincing myself that he wouldn't really kill us, that he just wanted to torture us before he just killed me. But now that Carrie was killed, I couldn't keep lying to myself. There was nothing to justify that her death was fake.

"One bitch down, six more to go," Luther said, rolling his shoulders before he turned and looked to me. "Looks like you better spend the rest of the day and night thinking about who you want to go next."

"You know I c-can't d-do that," I stammered, hiccupping in between my tears.

"Then you can prepare by the punishment you'll get. Your choice," he said and followed the remaining men out of the room.

The rest of us didn't say a word. What the hell could we say to what we'd just witnessed? After a few moments, Allison shook her head.

"I can't believe that just happened," she whispered. "We're really going to die."

"What the hell are we going to do?" Rebecca hissed under her breath. "We can't just sit around here like sitting ducks waiting to be killed."

Sarah glared at her. "Your ideas have gotten us into enough shit. Why don't you shut the fuck up for once?"

"I'm trying to help you," she fired back. "I know you're still upset about your pathetic ex-boyfriend, but we need to put our differences aside in order to make it out of this alive."

"I don't want to pick sides, but she has a point," Jamie interjected. "I thought he just wanted to freak us out, but I don't think he has plans of letting us out of here alive. We need to figure out how to get out of here."

I shook my head. They were delusional to think we'd make it out of here alive. Even if we made it out of this house, we had no idea what awaited outside. Luther had years to formulate this plan and get everything into place. He was a meticulous man, even when he was younger. Everything he did always had an order. His motto was that patience made no room for error and he'd been more than patient when waiting to strike. We had no idea where we even were, so an escape plan was impossible to make right now.

"Sevyn?" Rebecca called out. "Are you down?"

"No," I said.

"What? What do you mean no?" she snapped. "It's nice that you'll be last no matter what, but we don't want to die."

"There's no way out of here. You don't know what's outside or if there are people all over this property—"

"I didn't see anyone outside," Allison spoke up before looking over her shoulder to see if someone was returning. "Wherever we are, we're deep in the woods. Like, deep enough to where I know for a fact that we're not in Miami. Even if we got away from them, there's no telling how far from a store or civilization we are."

"And considering it took that guy forever to get Carrie's food, I have a feeling we're a long way from a town with Chipotle," Crystal added.

Sarah sighed. "So long story short, we're fucked," she murmured.

All of us sat in silence, as there was no doubt that we were royally fucked in this situation.

And there wasn't a damn thing that could be done to prevent it.

CHAPTER 8
LUTHER

I dropped the axe I used to sever Carrie's head and wiped my forehead on the back of my arm. Part one of seven was now done. I didn't want to just kill the woman, as that wouldn't do shit. I wanted to send a message to the judicial system of Miami and to all the rich fucks that thought their money made them untouchable. They may have thought they all got away with murder because of their money, but Carrie's folks were about to get a rude awakening when they received their daughter's head in a box.

"So, how do you want me to do this?" Ryan asked as he squirted lighter fluid on Carrie's clothes. "Who do you want me to send this to? The judge or the parents?"

"Not the judge. I think you should hijack the mail truck in thei neighborhood, get rid of the mailman—"

"Kill the mailman?" he asked with a raised brow. "Killing someone in broad daylight doesn't sound like a good idea in a high scale neighborhood."

"So, what do you suggest, genius?" I asked with a frown.

"How about I get in full disguise or something? Tell the mailman that I want to send a gift to my daughter for her birthday, but my ex-wife won't let me see her. I can just give them the package to them to give it to her parents or something. That way, the parents won't see me, and I'll have enough time to get the hell out of dodge before they realize what's really going on. If anything, they'll question the mailman, who still won't have an accurate description of me because of the disguise."

"That idea is actually dope as fuck if we're being honest," Jake said, nodding in approval. I couldn't lie; it was a genius idea. Ryan could be a major dick at times, but he was just as thorough as I was. He'd even thought about shit I hadn't even thought about. There was no need to kill the mailman, otherwise, he'd have to dump the truck somewhere. I didn't want anymore bodies on my hands aside from the ones I needed, so there was no need to tie an innocent person up into shit that had nothing to do with them. No need to let someone else die because of something we were trying to cover up.

"Then it's settled. What's your disguise though?" I asked. Because this house was our stomping grounds, we usually got ready here before we went out for our victims. That usually meant disguises to mask our appearance in the event we snatched them up from places that could possibly have cameras. Prosthetics, casts, wigs, fat suits, you named it, we had it.

"I'll have to look to see what we have, but you'll see it before I leave tomorrow."

"Sounds like a plan. In the meantime, wrap her up and put her head in the large freezer for now. Get the other girls to their room and you all can have a little fun with them if you want. I'll deal with Sevyn."

I struck a match and burned a wad of paper with a little gasoline on it. The fire quickly roared to life and I tossed the paper into the pit with Carrie. Her dress quickly caught fire before it finally consumed her headless body. We all stared at the raging fire in silence. The guys had taken off their masks at this point, the heat from the Florida sun beaming down on all of us.

"How much do you guys wanna bet that those bitches are trying to formulate a plan to escape?" Victor finally said, breaking the silence between us.

Curtis snorted. "There's literally nowhere to go, and that's if they can even navigate these woods to get to the gravel road anyway," he said.

This house was perfectly hidden. You couldn't drive all the way to it, which was why we needed the girls to be drugged to actually bring them here. We'd drove our cars to the end spot, so to outsiders, it would just seem like we were a group of people going camping in the woods because there was no house in sight. A nearly one-mile hike to the house could be hard when you had a fighting victim, and the last thing you'd want in a place like this was to have a victim run off. We had the safest path to the house memorized at this point, so navigating the woods was no problem for us. There was danger all around the women that they weren't even aware of. Bear traps, net traps, trip wire that activated weapons in trees that released tranquilizers. I mean I was an engineer after all. If anyone aside from me and the guys were ever brought to this house, they weren't leaving alive.

"Them trying to escape is the least of my worries," I said, my eyes still on Carrie's body. "They can't seem to come up with anything on their own without having to be up Sevyn's ass for approval."

"You'd think they'd get a clue on their own considering that Sevyn is the main reason they're here in the first place," Tony mused.

"Well, I'm not sure what you expect from a group of dense sluts," Ryan said, frowning as he watched Carrie's body burn. "Even though the girl was annoying as fuck, she was more bearable than those other ones."

"I don't care if she was better than the others. She got what she deserved," I mumbled. "It'll take time for the body to fully burn. Ryan, you can keep coming to check on it. The metal plate she's on will accelerate the burning process. Once she's burned down to ashes, you can put them in a container to dispose of in the ocean."

"You got it," Ryan said with a nod. "Since my girl is dead, I'm going to head into town to grab food."

"Can you actually get us something this time?" Tony asked with a frown. Ryan looked to me, but I only shrugged and grinned.

"Whatever, man," he said and sighed. "You need to get inside and write down what it is that you want. I don't want to have to drive all over town getting shit from different places."

And with the mention of food, the guys completely forgot about the fire and followed Ryan into the house, leaving me at the fire pit. A wave of satisfaction ran through me as I watched for a few more moments before looking up at the sky.

"Everything is going according to plan, sis," I said to the clear sky above. "Only six more to go before justice is fully served."

And I swore on my life that they'd all pay for what they'd done.

Once the guys gave Ryan their food orders, they each took their remaining girl and dragged them back to the rooms they'd occupied the night before. Sevyn wouldn't look at me. Her head was bowed, her hair hanging in her face as she sniffled softly. I ground my teeth. It pissed me off to see her so distraught over Carrie's death when she didn't show that same kind of sympathy when Logan died. Even to this day, my sister's room was still decorated as it was when she was alive. Pictures of her and Sevyn still covered her walls in that bullshit teen girl scrapbooking style. Even after all Sevyn and her clique did to her, she never got rid of those pictures.

I'd asked my mom about the pictures when I came home from school after everything happened. If I were Logan, there was no way I'd keep pictures of the bitch tormenting me no matter how close we were. My mom would always look at the picture with tears in her eyes before she'd answer with the same thing she did anytime I asked her that. "Logan always said that she wanted to remember the Sevyn she knew. She said that while she didn't like what Sevyn had become, she didn't want to get rid of memories she shared with Sevyn that made her happy."

I used to always get so pissed about my sister's forgiving nature. So many bitches took advantage of that and my sister would always forgive them with a smile on her face. She always had people's best interest at heart, and she hated seeing people hurt her friends. She and I got into a few sibling fights whenever she thought I was being an asshole to her friends. I ground my teeth when I thought about our last fight.

"What the hell are you doing?!" she shrieked when she burst into my room. The girl currently riding my cock jumped off of me, grabbing my sheets to cover her naked body.

"What the fuck?" the girl exclaimed, looking between me and my sister. I'd met her the night before at a party and couldn't remember her name to save my life. What I did remember was that she had amazing tits and a tight pussy that I wanted more of before I kicked her out. My main objective that summer was to fuck as many girls as I could before going back to college in the fall.

"Seriously, Luther, what the hell are you doing?" Logan asked again, glaring at me. I rolled my eyes.

"Trying to get laid, Logan. Get the fuck out," I retorted, throwing a

pillow at her. She caught it and threw it back to me, focusing her gaze on the girl in my bed.

"For your information, he's dating my best friend right now. If you don't want her to come over here and beat you to a pulp, I'd advise you to leave," Logan stated.

"Girlfriend? You said you were single, you prick," the girl said, slapping my bare chest.

"Ow," I protested. "I am single. It's not my fault my sister's high school friend has a crush on me. You don't have to leave, Ashley."

"It's Makayla, you dick," she mumbled as she snatched the sheets off the bed, exposing my hard cock as she quickly grabbed her clothes from the floor and ran off into my personal bathroom.

"Gross, you need to cover yourself," Logan said, putting her hand over her eyes.

"If you don't want to see it, then get the hell out," I snapped. "I hope you're happy with what you've done."

"Luther, you need to figure out what it is that you want. I won't let you hurt Sevyn," she said, her voice firm. "I wouldn't be a good friend if I didn't tell her what you've done."

"So, you'll throw your own brother under the bus?" I asked with a raised brow. She stared at me long and hard.

"I won't let you hurt her because you want to be a man whore, Luther. That's not fair to her. She doesn't trust guys often and for some messed up reason, she trusts you. And if she were to find out that you're doing this and that I knew you were doing this, she's going to hate me just as much as she hates you. I'm not going to allow that to happen!"

Tears burned in her eyes as she yelled at me, usually riddling me with guilt when she did that. I sighed and sat up, pulling on the pair of boxers I'd tossed to the side.

"I hear you, Logan. You're right; I don't want you caught in the middle of this shit. I'll talk to her," I promised.

"You better, Luther. I didn't even know the two of you were dating until she told me. If you're going to date my friend, you need to be faithful and stick to her. She's crazy about you; don't mess that up."

"Aye, aye, captain," I said with a grin. She didn't return it though, her mouth still settled in a frown as she closed my room door.

Makayla came out of the bathroom fully dressed. "Lose my number, asshole," she mumbled as she crossed my room.

I only watched her leave before flopping back on my bed. It didn't make a difference to me. I would've kicked her out eventually once she'd gotten me off. I chuckled to myself as I texted a couple of my friends to find out what party we were hitting up that night. I was headed back to college in a few weeks and I wanted to have as much fun as I could before school stressed me out.

Logan's words echoed in my mind though. Before I could do anything else, I needed to deal with Sevyn before Logan had another breakdown.

I sighed deeply as I looked at Sevyn. The aftermath of my last conversation with Sevyn before all this shit happened probably contributed to her targeting Logan in the first place. It just didn't make sense how someone could go from being attached-at-the-hip best friends to complete enemies. It had to be something more than the breakup that fueled that kind of hate and malice from her. I saw her at her most vulnerable. She'd shared shit with me in the few weeks we were together that I wasn't sure she'd shared with anyone else. I wanted to get in her head this week, to get to the root of knowing why she did what she did. I personally did care to know why; in my mind, she was the enemy that I had to destroy in the name of my sister. But reading my sister's diary after her death, the same question was repeated over and over again.

Why would Sevyn do this to me? I thought I did everything right to help her; why would she still do this to me?

For Logan's sake, I'd find out Sevyn's reason even if it were her dying words.

I untied Sevyn's feet, holding her up as I worked to untie her arms. She didn't try to fight me like I thought she was once she was fully untied. I put her on her feet and tightly gripped her arm, leading her to her room for the night. She walked alongside me silently, her head bowed and her hair hiding her face. I pulled her into a room empty of everything except a mattress on the floor. I watched her face as I put her wrists in shackles. She was blank of any visible emotion, just staring off into space with tears still rolling down her cheeks. When I finally let her go, she moved away from me, curling up into a corner and resting her head on the wall.

I tightened my jaw and stood up. There was a tiny sliver of me that wanted to feel a little guilt for the devastation I was sure she felt, but the loss I felt from my sister's death made it hard for me to sympathize with her. Despite whatever sliver of the old Luther that might've loved the pathetic excuse of a woman a long time ago, all I wanted from her now were answers before I took her life.

Walking out of the room, I stepped into the room next door and grabbed a wooden chair. I went back to her room and sat the chair in the middle of the room before sitting in it. She still didn't say anything or even look at me.

"Are you ready to tell me why?" I finally said after a long bout of silence.

"Tell you what?" she asked, her voice flat. She still had a blank expression on her face, her eyes making her look as if she was spaced out.

"Why you did everything you did to Logan?"

She finally cut her red, puffy eyes at me. "Would telling you stop you from killing anymore of my friends?"

"Nope."

"Then why does it matter?" she muttered.

I exhaled deeply, trying to contain the annoyance bubbling up within me. "It mattered to Logan," I said. "Matter of fact, hold on a second."

I walked back out of the room jogged up the stairs of the basement, heading to my room. One of the many weapons that I planned to used to on Sevyn weren't even things that could physically hurt her. Sevyn was a prideful woman who loved her friends fiercely; I'd already anticipated the fact that she'd take whatever punishment she could to escape having to choose which of her friends would die. To account for that, I had to bring another secret weapon along.

My duffle bag sat in the middle of my bed. I grabbed it and rummaged around in it until my hand hit the leather material of Logan's diary. It was one of the things of hers that I'd kept with me, using it as a way to feel close to her. On the outside, Logan always had this happy-go-lucky attitude about life, which sometimes made me jealous of her. But her diary described her real feelings. Her sadness, her pain, her loss. The things she wouldn't say to others in order to not "burden them with her problems" were all chronicled in her diary.

I clutched the diary in my hand and made my way back to the basement. Sevyn raised her head to look at me when I re-entered the room and sat in the chair. She didn't say a word as she watched me, her eyes trained on the diary as I flipped through the pages of it.

"Ah, here's a good one. Let me show you the kind of friend that my sister was to you," I said and cleared my throat.

Dear diary,

The craziest thing happened today. Sevyn admitted that she's been messing around with Luther. Can you believe that? Apparently, this has been going on for a few weeks right under my nose. A part of me was upset. I mean I don't want to get in between my best friend's happiness, but I know how my idiot brother can be about girls. I just feel like this is going to end in disaster, which will somehow affect my friendship with Sevyn. The worst part? I know for a fact that Luther has been with other girls. He parades them around the house when Mom and Dad aren't here and according to Sevyn, they'd been dating in secret for a little over a month. I feel like I'm stuck in the middle of this situation because I'm loyal to both my best friend and my brother. I know I'll have to talk to Luther about this, but Sevyn made me promise not to say anything to him in case he gets mad at her. What in the world am I supposed to do now? Ugh. I guess I'll figure it out. I seem to always have to figure everyone's crap out.

Xo, Logan

"Do you blame her for me breaking up with you?" I asked when I finished reading it.

Sevyn raised an eyebrow at me. "It's pretty self-centered to think that anything is about you," she said, her voice flat.

"All this bullshit you did to her seemed to happen after I broke things off with you. It's the only logical explanation that you took your anger out on her because you knew she cared about your friendship so much that she'd be your human punching bag," I snapped.

She rolled her eyes. "I don't know what you want me to tell you, Luther," she said. "There was more than just us breaking up that'd happened that summer."

"Then what else happened that made you do the bullshit you did?" I asked, trying to keep my anger in control. She was fucking infuriating, that same smug attitude she'd have seven years ago in court now rearing its ugly head again. She was so devastated when Carrie died, sobbing her pretty little head off in grief, but the mention of Logan sent her back to her "whatever" attitude that she had about shit she didn't care about. It pissed me the fuck off that she could appear unbothered by the death of someone who she'd been friends with for years, probably longer than any of the bitches that helped her push my sister to the edge of a mental cliff before she pushed my sister into throwing herself over the edge, unable to deal with the torment anymore.

"It was seven years ago," was her only reply. "I'll admit that the reason was immature at best, but what did you expect, Luther? We were idiotic kids back then that didn't think about the long-term consequences of our actions. All I can say is that I'm sorry for what happened to Logan. No, she didn't deserve any of the shit we did to her, but we can't take any of that back. We're not the same girls we were back then. You're so stuck on your revenge that you won't even see that."

I ground my teeth as I stared at her. She had some fucking nerve. It wasn't even the complete fact of what they'd done. I couldn't take back any of the shit they did to my little sister any more than they could. It was the fact that no one was punished for it. No one had to pay for their part in my sister's death. Every single one of them went on with their lives completely unaffected. They went to college and graduated. They created memories and lived their young adult lives as if they hadn't bullied an innocent girl to suicide. It wasn't fucking fair at all. And to have Sevyn sit here with her smug ass "We're different people and you're just stuck in the past," bullshit definitely didn't sit well with me.

I closed the space between us in a second, grabbing her by the throat and squeezing. "You know what pisses me off about you?" I growled in her ear. "The fact that you don't even care. You don't care that you destroyed my sister, destroyed my family, destroyed me—"

"As if you didn't destroy me," she fired back, tears glistening in her eyes.

"By fucking breaking up with you?" I scoffed. "Heartbreak happens in life, Sevyn. I'm sure you're well acquainted with breaking hearts yourself."

"It's not the same," she ground out.

"It doesn't even matter," I snapped back. "Maybe it's best that you don't care. It'll be so much easy to fucking break you and not feel any kind of guilt." She tried to wiggle out of the grip I had on her throat as I unbuttoned my jeans. "You're lucky I don't like to share, otherwise there'd be two more guys in here to take turns on you."

"No!" she squeaked out, gasping for air.

"Logan also told them no, even begged them not to do it because she was a virgin," I reminded her, anger coloring my vision red. Even though I couldn't bring myself to watch the video long enough to see the actual assault while in court, I couldn't block out her screaming. Her pleading. Her begging while those fucks tore her apart. I held onto that guilt for the first few years after I'd learned everything that'd happened to her. Her big brother wasn't there to protect her like I promised her I would. Listening to those fucks taunt her with, "Where's Lunatic Luther now?" when they were finished with her lit a rage that I knew wouldn't disappear until every single one of them were dead. And to know that the woman laying beneath me and her squad of bitches were responsible for putting that in motion, I wanted to make her hurt. I wanted to make her scream, make her beg, and make her bleed just as those three fucks did to Logan.

"I said I was sorry!" she rushed out when I finally let go of her throat.

I ignored her, grabbing her legs and pulling her down the mattress until she was flat on her back, the chain attached to her cuffs tightening when she was where I wanted her. She tried to kick me as I pulled my hardening cock from my boxers, whimpering when I grabbed her throat again. The only thing I wanted her doing was screaming and begging for me to stop. She let out a blood curdling scream when I forced myself into her. Her body tightened, her walls squeezing my cock as she tried to wiggle away from me, but she was trapped. With my free hand, I lifted her right leg and pinned it to the mattress, opening her up to me. She sobbed in pain, pleasure streaking up my spine.

"I'm sorry if I'm hurting you, Sevyn," I said sarcastically, pounding into her as she cried. "Let me make it better for you. Does it still hurt now?" I slammed into her, relishing in the fact that she sobbed so hard that she couldn't speak. The more she cried, the more pain I gave her. I let go of her throat and pinned her left leg to the mattress, fully opening her to me.

"Please stop!" she begged, but I was only getting started. She was completely trapped under me, nowhere to run to. She jerked at the chain that bound her, trying to pull herself back from me, but she wasn't going anyway.

"Your pussy has always been amazing, doll," I groaned as I pounded into her. The scent of blood slowly started to permeate into my senses, turning me on even more. "It's even more amazing as I destroy it."

"Please stop," she cried. "I'm sorry!"

"I don't give a fuck about your sorries," I growled. "All I care about is hearing you scream and beg while I tear you open."

And that was what I did. She screamed until she went hoarse again. Every rough stroke I put inside of her melted the current anger that I had. I'd admit that it was a bit strange to have Sevyn under me in this way. The last time I had her on her back was the night before I broke up with her. We'd had sex for the last time, with her having no idea I was breaking up with her the next day. She'd looked up at me with adoration in her eyes, a soft smile on her lips as she asked me what I was waiting for. To see her below me with puffy red eyes and snot and tears all over her face, it was a complete different experience with her.

I pushed back any past memories of us because they no longer mattered. She wasn't that teen girl that I had a summer fling with anymore. She was now the enemy that had to pay for what she'd done, no matter how much I had to hurt her. *The pain is mutual*, I reminded myself. At least for her, the physical pain would eventually go away. And pretty soon, she wouldn't be alive long enough to worry about any mental pain this would leave her with.

When I felt myself nearing my end, I let go of one her legs and grabbed her throat again and squeezed tight. She bucked against me, adding more friction that pushed me further to my end.

"That's it, pretty girl. Fight me all you want," I panted, pumping

EMBER MICHAELS

harder and quicker inside of me. "It feels so much better when you fight me."

She jerked and gasped, unable to get her neck out of my grasp. Her walls contracted around my cock tightly when she tried to bow her back, pulling a groan from my lips. Not soon after that, her eyes fluttered as her body twitched beneath me, bringing me to my end. My balls drew up and I emptied myself inside of her with a moan that echoed off the hollow walls. I panted and bowed my head, sweat rolling down my face. Sevyn was limp beneath me, her pulse weak beneath my fingers. I slowly let go of her throat and pulled out of her. Her blood leaked out of her and onto the mattress, the red tint of it all over my softening erection and my boxers.

Despite the fact that I achieved what it was that I wanted from her, I definitely didn't feel as good as I wanted to. I fantasized about a moment like this for years; I should've felt victorious, vindicated, in control. But I felt...nothing. I definitely didn't feel guilty; she got what she deserved, but I didn't feel anything I thought I would, which pissed me off all over again. A part of me wanted to wake her up and do something else to her to see if it would change my lack of feeling, but finally decided against it. Tomorrow would be even more difficult than today was, so she'd need all the rest she could get.

A solid knock sounded on the door, pulling me out of my musings. "Got food," Ryan said on the other side.

I forced myself to my feet and stuffed myself back into my jeans. I watched her for a few more moments. She took shallow breaths that at least told me she was alive, but it frustrated me to no end that this didn't make me feel anything. With a sigh, I finally pulled my gaze away from her and walked out of the room, running into Ryan. He leaned against the wall and held a bag out to me, a smirk on his now unmasked face.

"Have fun?" he asked when I took the food from him.

"Define fun," I muttered as he followed me back up to the main floor.

"Definitely heard her screaming while I was giving everyone else their food. What happened in there?"

"Doesn't matter. It didn't make me feel shit that I thought I would," I muttered.

Ryan nodded. "Sometimes that's just the collateral damage that comes with revenge. Even if you kill all of them and get justice for your sister, there's a high chance that it won't change anything that you feel or make you feel any better."

"Then what's the point?" I opened the bag and grabbed a few fries. "What's the point in doing all this shit if I won't feel shit? She's the main one I want to hurt and I've yet to feel anything when I've hurt her. I didn't feel anything but a tiny bit of satisfaction when I beat her earlier and that faded just as quickly as it came. I made her scream and beg me to stop while I raped her and it did nothing for me."

"Did you feel the same when you killed Carrie?" he asked.

I shook my head. "No. That was the first time I felt something. Hell, I still feel good after that."

"So...do you think that you can't feel what you expect to feel because you used to have a thing with Sevyn?" he asked cautiously.

The thought alone made my body tense with annoyance. There was always that possibility. The way I'd freeze up when memories of better times would creep into my mind. But she didn't deserve that Luther. The only version of me that she'd get was the raging savage that I'd become. She'd see that soon enough.

"If that were the case, I'd at least feel guilt. But I don't feel shit. Nothing at all."

"You feel that she deserves it; that's why you don't feel guilt. But it's hard to feel happy about someone you may care about even after all these years. Negative and positive shit cancel each other out. I think your hatred and past feelings for her are canceling out, which is resulting in feeling nothing at all. But I don't know, man. It's just a theory."

"Seriously doubt that." I closed up the bag of food after grabbing a couple more fries and stuffing them into my mouth. "I need to take a shower. Good talk, though."

I left him in the living room shaking his head, pondering over his words. The only feelings I knew I felt were hate for this woman, no matter the history I had with her. I mean I couldn't still have feelings for her…could I?

I scoffed to myself as I headed to my room. I needed to get my head in the game and focus on what I needed to do.

One fuck up could cost me everything, and I couldn't afford for any unexpected situations.

The livelihood of my guys and myself depended on it.

CHAPTER 9

SEVYN

I looked around Logan's old room, unsure of what I was doing here. Everything looked as it did the last time I was here. She was such a girly girl, her gorgeous canopy bed against the far wall, a thick purple comforter made up on it with matching pillows and white accent pillows. Her walls were covered in posters of Zayne, Twilight movie characters, and photos of her friends. I walked over to a wall that was covered in nothing but pictures. A small touched my lips as I looked at all of them. She wasn't close with the other girls I was friends with because she thought they were "no good." Sometimes I wished I'd listened to her.

A particular picture of the two of us stopped me in my tracks. We were both in bikinis on South Beach, living our young, teenaged lives in the sun. With our ridiculously large sunglasses and floppy sunhats, we each *held a canned soda in the air with one hand and held up the peace signs with our other hand. The bright smiles on our faces made my chest ache with grief. I hadn't seen a picture of her in so long that it hadn't hit me just how much I actually missed her. Even halfway through everything we'd done to her, a part of me wanted to stop when I thought we'd gone too far, especially when she was raped, but we'd already crossed the line.*

"We had so much fun that day, right?" a soft voice said behind me. I whirled around on my heels to see Logan standing there with a small smile on her face. She looked as pretty as she always did, and forever seventeen. She wore a white dress with small yellow sunflowers on it, her dark chestnut hair swishing over her shoulders. It was her favorite dress in life, one that I'd heard she requested to be buried in when she wrote her suicide note.

She walked over and stood next to me, looking at the picture. "I can't believe we thought that was stylish back then. We looked so dorky," she said and giggled.

Tears burned my eyes as I looked back at the picture. "It was," I said, my voice cracking. "But it was fun. That was all I cared about, I guess."

"Yeah, me too," she said with a small sigh. "Oh! You remember this one?" She pointed to one of us wearing life jackets, our hair soaking wet. I giggled. She'd convinced me to go kayaking with her family for the weekend. I'd never done anything like it, but I went because it was a nice escape away from the bullshit going on with my family at the time and a good enough excuse to be around Luther.

"I nearly drowned that day, you know," I said, remembering how I flipped out of the kayak trying to get my tennis bracelet from the water

that'd slid off my wrist while I swished my hand around in the water.

"You were wearing a life jacket," Logan said and laughed, the sound making tears roll down my cheeks.

I laughed and shook my head. "That was still scary as hell, Logan," I said and released a light sigh. "It was fun though." I looked at her, watching as she grinned, her eyes traveling along the pictures. "I miss you, you know."

She looked at me and smile. "Duh. I'm a missable person," she joked. Her smile faltered a bit the longer she looked at me. "I didn't tell him your secret."

I swallowed the lump forming in my throat. Of course she didn't. It was one of the things I'd blamed her for. I made her swear that she wouldn't tell him, as I wanted to do it myself. So, when he broke up with me a few days after I'd told her, I was livid. Hurt. Betrayed by my best friend that I thought I could trust. But I should've known Logan would never do anything like that. I was so caught up in my own emotions that I didn't think logically. Now, my best friend was dead, her brother was out to kill me and my friends, and it could've all been prevented had I actually just asked her if she did instead of assuming.

"I'm sorry," I whispered, a single tear rolling down my cheek. She reached up to brush it away, giving me the bright smile that she was known for.

"I know you are," she said. "And you also know I can never stay mad at you."

"How can you forgive me so easily? I basically ruined your life."

"Yeah…you did," she said slowly, her shoulders sagging a bit. "But I know the real you, Sevyn. You were acting out of anger and pain, especially *after everything that happened after you and Luther stopped seeing each other." She was quiet for a moment. "My mom always said that sometimes people lashed out in pain when they couldn't really communicate what they felt. That's how I look at what you did."*

I gave her a watery smile and shook my head. "You didn't deserve that though, Logan. I know it won't mean much now, but I truly am sorry for everything. There hasn't been a day where I haven't thought about you."

"Is that why you cut yourself?" she asked. I looked down at my legs, seeing that I was still naked here. The scars of my self harming phase were visible on my skin, so it wasn't like I could lie about it. I looked back up into Logan's sad eyes. "I wouldn't want you to do that."

"But you did," I countered.

"I did because I was in pain. You did a lot of cruel things, Sevyn. And while I forgive you, it wasn't something that I could keep living with. You guys ruined me. You ruined my future. My reputation. You got me expelled from school during senior year, which meant that no college would accept me. I did what I did because I was hurt by someone I loved like a sister, someone that I'd do anything for. Why didn't you just ask me if I'd told him or not? I would've told you I didn't," she said.

A few tears rolled down my cheeks as I looked at her. "I don't know," I confessed in a whisper. And it was the truth. Once Luther broke up with me, my world shattered. The time I spent with him was the peace I needed from my stressful life. He didn't care about my family's status or our money, just like Logan didn't. She and I were so different and alike at the same time and being around her, around him, made me feel so…normal. It was almost pathetic in a sense, the rich girl with everything she could want being jealous of her friend for having a normal life. For having normal, loving parents. For having normal struggles. Creating normal memories that my family would turn their nose up at. Her family made me feel like one of their own, which was why I spent more time at her house than I did at my own. It was even to the point to where my other friends couldn't understand why I was friends with her in the first place.

"Isn't she, like, poor or something?" Rebecca had said once. "Is she one of your charity cases?"

Like an idiot, I didn't defend her. I let my rich friends talk shit about her, smiling in her face while they stabbed a knife in her back. But after what I did to her—what we all did to her—I was no better than they were. In fact, I was the worst of all because Logan didn't expect something like that to come from me.

"I didn't deserve you as a friend, Logan. I can't express how sorry I am for how things ended," I finally said, wiping my eyes.

"Shit happens, right? Isn't that what you used to always say when bad things happen?" she asked. I giggled. Logan didn't curse often and when she did, it was usually to quote something I'd said. The only "curse" word she'd use was hell, and that was only when she was angry. Either way, it was always amusing when she said them. She'd always blush when she said a "bad word" and then giggle, as if it tickled her to be "bad." God, she was just too good of a person, which was the main reason I carried my guilt about what broke down our friendship for so many years.

"Yeah, shit happens," I said. "Your brother's going to kill me, you know."

She sighed. "Luther has always been an angry guy. He's not as forgiving as I am," she said.

"Then I guess I'll be seeing you more often soon enough. Once he's killed all my friends in the next few days, he'll do the same to me."

"Are you scared?" she asked. Her question caught me off guard. I wasn't sure how I felt. I think I was more afraid of watching my friends die than I was of my actual death. I'd attempted to take my life a few times but was too scared to go through with it. A part of me was glad that Luther had finally caught me. I was so exhausted from constantly watching over my shoulder for him. I couldn't take the nightmares anymore, the hallucinations, the paranoia that plagued my life. Maybe I was ready for him to make me pay so that I could finally release my guilt. Maybe I was ready for him to do what I couldn't bring myself to do. But as I looked at Logan and thought about all the things she'd missed out on so far, like turning eighteen, going to college, growing up…I thought of how selfish it would be to want the easy way out after all I'd done.

"I don't know," I finally said. "It's easy to want to die when you feel like you have control…but it's hard to know what to feel when you're actually staring death in the face." I was quiet for a few moments, my gaze focused on the floor. "Were you scared?"

I saw her nod in my peripheral. "Yeah." She was quiet for a moment. "The scariest part was right before I did it. But with my phone going off on the bathroom counter while I sat in the tub was just too much to handle. I thought if everyone hated me so much, maybe I was better off not being here."

Sadness laced her voice and my heart broke knowing I'd caused that. She sighed and bowed her head before she continued speaking.

"But once it was done and I was laying there waiting for the end,

I was sad. Sad that I wasn't strong enough to get through to the other side. Sad that my parents were going to discover me and that would forever be a traumatic thing for them. Sad about what it would do to my only brother. Sad that you thought so little of me that you thought I'd do something to hurt you. Sad that you hated me so much that you'd hurt me like that."

"I never hated you, Logan," I said, a sob escaping from my lips. "That situation was 100% on me. It never should've happened, and I don't know if I can ever forgive myself for it. I live with that guilt every single day."

"Well, we can't change the past. All we can do is learn from it." She reached up and gripped my arms, giving them a gentle squeeze. "You have to learn to forgive yourself, Sevyn. But now, you have to wake up."

"Wait! Logan—"

I opened my eyes and took a deep breath before going into a coughing fit. Every part of my body ached, a burning sensation settling between my legs as the fog of sleep lifted. My throat hurt each time I swallowed, and it hurt too much to move in any direction. I tried to close my legs, whimpering when the pain down there nearly took my breath away. My entire body ached being on this uncomfortable mattress. My joints were stiff, and my muscles ached all over. It seemed like yesterday when I was in my own plush bed only having nightmares of the shit I was now experiencing. But no matter how many times I squeezed my eyes shut and chanted that I'd just had a bad dream, it didn't change my current reality of being in my own personal hell.

Staring up at the chipped pain on the ceiling, tears burned my eyes. If death awaited me, I wished it would go ahead and come. *You don't deserve a quick and easy death,* a small voice reminded me. I thought about my dream. Logan was so vivid in it and it felt so real. I didn't realize how much I really missed her. I did think about her from time to time, mostly trying to push thoughts of her to the back of my mind. But to be in her room in my dream, to actually see her face again, it was soul crushing even though it was just a dream.

The door to the room opened, but I didn't bother to look. I already knew it was Luther. I couldn't bear to look at him after what he'd done to me. I wasn't sure how long I'd been out. There were no windows in this room to know if it was day or night. His footsteps echoed in the relatively empty room until they came to a stop next to me.

"You slept all night," his deep voice said. I didn't say a word. It wasn't like I could. I felt as if someone had scrubbed the inside of my throat raw with the coarsest sandpaper they could find. He stood next to the bed, his hands in his pockets as he looked down at me with an expression that I couldn't quite interpret. "Ready to choose which one of your friends will die today?"

I shook my head. I just couldn't take on that responsibility. Seeing Carrie die yesterday was too much for me to bear and I wasn't even the one who'd chosen her.

"Please don't make me," I croaked, my voice coming out barely above a whisper.

Luther only frowned down at me. "It's so funny how you easily chose my sister as a victim with no hesitation, but you want to be a saint now and not be the cause of anyone's death," he stated, his voice tight. "Unfortunately for you, it doesn't work like that. The rules are the same as yesterday. Either you choose someone, or you'll face another punishment." He looked down at my battered pussy and smirked. "And I'm sure you can't handle my cock for a second day in a row."

He was definitely right about that. Being a saint wouldn't earn me any favors here. All that did was make my hell a lot worse. I couldn't even say not picking anyone would mean that I wouldn't have blood on my hands because that wouldn't be true. I had blood on my hands the moment I wrangled my friends into my plans. Their blood was on my hands when my parents paid off a few jury members and the judge. Their blood was on my hands when Luther winked at me, promising me that he'd make me pay. It didn't matter if I chose them or someone else; someone was going to die today just as someone did yesterday.

I swallowed hard, wincing. I'd have to think long and hard about what I wanted to do. Luther broke into my musings when he unlocked the cuffs around my wrists and yanked me to my feet. I cried out, the sound coming out weak and pathetic. My pussy burned like hell, my blood crusted on my thighs and on the bed.

"Before we do anything though, you need a shower," he said as he pulled me along. "I can't fuck a filthy whore in front of an audience if you make the wrong decision, now can I?" he taunted.

My eyes were sore from all the crying I'd done before. Even

though I wanted to cry, I couldn't even produce any tears. I stumbled alongside of him, pain coursing my body with every step I took. *You have to choose someone today*, I thought to myself. After what he did to me yesterday, my body couldn't take anything else today. If choosing someone today meant that whatever he had in store for me wouldn't be so severe, it was a possibility I had to consider. Taking my punishment yesterday didn't stop Carrie from being killed. Luther made everything crystal clear; it was my own fault if I made things harder for myself.

Tears sprung to my sore eyes when we walked up the steps to the main level of the house. Every time I stepped up, I felt as if I was ripping myself in half. Luther only looked at me with a raised brow when I grunted but made no kind of effort to actually help me. *Why would I even expect him to? He's the one that did this to me in the first place,* I reminded myself. I ground my teeth and did my best not to focus on the pain, practically holding my breath until we were finally on the main floor. He pulled me down a short hall to a fully decorated bedroom. The bed frame was a dark wood poster frame, a soft queen mattress calling out to my aching body.

Luther chuckled when he saw what'd caught my attention. "Looks good after a night in the basement, huh?" he asked. I nodded. He stared at the bed before running a hand down his face. "I'll tell you what. If you choose someone to die today, you can rest in it until tomorrow morning."

I looked up at him. The amusement that colored his face frustrated me. He was playing on my pain and emotions to get me to do what he wanted me to do. It wasn't fair in the slightest, but wasn't that the whole point of this? To show us how unfair it was to his family that we basically got a slap on the wrist for what we'd done? I looked at the bed again. *I can't save anyone being a saint. After everything I went through yesterday, I definitely need it,* I thought to myself.

"Just imagine it: getting to eat in a comfortable bed and actually eating a real meal instead of sandwiches like the rest of the girls. All you have to do is give me a name," he said.

I frowned. How did I know this wasn't a trick just to get me to choose? "Why would you reward me with a decent bed?" I croaked.

"Because watching your face when I kill whoever you choose will be the best reward you can give me. I feel it's only best to return the favor, even if it's something as simple as a bed for a couple of nights until I eventually end your life, too," he said with a shrug. "I'll give you some time to think about it when you shower."

He pulled me into his bathroom. It was just as big as my bathroom in my condo. I wasn't entirely sure what Luther did for a living exactly, but if he'd purchased this house, he definitely had a lot of money now. He didn't say anything as he led me over to the large walk-in shower. I watched him as he turned on the water, a bit nervous about getting under the spray. With how sore my body was, the water almost looked painful. Considering the nonchalant look he had on his face, I assumed he didn't care about my pain as long as I got clean. My eyes traveled around the room. Everything was white and sterile with black accents. Black towels. Black abstract pictures on the wall. Black wash cloths. Black cups on the sink holding a single toothbrush. The sunlight filtering into the bathroom caught my attention. *A window,* I thought, a bubble of hope growing inside of me.

"There are bear traps under every window of this place. The only safe place is out of the front and back door, and that's only if you have the key to unlock it from the inside," Luther said, as if reading my mind. He held his hand under the steaming water before nodding toward the shower. "Get in."

I swallowed hard and slowly inched into the shower when he let go of me. The heat of the water was comforting, but it burned my open cuts and wounds. I jumped out of the water as Luther closed the shower door behind me. I could see his silhouette leaning against the bathroom counter, essentially blocking me in here. With a sigh, I grabbed a washcloth that was inside, the cotton material soft in my hands.

The water pounding against the bruises on my entire backside hurt like hell as I forced myself to stand under the spray. I winced as my hair became soaked, my scalp burning when the water hit the cuts on it thanks to the crown of thorns Luther made me wear yesterday. There were cuts and bruises to places I didn't even realize until the water hit it. The back of my neck. My calves. I held back tears as I tried to wash the dried blood from between my legs. The soap burned even more. The pain felt as if I were washing myself with soap laced with acid or some kind of chemical meant to burn me even worse. Knowing Luther and his intention to hurt me in any way he could, I wouldn't doubt it.

When I thought I was clean enough, I just stood under the water. I wasn't sure when my next shower would be or if I'd get another one at all. I wished I was in my shower at home, that when I got out, I'd go into my bedroom, get dressed, and start my day. But the only thing waiting outside the shower door was a man who'd want to know what decision I'd make today; one I wasn't ready to make.

A gust of cool air rose goosebumps on my skin before the water turned off. "Let's go," Luther ordered. I shivered a bit, wrapping my arms around myself as I got out. He roughly dried me with the plush black towel. Silent tears rolled down my cheeks as he ignited my pain all over again, especially between my legs. He finally finished and tossed me another towel to dry my hair. My shoulders were still a bit stiff and sore from being bound above my head all night, but I dried my hair the best I could. He stared at me as I did, his face wiped of any emotion. I passed him the towel and he tossed it into a black laundry hamper.

He nodded toward the counter. "Put that on," he said, his voice low. A white, silk nightgown and a pair of panties were there. I picked up a pad that sat on top of it and looked to him. He only shrugged. "I'd rather not have you bleeding all over the place while you're wearing white."

I ground my teeth. *It's your fault I'd be bleeding in the first place, asshole,* I bitterly thought to myself, but I just put everything on as he instructed. I had bigger things to worry about, like what was on the agenda today. I had no idea what kind of painful death I'd be submitting one of my friends to by making the choice, which was even worse than the actual choice.

Luther led me out of the bathroom and through the bedroom until we were back in the hallway. My friends were being pulled from the basement, all of them looking a lot rough than they did the night before. I wasn't sure what happened to them but based on the bruises on their faces and throats and the way some of them limped, they probably suffered the same way I did, which made my heart heavy. He waited until they'd all passed me before he tightened his grip on my upper arm and led me into the living room with the rest of them. The cross that was there yesterday wasn't there, only a chair like the rest of my friends sat in. I fought the urge to whimper in pain when Luther pushed me into the chair and secured the cuffs around my wrists and ankles, putting the painful crown of thorns on my head as well.

"Welcome to day two, ladies," he finally said when everyone was situated. No one said a word, so he continued. "Since I feel like I've established that Sevyn isn't a god despite how you worshipped her, I didn't think the cross was necessary."

"You're fucking psychotic," Crystal mumbled. Her olive skin was covered in bruises: her neck, face, and arms sported blueish-green bruises, still fresh as the edges of them started to darken.

Luther chuckled. "I think everyone in this room is psychotic. I mean there's no way you could've done what you bitches did and not think you also weren't psychotic," he mused and then looked to me. "But let me make this quick. I'm sure some of you had a rather

THE DESTRUCTION OF SEVYN

eventful night last night and would much rather be in your rooms resting instead of being up here all day. So Sevyn, have you come to a decision?"

Anxiety overwhelmed me as I looked to my friends. I still didn't know if I could trust Luther to keep his word. How in the hell was I supposed to pick? I cared about all of them and felt as if I were close to all of them. I didn't know if I was strong enough to pick one of them now that I sat before them. I weighed the options I thought I'd have, but in reality, there were no options. Whether I chose or not, Luther would choose someone himself and kill them anyway. The only thing I'd get was another punishment and having to sleep on that hard bed in the basement.

But even if he doesn't keep his word about the comfortable bed, I'll still escape a punishment, I reminded myself. Luther snapped his fingers in front of my face.

"Hey space cadet, you wanna come join us back on Earth? Who's your choice?" he asked. His voice has an edge of impatience and I knew if I didn't choose one of my friends or choose to take another punishment, he'd make the decision himself.

I looked amongst my friends. I thought back to everything that happened yesterday. Remembering how my friends turned on each other at a drop of a hat. Then I remembered how Jamie basically said she'd used me because her parents needed the connections my family had. She was only going along with whatever I said to help her parents get ahead. Fucking typical for majority of the friends I'd ever had except Logan.

"Jamie," I finally said, my voice trembling as I said her name loud enough for Luther to hear.

He smirked at me. "Look at you finally growing a pair of balls and doing what you're supposed to," he taunted and then looked to Jamie. "Looks like you're the next contestant on *Paying Luther's Price*."

Jamie glared at me. "Of course you'd pick me," she scoffed under her breath. I narrowed my gaze at her.

"Why are you surprised? I mean you were only friends with me to help your own family. Why should I care about someone who admitted to using me?"

"That was back then, Sevyn. I don't think that way about you anymore," she argued. I shook my head. That was what they always said when they had to face the consequences of using me. They of all people knew how spiteful I was. There was nothing I hated more than people using me or toying with my emotions. Now that I knew what I knew about her, I wouldn't feel all that sorry when it was her time to go.

"You know the drill, Jamie," Luther said. "Last meal request?"

"Fuck you! And fuck all of this! I don't want your stupid last meal that'll only make me have to wait in fear and anticipation before you decide to finally kill me," she screamed, tears brimming her eyes.

Luther raised an eyebrow and looked around at his masked guys before looking back to her. "So...does that mean you want to just skip to being killed or...what? I mean I'm down with getting to the good part if you want to," he said and chuckled.

Jamie's face turned beet red as she stared at him, her bottom lip trembling. "You make your sister appear to be some saint, but not once have you acknowledged what she did to Sevyn," she fired back.

"Sevyn won't even tell me the real reason, so what do you expect me to think? If anything, I just think you bitches were jealous of her and wanted to get her out of the way."

"Sevyn did it because she was angry at you for cheating on her and then having the nerve to break up with her," Jamie stated.

"Wait, what?" I asked. I'd never heard of anything official about him being with other people. I thought back to our conversation that day, flipping through my memories to see if he'd told me he was already seeing someone else.

"This sunset is so beautiful," I said as we sat in the park. He nodded, his hands clasped in front of him as he rested his elbows on his knees. He'd seemed distracted all evening, almost as if he had somewhere else he'd wanted to be. "Why're you so quiet?"

He sighed deeply and leaned back on the bench. "Trying to figure out the best way to tell you what I need to tell you," he said, his voice low. My heart skipped a beat. Was tonight the night he'd finally tell me he loved me or something? We hadn't been officially dating for very long, but I'd known him for years. Everything felt so natural together and I ended up spending many nights with him, even some nights that Logan didn't even know about as I fucked her brother right under her nose. Our secret relationship felt like something sexy and dangerous, and I craved him in ways that I couldn't fully understand. Just like him, I also had something

I wanted to tell him. I wanted to tell him how I felt about him as well, along with a little secret that I wasn't sure how he'd react to.

"What's up?" I finally asked, deciding to test the waters before dropping the four-letter word.

He looked ahead and slumped down on the bench a little. "So, you know I'm returning to college soon, right?" he started.

I slowly nodded. "Yeah? I mean we can do video chats and stuff and I can come visit you on the weekend or something—"

"I think we should break up," he interrupted.

"Long distance relationships aren't...what?" I said when my brain finally caught up to what he'd just said. The muscle in his jaw ticked as he dropped his gaze to his lap.

"I think we should break up," he said, his voice a bit louder and clearer now. I should my head in confusion. I didn't understand. How we'd go from being intimate to him now wanting to end things?

"I don't understand," I said slowly, rolling the words around in my head. "Did I do something wrong? Are you mad that I told Logan about us?"

"It's not you. I just think that since I won't be in high school anymore and I'll meet new people in college, I think it's best we end whatever it is going on between us. I think it'll be a less likely chance for me to hurt you if I go ahead and end this now."

"Luther, you can't be serious right now," I asked in disbelief. "What happened since the last time I saw you? Is it someone else?"

"It's no one, Sevyn. I just think it's just the best for me right now," he said.

"Is fucking Logan behind this? You at least owe me an explanation,"

I fired back, tears burning my eyes. He only stood up in response, his hands in his pockets as he looked in the ground.

"I just don't want to be with a high school girl. You were cool to mess around with this summer, but I think we both need to move on," he said.

"You're fucking unbelievable," I scoffed and grabbed my purse. "Lose my number and don't ever talk to me again."

I stormed past him, purposely bumping him. He didn't bother trying to stop me or telling me that he was kidding. My blood boiled as I stomped across the grass to the parking lot, hopping in my Audi and speeding out of the parking lot. I broke down in my car while stopped at a red light, confused, heartbroken, and devastated. But despite the pain I felt when he just dropped me like a hot potato, I couldn't help the overwhelming anger I felt toward Logan. I'd made her promise me that she wouldn't say anything to Luther about the thing I kept from him because I wanted him to hear it from me and not his friends or anyone else. I thought Logan had ruined all of that. Ruined my future with the one guy who'd ever had my heart. All I could think in that moment was that Logan was going to pay for ruining one of the best things I had in my life at the time.

"You'd be stupid to think Luther was really exclusive to you while you were together," Jamie stated, a smug look on her face as if she thought she'd hurt me somehow. Luther was no longer the guy I remembered for me to really be sad about what he'd done to me years ago. When I didn't react, she frowned and went quiet. Luther turned his attention on me.

"So that was your reason after all, huh? You thought Logan was the reason we broke up," he stated. I knew he'd keep asking me about it if I didn't give him a reason. It was part of the reason, but not the main thing that sent me over the edge.

"I guess it was," I said, my voice flat. He studied me for a long moment.

"Do I look today or yesterday years old?" he asked as he rolled his eyes. "You have to think I was an idiot to believe that."

"Is it impossible to even consider the thought that you meant everything to me?" I asked. He shook his head.

"For someone to be so important, you could get any guy you wanted. You can't expect me to believe that you were so hung up on me that you decided to go after my sister." He stroked his bare jawline, his eyes never leaving mine. "I'll find what the reason was even if I have to beat it out of you. But it won't be today." Peering at Jamie, he asked, "Last meal request; final offer."

"I don't want a fucking meal," Jamie snapped. "You're not about to torment me with waiting.

"Suit yourself," Luther said with a shrug and then turned to his men. "Get the wheel. I think I'm in the mood for a little knife throwing."

CHAPTER 10

LUTHER

Adrenaline rushed through my veins once again once Jamie was strapped to the wheel. I couldn't even stand still, opting to bounce from foot to foot as if I was preparing for battle. This was the feeling I craved, that excitement and anticipation of spilling blood. I couldn't wait to relish in her screams, her tears, her pain. I couldn't wait to see the look on Sevyn's face when she saw the impact of her decision this time around. I was surprised that she caved so quickly. Who would've known that all it took was the offer of a soft bed that she wasn't actually going to sleep in to make her cave so easily?

Tony handed me a bag of sharp knives, ones we always threw at the targets on the trees outside. This would be my first time actually using them on people and I'd be lying if I said I wasn't overly excited.

"Anything you'd like to say to your friends?" I asked as I took a few knives from the bag.

"You're going to burn in hell for what you're doing," she said. I rolled my eyes.

"Anything you'd like to say that I don't already know?" I asked sarcastically.

She glared at me. "Your sister was a bitch who got what was coming to her," she fired back.

My body stiffened, the playful mood I was in morphing into anger. I would have so much fun ending this bitch now. "Pissing me off before I kill you isn't the smartest thing you want to do," I warned.

"As if I care. I'm going to end up dead anyway. So, fuck you! Fuck you! Fuck you! Fuck you! You're all a bunch of dicks who'll rot in hell."

"We'll rot right next to you. You're no saint either, bitch." I looked to Tony. "Spin the wheel." He nodded and walked over to it. When he reached up to give it a good spin, Jamie's eyes went wide.

"Wait, wait, wait!" she exclaimed, but I didn't want to hear anything else except her screaming. Tony spun the wheel she was tied to and she screamed. I closed one eye and lined up the knife with her center, trying to focus on the place I wanted to hit. After a few moments, I threw it as hard as I could and caught her in the upper thigh, just as I wanted it.

"Have you been practicing? You used to suck ass at this game

THE DESTRUCTION OF SEVYN

when we're outside," Victor teased behind me.

I chuckled. "Shut up, asshole. Maybe I liked letting you win," I retorted.

"Bet you $20 he won't hit another one in a row," Jake said to the guys.

"Then get ready to pay up, Jake-y boy," I said as I repeated my earlier stance, closing one eye and lining it up. Tony gave the wheel more momentum as Jamie screamed in pain.

"No!" she screamed just as I threw the knife. I grinned in satisfaction when the blade drove into her bicep. She wailed in pain, jerking against the ropes that held her as if they'd give out and free her from the wheel. I turned to face the guys, giving a slight bow as they all clapped.

"I'll round up any money I've won when this is over, so please, do keep betting," I joked.

"Hell no. I'll be broke by the time this is over. I'll stick with the $20," Jake said with a chuckle.

The girls watched in horror as I threw knife after knife, hitting Jamie in various places. Her other bicep. Her forearms. Her stomach. Her chest. Soon her screaming stopped as blood leaked from her mouth, her body growing limp as she lost more blood.

"Go for the jugular!" the guys chanted in the background. I grinned at them over my shoulder.

"Eh....I don't know. Think I can hit it?" I asked.

"If you could, that'll be a kill for the history books," Curtis said. Tony gave the wheel an extra spin. If I was going to do it, my window was closing fast. It wouldn't have the same effect if she died before I actually had the chance to do it.

"Throw it! Throw it!" Paul exclaimed, bouncing from foot to foot in excitement. I took a deep breath and threw the knife with as much power as I could muster, satisfaction filling me when the knife went through the center of her throat, pinning her head to the wooden board. A grin slid across my lips as the guys all cheered in the background. All the feelings I wanted to feel when hurting Sevyn flooded me all at once, making me high on the thrill of the kill. The wheel slowly came to a stop. Jamie's blood dripping onto the plastic on the floor, the scent of copper quickly filling the space as she bled out.

"Oh, my fucking god!" one of the girls screamed. Someone sobbed behind me, but my attention was on Sevyn's face. She looked a bit green around the gills, her face wet with silent tears. A mixture of guilt, regret, and sorrow swirled in her eyes as she gazed up at Jamie's body. But unlike the other girls who sobbed and cursed in shock, Sevyn didn't say anything. In a sense, it seemed as if she was accepting the fate of everyone here, knowing that her time was coming in five more days. The sound of retching made me cringe. I turned to see Crystal throwing up in her lap, her face covered in snot and tears at the scene before her.

"Fucking hell. You bitches act like you've never seen a dead body before," Victor mumbled.

"I mean not in the extent that we have," Paul reminded him. "We're actual killers. The only time these sluts have seen a dead body is at a lame funeral."

"What a sad life they must've lived then," Victor said and shrugged.

Sevyn finally met my eyes and I grinned. "Was the choice worth it?" I asked her. She didn't verbally answer. She only bowed her head, her shoulders shaking softly as she cried at the loss of another friend.

"You guys are fucking sick," Sarah fussed.

"I'll show you what's really sick," Curtis said as he grabbed his phone from the charger near the mantle. "I need to get a picture of this masterpiece. Everybody gather round."

We all huddled around Jamie's body, everyone giving a cheesy thumbs up to show just how unaffected we were. One of the women scoffed in disgust, but I didn't give a fuck. They should be glad that they had more time left instead of whining about how sick we were.

"Are you ladies ready to eat then?" Jake asked sarcastically.

"You know, you and Ryan are the only people I know that immediately start asking about food after a kill," Curtis joked.

"Well, all that excitement and action gives me a hell of an appetite," Jake responded, patting his rock hard abs. "So how about it? I make a food run after we dispose of the body?"

I frowned and looked around the room. "Speaking of bodies, where the fuck is Ryan?" I asked.

"I think he's getting his disguise ready. I saw him going outside this morning," Paul answered. I relaxed a bit and nodded.

"Has he decided on one yet?" I asked, just as the front door opened and closed.

"I guess we're about to find out," Tony said, our eyes moving toward the foyer. Ryan came into view and I snorted so hard I hurt my face. He'd transformed himself into an old man that could pass off as an innocent grandpa. He wore a wig that made him look like he was balding at the top, using prosthetics to create wrinkled skin and a nose bigger than his actual one. He had a bushy mustache and eyebrows, which were furrowed at us as we laughed at him.

"I take it that it's a good disguise?" he asked, tap dancing a few steps. Even his voice sounded like an old man. He had one of those "get off my lawn" grumpy grandpa voices and I couldn't control myself the more he spoke.

"You don't even look like yourself, man," Victor said, wiping his eyes as he laughed.

"That's the whole point, genius," Ryan replied sarcastically before looking to me.

I tried to contain myself long enough to answer him and nodded. "It's definitely a good one, Gramps. You're definitely getting into character with the whole voice thing," I said. All of Ryan's experience in theater made him the king of disguises. He usually did everyone's disguises if we all needed one, but he was amazing at doing his own. "Looks like you're ready to rock and roll."

"Always," he said and cocked his head when he saw Jamie's body. "Pretty damn impressive. I didn't know you were bringing the wheel out. Wish I didn't miss it." His voice had reverted back to his usual one as he admired my work.

I shrugged. "I was in a knife throwing mood, I guess," I said and grinned. "But you're already slipping out of character, Grandpa."

"Oh, sorry, sorry," he said, his voice matching his disguise again. "Do you want me to wait for her or do you want me to go on with Carrie's?"

"Just worry about Carrie. Tony will be responsible for Jamie's head," I said.

"Sounds legit. I'll call you once the box is out of my hands," he said and left again with a parting wave.

"Can you imagine asshole Ryan as a grandpa?" Paul asked.

"I'm not even out of the house yet, you dickhead!" Ryan threw back from the foyer.

"Whoops," Paul snickered when the front door opened and closed again. "That guy's always so uptight."

"You're always fucking with him. Ever consider that possibility?" Curtis asked, smirking.

"Just messing with him. He's so easy to get riled up. Him and Luther, actually," Paul said and grinned.

I shook my head. "Just shut up and held me get this body off the wheel," I said.

"Are you fucking enjoying this or something? You haven't said a single word or had a single reaction," one of the girls said. I looked over my shoulder to see what she was going on about and saw Rebecca just sitting there. She didn't cry like the rest of them or have any kind of emotion on her face. She looked as if she was bored, as if she didn't just witness the murder of one of her so-called besties. Considering the animosity between the girls right now, they were all probably just thinking of their own self-preservation.

"It wasn't like Jamie and I were close," she drawled. "Just because I'm not crying a river like the rest of you, it doesn't mean that I don't care."

"You're even more of a psychopath than they are," Sarah grumbled under her breath.

"Now isn't the time to fight with each other," Sevyn ground out. "We're all upset, okay? Besides, Rebecca isn't an overly emotional person."

"Really? I couldn't tell," Paul said with a scoff. Sevyn narrowed her gaze at him and frowned.

"I've known her a lot longer than you have. I think I'd know what she was like," she snapped.

"She was crying crocodile tears yesterday when you were beaten. And let's not get started on how she reacted when she heard you screaming. Guess Luther was going to Pound Town on you then."

"Awww, how sweet is it that she's concerned about her girlfriend," I mused. I walked across the sheet of plastic and stood behind Rebecca. Moving her hair over her shoulder to expose her ear, I leaned down until my lips were leveled to it. "I bet you enjoyed seeing her naked yesterday, huh?"

"Shut up," she ground out, keeping her eyes forward. I locked eyes with Sevyn, who had a mixture of worry and annoyance in her gaze. I didn't break eye contact with her as I continued whispering to Rebecca.

"I bet you wish I would've let you loose for you to have your way with her because you know she wouldn't be able to refuse. You probably daydream about what it'd be like to have her ride your face, don't you?"

"No," she stated, though her voice wasn't as confident as it usually was.

"Too bad you missed it last night. She's so tight and juicy…and I bet she tastes just as sweet as she used to when I used to fuck her over every inch in my house."

"Fuck you, you asshole! Shut up!" she exclaimed.

"I'm sure you heard the way she screamed when I tore her apart. No matter how hard she tried to get away from me, I still destroyed the pussy you want so badly."

"I don't," she said through gritted teeth, tears glistening in her eyes.

"And you want to know what'll happen before you die? Just take a wild guess," I taunted. When she didn't say anything, I chuckled. "Come on. Take a guess."

She ground her teeth and expelled a long breath. "What?" she finally said.

"You're going to watch me fuck her and make her come. You know why? Because that'll fuck with you more than any torture device I could create. How does it feel to know that you'll spend your last moments watching me fuck the woman you want but you're too much of a pussy to tell her?" I asked. Her body vibrated with anger, a single tear rolling down her cheek. I grinned at Sevyn. "You sure she's not an emotional person?"

"There's no telling what you said to her," she replied, glaring at me. I gestured toward Rebecca.

"Then ask her yourself," I suggested before looking to my guys. "While Rebecca decides whether or not she's ready to reveal her true self, let's get this shit cleaned up."

They nodded and moved over to the wheel and carefully laid it back. Once we untied her from the wheel and moved her body over to the sheet of plastic that already held puddles of her blood, Tony moved toward her head.

"I want to remove the knife from her throat," he mused. He put his booted foot on her forehead to keep her head from moving and reached down, grabbing the handle of the knife and pulling. Blood oozed out of the wound and I couldn't help but to smile. Had to admit I was rather proud of this handiwork and was even more amused when the girls reacted in disgust with each knife we pulled out. By the time we'd removed all of them, Crystal had thrown up at least two more times.

The guys and I took the body outside to the concrete slab on the side of the house, where I gave Tony the honors of beheading her. Just when Tony raised the ax over his head, an even better idea came to me.

"Wait!" I bellowed. Tony frowned at me, all the other guys appearing confused. "I don't think I want to do a simple beheading."

Tony released a dramatic sigh. "Seriously, man? I was really looking forward to this," he complained. I shook my head.

"You'll still need the axe for what I'm going to request of you." I grin planted itself on my lips just at the thought of it. With Jamie's last words insulting my sister, I wanted to insult her in death also.

"What're you thinking then?" Victor asked as he rubbed his hands together.

"I think she needs to be on display for everyone to see, not just her parents. I'm thinking…." I tapped a finger against my chin for a few moments, purposely leaving the guys in suspense. "I'm thinking I want to recreate Elizabeth Short's crime scene."

"Fuck yeah!" Tony roared. "I'm 100% down with recreating the Black Dahlia scene. Cutting her in half will be so much more fun than just cutting off her head."

"I get dibs on creating her permanent smile," Curtis stated as his hand shot up in the air.

"How are we going to transport the body?" Jake asked.

"I'll put it in the bed of one of the pickup trucks and make sure I cover it with a bunch of disposable plastic. In the meantime, maybe we can store her in the glass box and just put it in the walk-in freezer once the blood drains? I mean a whole body won't fit in the other freezer that we held Carrie's head in."

"Yeah, that's fine, but you need to be meticulous about how you cover the bed of that truck. A strong gust of wind can blow your entire cover," I warned. "You'll also need to do this in the middle of the night."

"Duh. I'm not going to just dump a severed body onto someone's lawn in broad daylight," Tony said, rolling his eyes.

My phone rang, ceasing all conversation around me. Pulling it out of my pocket, I saw Ryan's picture and immediately picked up.

"What's up?"

"I've been tailing the mailman for a couple of streets now. Get ready to get the link to my body cam to view the package transfer," he said and hung up. Seconds later, a link appeared in my texts.

"Looks like he also snuck a body cam into his disguise," I said as I opened the link. The men all huddled around me and focused on my phone screen. We watched as Ryan got out of an old station wagon, pretending to hobble along toward a mailman that was returning to his truck.

"Excuse me, sir," Ryan started, his voice raspy and light. "I have a favor to ask of you."

"How can I help you, sir?" the cheerful postal worker asked.

"Well, you're about to deliver mail on Canyon Street, right?"

"Sure am." We saw him look at the box Ryan held.

"Well, you see, today's my daughter's birthday. We don't have the best relationship these days and I know if she saw it was addressed from me, she wouldn't accept it, so I can't quite mail it to her," he'd said. I chuckled. Ryan was definitely playing the hell out of his character. "I just...I wanted to give her something that her mother would've wanted her to have, but I don't want her to throw it away before she actually gets it, you know?"

"I understand, sir, but I'm not really allowed to do something like that—"

"Please, sir? It's so important to me. Here..." Ryan struggled for a moment before the mailman gave him a sympathetic look.

"Here, let me hold that for you," the man said.

"Oh, thank you so much," Ryan said, and we all snickered. Ryan rarely ever said thank you and never used a tone that would imply he was grateful for whatever he was thanking you for if he said it in the first place.

"This is a bit heavy," the mailman joked, lifting the box up and down as if to test the weight.

"Yeah, it has my wife's urn in it. The urn itself has a good bit of weight in it. It's why my daughter and I were fighting. I feel like if she sees it, it may fix what's broken between us before it's my time too."

"Man….I'm really sorry to hear that."

Ryan suddenly pulled out a wallet full of cash and opened it, revealing it to the mailman. "If you can do this, you can have all the money in my wallet. I just need my daughter to get this. It's really important," he pleaded. I covered my mouth to stop myself from smiling. I wished I could see Ryan's face as he said half of this shit. I'd have to make him reenact this when he got back here.

The mailman looked around to see if anyone was watching before turning to Ryan. "Okay, but you can't tell anyone about this. I can lose my job."

"You have my word, young man," Ryan promised. The mailman looked around one more time before pulling the wad of cash from Ryan's wallet. "I trust that you'll keep your promise to deliver it. I need to get out of here so that she doesn't see me or suspect anything."

"That's a good idea. And remember—our little secret, right?"

"Of course, young man," Ryan said and hobbled back to the car. The mailman put the box in his truck and drove off, Ryan taking off the body cam when the truck was out of view. "And that, fellas, is how a pro works. Switching cars and then I'll be on my way back."

The camera went dark signaling that the feed was cut. "Bravo, bravo," Paul said, clapping his hands. "I gotta hand it to him; the guy is good at what he does. All that training being a theater dork really paid off."

"Indeed it did," I said and put my phone back in my pocket. "Well, let's get to work. It's hot as fuck outside and now I'm actually getting hungry."

The men and I all jumped into action, excitement coursing through me. With the package now being delivered, I knew I'd at least have something interesting to watch on the news soon.

An hour and a half later, the guys and I finally put the dismembered body in the glass box and put it in the walk-in freezer.

"You know, it was a good idea when you think of it as a whole, but fuck, that was a lot of work," Paul panted, bending over to put his hands on his knees.

I had to agree with him there. Aside from cutting her in half, we also had to drain her blood and cut a permanent smile into her face. While it wasn't extremely difficult, the Florida sun beaming down on us the entire time definitely didn't do us any favors. We all still stood in the freezer, trying to cool off. My black t-shirt was drenched in sweat, the wet fabric sending chills up my spine as the cold air of the freezer licked my skin.

"Now I've really worked up an appetite," Victor said.

"Same. Kind of want pizza though," Jake said.

"I second pizza," Curtis panted.

Paul nodded, "Third."

"And you can count me as the fourth," Tony said.

I nodded in agreement. "I can do pizza, but...who's going to pick it up?"

Tony raised his hand. "Since my girl is now dead, I can get it. Everyone want their usuals?"

"Yeah," we all said in unison.

"Cool. I'll order Ryan one just in case. Be back in a bit," he said and took in a deep breath. "Fuck, I'm not ready to go back out in that heat, but my stomach won't allow me to keep standing in here starving to death."

"Then get moving," Curtis chided. "Well, at least the hard part for the day is over with. Once I eat, I could use a nap."

"Make that the both of us," Victor said and focused on me. "Should we go ahead and feed the girls so we can lock them back up until tomorrow?"

"Probably best," I said. We all filed out of the freezer and I closed and locked it when the last person exited. I could already taste the cheesy pizza loaded with toppings and the ice cold beer I'd enjoy with it, my stomach growling at the thought of it. The women all sat in silence by the time we returned to the living room. "On second thought, let's take them downstairs. They can eat in their rooms."

The men strolled over to the remaining women, only five pathetic wastes of space that I had left to deal with. Sevyn almost looked a little relieved to learn that we were taking them to their rooms, but she was about to be in for a rude awakening.

I made sure to put us at the back of the line as we made our way toward the basement. I could feel her eyes on me when we passed the small hallway that held my room.

"Wait, I thought—"

"You thought I was actually going to let you sleep in my bed?" I asked with a chuckle. "You make it so easy to manipulate you with how gullible you are."

She bowed her head slightly and didn't say another word as she limped alongside me. As we continued down the steps, so many thoughts crashed around in my mind about her. A part of me wondered if I pretended to care or made her think that I was softening around her, she'd tell me the truth behind why she did it. So far, killing her friends in front of her or even punishing her wasn't doing much in the way of getting me closer to a confession. Ryan's words bounced around in my head. I needed to get to the bottom of whatever was fucking going on with me or else I'd never achieve the feelings I'd wanted to experience once I'd gotten my revenge against her.

I just needed to figure out where the hell to start.

She was silent as I put the cuffs back around her wrist. I sat in the chair as she curled up in the corner again, her head resting against the wall as she drew her knees to her chest. I'd give her a tiny olive branch of false security until she gave me what I wanted. Maybe I couldn't feel anything when I hurt her because I didn't know the real reason behind her actions back then. It made me uneasy when she kept making it a point that I wasn't innocent either. A breakup didn't justify all the shit she and her friends put Logan through, so something else happened that was much bigger than the breakup.

I pulled my wet shirt off and draped it across the back of the chair. Sevyn cut her eyes to me before pulling her knees tighter to her chest. I rolled my eyes.

"I'm not going to touch you if that's what you're thinking," I drawled, slouching down in the seat. "At least not yet." She still didn't respond. Her eyes darted from my tattoos and back to the wall when she thought I was looking at her. After a long bout of uncomfortable silence, she slowly shifted a little on the bed.

"When did you start getting tattoos?" she asked. Her voice was still hoarse and raspy when she spoke, her brown eyes studying me as she waited for me to answer.

"After Logan died."

She nodded. "I didn't think you were the type to cover yourself in tats like that."

"Going under the needle was therapeutic for me," I said with a shrug. "I didn't take you to be the type to cut your thighs up in private, but yet, here you are."

She lowered her eyes, shame shading her cheeks. "The pain was therapeutic for me, too," she mumbled.

"Apparently so considering how many scars you have," I mused. She was quiet for a moment before she finally spoke. "What exactly do you do?"

"Why does it matter?"

"I'm just trying to make conversation since you're just sitting there staring at me," she said on a sigh.

"Mechanical engineer," I finally answered.

"Sounds very 'you.'" She sighed inwardly. "Though I don't even know how true that is considering you aren't the same person I remember."

"I don't think any of us are the same people we remembered," I said. She narrowed her gaze at me and frowned.

"If you can come to that conclusion now, why is it so hard for you to believe that we've all changed from the immature teenagers we were back then? I know I have."

I shook my head. "It's the principle of it all, Sevyn," I explained. "I'm more upset that you all got to carry on with your lives as if nothing happened. You guys have to be held accountable for what you've done in some way."

"Killing won't help; it won't bring Logan back."

"I'm not worried about whether or not it'll help. We're just evening the score. An eye for an eye and all of that."

"What did you say to Rebecca?" Sevyn asked suddenly, shifting the conversation in another direction without warning.

I smirked, tipping the chair back onto its two back legs. "Just stuff."

She rolled her eyes in a way that used to remind me of the old her. "I always hated when you'd say that," she said and shook her head.

"Some things never changed," I said.

"Do you live close to Miami then?"

"Something like that."

"Then where've you been all this time?"

"Minding my business and planning for this week," I said. Fear colored her features before she bowed her head. "Are you scared?"

"Of?"

"The inevitable." I put the chair back on all fours and leaned forward on my elbows. "Are you afraid to die?" She didn't say anything for a long moment. "I'm surprised you're not thinking of some kind of plan to try to convince me that you should live."

She frowned, her brown eyes boring into me. "Why should I?"

"I'd think self-preservation should be kicking in now that you realize the danger you're in," I said and tsked.

She shook her head. "I won't beg for something I don't think I deserve," she said. I raised an eyebrow, slightly confused by her statement.

"You don't think you deserve to live?" I asked slowly.

"Why should I?" She rested her head back on the wall. "I had a dream about Logan last night. I don't know how true it was, but she'd said that she never told you what my secret was."

"Secret?" I thought back to the last conversation I'd had with Logan about Sevyn, but I don't remember her telling me about any secret.

I walked through the door and let out a deep breath. Part of me felt bad that Sevyn was so upset. The visual of the way her face fell when I'd broke up with her was seared into my mind. I'd admit that I felt a little guilty for toying with her emotions just to sleep with her. How the fuck was I supposed to know that confident, self-absorbed Sevyn was a big softie when she fell in love? It was supposed to be a secret thing for the summer before we both went our separate ways. I could tell that she'd wanted to talk about something, but with how giddy she was, I didn't want it to be a conversation about us going public with our relationship. She'd hinted about it a few times, but I'd always shut down the conversation, occupying her with something else until she forgot about the topic entirely. Logan was on the couch when walked past the living room. She jumped up to her feet and followed me into the kitchen.

"So?" she asked.

I opened the refrigerator door and pulled out a canned soda. Cracking it open, I took a long sip before I met her curious gaze. "So what?"

"I mean you and Sevyn talked right? How do you feel about what she told you?"

I furrowed my eyebrows in confusion as I looked at my sister. Her body language was odd. She seemed…nervous as she stood before me, wringing her hands in front of myself as her curious eyes traveled along my face.

"What she told me? What was she supposed to be telling me? That she wanted to go public with our relationship?"

"What?" Logan shook her head. "So, she didn't tell you? I thought you said you talked to her."

"I did."

"Okay, then what happened? Because I'm assuming that something *bad must've happened if she didn't tell you what she was supposed to."*

I shrugged. "Probably because I didn't give her the chance to. I broke up with her," I said nonchalantly and took another swallow from my can. Logan's face paled.

"You did what? Luther, why would you do that?"

I scoffed. "What do you mean why'd I do that? I listened to what you said, and you were right."

"I told you to stop screwing around with other girls, not break up with her! What's wrong with you?" she all but screamed.

"I don't know what you want me to say, Logan. Besides, I'm about to go back to college. Having a high school girlfriend wouldn't be a good idea when I'll be surrounded by hot college girls."

"Do you not know how to be a faithful boyfriend? Or do you only work in 'douchebag' mode?" she asked with a frown, folding her arms across her chest.

"Apparently not, but you know that already considering that you walked in on me," I said and smirked. "You should really try knocking sometimes."

"Luther, this isn't funny," she snapped.

I chuckled. "Fine, fine. No need to turn all red and get upset. I just didn't want you to be put in the middle like you mentioned the other day, so I just thought it was best to just end things off with her. I thought you'd be happy about that."

"Well, how'd she take it?" Logan asked.

"She was pissed. I mean she just got dumped. How'd you think she'd take it?"

"Like, what did she say? Did she tell you anything?"

I shook my head. "She started saying something, but I may have interrupted her to dump her. I think she was going to bring up being exclusive again and that was the last thing I wanted with her."

Logan glared at me, her lips pursed. "You know, you can be such an idiot sometimes," she muttered. "If anything, she's going to think I had something to do with it."

"And why's that?"

"Because she told me you and her were dating and then you go and dump her soon after that. So, thanks a lot," she snapped and stomped off to her bedroom. I sighed and finished off the rest of my soda.

"Women, I tell ya," I muttered to myself before leaving the kitchen. I pulled my phone from my pocket with the urge to text Sevyn just to tell her that Logan had nothing to do with my decision. After a split second, I shook my head. She was probably still pissed. Texting her would do nothing but initiate another conversation that I wasn't in the mood to have with her.

"She never said anything about any secret," I finally said. "She was just really upset that I'd broken up with you." I was quiet for a moment. "She mentioned a secret a lot in her diary though. Care to tell me what it is?"

She shook her head. "No. It doesn't matter anymore anyway."

I ground my teeth. I wanted to know about this secret that was so fucking bad that it made her do the bullshit she did. Maybe her reason why would give me the fresh, new rage that would allow me to finally feel something when I ended her life. But her refusal to answer my question pissed me off.

"Don't you think that's the least you can do?" I finally asked, doing my best to keep my anger in check.

She cut her eyes at me briefly before slightly rolling them and looking away. "The least I can do? Whether I tell you or not, you're going to kill me. Telling you won't do anything."

"It could possibly save your life," I bargained, but she and I both knew that was the furthest from the truth.

She scoffed. "As if you're someone to trust right now," she muttered.

"You only have a few days left before I kill you, Sevyn. Do you want to spend those few days suffering?"

"I'm already suffering. What's a few days more?"

I narrowed my eyes at her, a sinister grin tipping my lips. "Be careful what you're asking for, Sevyn. I'm sure you're more than aware of what I'm capable of."

"Then do what you feel you need to do, Luther. The end result will be the same; I'll be dead soon. You can't hurt me more than I've already hurt myself," she said, though she wouldn't meet my eyes.

"You don't think I can?"

"No."

I chuckled. "Well, challenge accepted."

CHAPTER 11

SEVYN

My heart sped up in my chest as he slowly stood. "I wasn't trying to challenge you," I protested. After what he'd already done to me yesterday, I wasn't sure if I could handle him doing anything else. Despite the fear coursing through my body, a tiny part of me wanted the punishment. For years, I'd tried to punish myself, to make myself hurt in an effort to feel anything other than guilt. It was a different ballgame when you no longer had a choice of your pain.

And it was no longer appealing when you no longer had a choice in whether you lived or died.

"It sounded like you were, so I took you up on it," he said and shrugged. The muscles in his chest twitched in warning, the danger and pain that was yet to come. I had no idea what he had up his sleeve but waiting for the inevitable made it worse. I watched him as he just stood there, his head cocked to the side.

"Look, I'm sorry, okay? I was only saying that I've beat myself up for so long about this that—"

He turned and walked out of the room before I could even finish my sentence. I held my breath, waiting for him to close the door behind him, but he didn't. That only meant that he was coming back. My breaths came in quick as I waited, a woman's voice sounding in the hallway.

"Get off of me, you fucker!" the voice exclaimed and I froze. What the hell was he bringing Rebecca in here for if he was going to punish me? Confirming my suspicions, Luther pulled Rebecca into the room as she tried to pull herself from his grasp, freezing when she saw me. "Sevyn?"

"What is she doing here?" I asked Luther. I had no idea what he had up his sleeve, but I didn't like it. He didn't say a word as he closed the door and locked us in before dragging Rebecca over to the chair he'd occupied moments before. "Luther, what is she doing here?"

He cut his eyes to me but still said nothing as he put a collar around her neck and pointed to the chair. "Sit."

"Fuck you," she spat, spitting at his feet. He only gave her a dangerous smirk, reaching into his pocket to pull out a remote. Within seconds, Rebecca was on the ground and convulsing at his feet until he took his finger off the button.

"Bec!" I called out, reaching out to her but stopped by the chains on my wrist. I glared up at Luther. "What the fuck is wrong with you?!"

"Shouldn't talk shit with a shock collar on, bitch," he growled, looking down at her while still ignoring me. "Ready to sit down and shut up?"

Rebecca groaned on the floor, taking in big gulps of air in between hiccupping sobs. I glared up at him.

"Are you going to answer me as to why the fuck she's even in here?" I asked again.

He frowned at me. "I don't owe you shit, Sevyn. Your best bet is to sit there and shut the fuck up until I'm ready to tell you both what's about to happen," he stated. The cool demeanor that'd been present in his eyes and body language was gone the moment he'd walked out of the door. The dark look in his eyes made me uneasy. I moved as close to the wall as I could, as if it would save me even though I knew nothing could save me in this place.

The fact that he only wanted Rebecca to sit gave me a small bit of relief. If he was going to punish me, I'd rather him just do it to me instead of to her. *But what if she's here to make me reveal the truth,* I thought, which disintegrated any relief I'd previously had. He could've brought her here to threaten harm against her if I didn't tell him what he wanted to know.

I shook the thought from my head. He wouldn't have to use her for that; he'd wanted to hurt me by his own hand. As if reading my thoughts, Luther nodded toward me as he looked at Rebecca.

"You remember what I told you earlier about Sevyn?" he asked with a grin. I looked between him and my best friend.

"Told her what about me?" I asked slowly.

"Why don't you tell her?" Luther taunted.

Rebecca's eyes darted between me and him before she finally looked up into his eyes and shook her head. "I...I can't," she finally said.

"Bec, what did he say?" I asked, trying to keep my voice soft. She wouldn't look at me, only bowing her head to look at her lap.

"Yeah, what did I say?" he mocked.

"Shut up, Luther!" I focused my gaze on my friend, who still wouldn't look at me. "Did he say I did something? Whatever he told you was a lie—"

"It wasn't about you," she murmured.

I furrowed my brow in confusion. "But he just said that he told you something about me," I said, my tone flat. "What did he tell you then?"

"It was more so about me," she said.

"Tell her what I said, Rebecca," Luther said as his tone grew impatient.

"You can tell me, Bec," I coaxed. I hated that I couldn't hug her. Comfort her. I wasn't sure what he'd said that'd made her shut down, but it made the hairs on the back of my neck stand up as nervous energy flowed through me. "I promise I won't be mad."

Her shoulders sagged a bit, but she still wouldn't look at me. "He said that he was going to have sex with you and force me to watch," she finally admitted.

I narrowed my eyes at him. "That's it? You want her to watch while you rape me, you sick fuck?"

221

"Tell her why," he responded, ignoring me.

"Look, I told her what you—"

"Tell. Her. Fucking. Why," he ground out.

Her nostrils flared as she brought her gaze up to his. They stared at each other for a long moment, as if exchanging thoughts before Rebecca finally tightened her jaw and dropped her gaze.

"Bec?" I called out with a raised brow.

She released a deep sigh. "Because he said it would hurt me more than anything else he could do to me," she finally admitted.

"And why would it hurt you more?" Luther pressed. "And tell her about Logan while you're at it. Logan wrote about it in her diary, too, so I'd advise you to tell the truth while you have the chance to."

A single tear rolled down her cheek, which made me a bit worried. I had no idea where Luther was going with this. None of this made sense and the only thing it was doing was frustrating me.

"Can somebody just say it already? The suspense is worse than what I already know is coming," I finally said.

"Ten seconds, Rebecca," Luther announced. "Ten. Nine. Eight."

"Just say it, Rebecca," I begged.

"Oh no. If she doesn't say it, I'll just go ahead and kill you," Luther said as he pulled a gun from the back of his waistband and pointed it at me. "Seven. Six."

"No!" Rebecca screamed.

"Then say it," Luther ordered and continued counting down. "Five. Four. Three—"

"Okay, you asshole!" she exclaimed. Luther moved closer to me and pressed the gun to the side of my head as he fisted my hair.

"We're listening," he said.

Rebecca looked at me with tears in her eyes. "Because he was right about me being in love with you. I'm sorry," she said.

"Wait, what? Since when?" I asked. If she were telling the truth, I'd never noticed it. Sure, she was always very protective over me and would always act weird whenever I showed a guy too much attention or dated anyone. I never took it as her being in love with me; I just thought she was just selfish with her friends.

She bowed her head and sniffled. "I don't know. I think since we first met. And when you shot me down—"

"You never told me you were into girls. You asked me if I'd ever date one and I said no," I corrected her. "That's not you telling me you're gay or bi or whatever."

"Now tell her where Logan comes in," Luther stated.

I narrowed my eyes at her. "Were you and Logan a thing?" I asked. Now that I was hearing this for the first time, it made me wonder how well I knew the people I called my best friends. I'd only seen her dating guys; I'd never seen her with a girl to even have an idea about her being attracted to women. To hear it now—and to know that she was in love with me, no less—was blowing my mind.

"No," she admitted. "That night at the party, I had a little more to drink that I should have. Logan looked really out of place, so I went over to her to keep her company. I tried to make a move on her—which was stupid—and she practically screamed 'I'm not into lesbian stuff' to where everyone around us heard."

"Bec...did you..."

"I was angry, okay?" she immediately said. "I was embarrassed and upset because she'd practically outed me to a group of people that you know aren't very accepting of people like me." She swallowed hard. "I was the one that told Josh, Hunter, and Tyler that Logan was looking for a good time and was 'that kind of girl.' They were already drunk themselves, so it didn't take much convincing."

"What the fuck is wrong with you?" I exclaimed.

"Don't act like you're so innocent either, Sevyn," she snapped. "When I mentioned it as a plan before the party, you were all for it."

"I told you that was extreme! I didn't give you a fucking green light to have her raped," I shouted back at her. I couldn't believe the person sitting feet away from me. While I was disgusted by her reasoning, I couldn't judge her. I was no better for my part in Logan's suicide either. She and I were both guilty for all we'd done, my rage, hurt, and betrayal being a leading catalyst for my friends' involvement.

But Luther was the origin of it all. Too bad I couldn't get him to see that just yet.

"Well, it doesn't matter anymore because now she's dead," Rebecca said, her face wiped of the earlier emotion that was once there.

"And you'll be following suit soon enough," Luther growled. He was quick when he let go of my hair and gripped my leg. I squeaked in surprise when he roughly yanked me until I was flat on my back, slightly hitting my head on the wall when I went down.

"No!" I screamed, kicking him with my free foot. He only

grabbed it as he got down on his knees, a sinister smile on his face.

"I already told you what fighting me will do, Sevyn," he teased as he secured both of my legs with one arm. I tried my best to wiggle out of his grasp, but it was no use. Tears burned my eyes as he reached under my nightgown and grabbed the hem of my panties, yanking them down my closed legs.

"You bastard!" Rebecca screamed as she jumped out of her chair. Luther raised the gun and shot her in the thigh, sending her down to the ground before she could even move toward us. She cried out in pain, clutching her wound.

"I told you not to move. Move another inch toward her until I tell you to and the next bullet will go in your head," he warned before turning back to me. "You claim that I couldn't make you hurt more than you hurt yourself. That's only because you have no idea how I plan to hurt you."

Before I could even respond to him, he pressed my legs to my chest before putting the barrel of his Glock inside of me. The metal was freshly heated from the shot he'd just let off, but it felt as if it was 100 degrees the way it burned going in. The pain rendered me silent, my mouth opening to scream but nothing would come out. My breath caught in my throat, my entire body freezing as a burning sensation slid over my nerve endings and strangled them. It made me dizzy and nauseous at the same time, my body unable to process the amount of pain.

Tears swam in my eyes as Luther looked down at me, his gaze dark and angry as he shoved the gun in and out of me. I could hear

Rebecca screaming, but it sounded as if I was underwater. By the time everything cleared in my head, I realized that I was the one screaming.

"Still sure I can't hurt you more than you've already hurt yourself?" he taunted. "I'm pretty sure this gun shoved in your pussy hurts a lot worse than those pathetic cuts you've put on your body."

"You're a sick bastard!" Rebecca screamed, but she didn't dare move toward me. All Luther needed was a reason to shoot her again just to heat up the barrel of the gun some more. I pulled at the chains, trying to twist and turn my body out of his grasp, but he only moved with me.

"Everyone in this house is sick, including you," he replied back to her, but he never took his eyes off my face. A look of pure satisfaction filled his eyes each time he pushed the gun as far as it could go inside of me, a grin tilting his lips. "It would be unfortunate if this gun were to go off inside of you, wouldn't it?"

"Please, no!" I wailed. He took the gun from inside me and let go my legs, optioning to grab my face instead.

"Open your mouth," he growled. At this point, I'd do whatever it took to get the pain to stop. His hand firmly gripped my cheeks, forcing me to open my mouth. I whimpered when he shoved the barrel into my mouth, the metallic taste of cooling metal and blood assaulting my tongue. "That's what your fear, your pain, your desperation taste like."

I tried to shake my head out of his grip, but he only turned the gun's barrel side to side in my mouth, making sure I got as much blood of it as possible. He finally pulled it out and quickly put a hand over my mouth.

"Swallow," he demanded. Tears rolled down my cheeks as I fought the urge to, but he wouldn't uncover my mouth until I did. When his hand moved as if to put the gun inside of me again, I did as he asked, letting out a sob as nausea pooled in my belly. I almost breathed a sigh of relief when he put the gun on the mattress, but I should've known better. He kept his gaze trained on me as he unbuckled his belt and unzipped his jeans.

"No, no, no," I begged. "Please! Not after yesterday."

"Oh no, I'm not fucking your pussy today," he said and chuckled. I didn't have to wonder what he'd planned to destroy today as he roughly flipped me over on my stomach, causing my arms to cross over my head.

"Please don't, Luther," I begged. "I'll tell you whatever you want!"

"Too late for that right now," he only said in response. I sobbed as he forced my hips up and spread my legs. I squeezed my hands into fists, waiting for the inevitable. I tried to take my mind to any other place other than being on this dirty mattress with a monster who kept my heart hostage even after he'd broken it years ago. But nothing could rip me away from the searing pain that licked up my spine as he forced himself into my ass. I squeezed my hands into fists so tightly that my pointed nails cut into my skin. I couldn't make a single sound, only silent tears leaking out of my eyes and onto the mattress. With every pump he put into me, I disappeared further and further into myself. I wanted to be dead already. I wanted this to be over. I hated that he was going to drag this out for a whole week before he finally killed me, punishing me in every way he could possibly think of. I forced my mind to drift off to a better time as the pain slowly wrapped me up in its unforgiving embrace.

"I don't know…I've never done anal," I told him as we lay in his bed. He stroked my cheek, looking at me with soft eyes as he gave me a mischievous grin.

"Have I hurt you yet, pretty girl?" he asked. I shook my head. "So anal wouldn't be any different."

"I'm sure it'll hurt. My asshole is a lot tighter than my pussy," I protested with a frown.

"I promise I'll take good care of it," he murmured and pressed a soft kiss to my lips. "Just trust me."

I sat up a little and looked over at both of his nightstands. "Do you have lube or something?"

"All the lube I need is going to be right here," he said, his voice husky as he cupped my clothed pussy. A shiver of pleasure washed over me as his knuckle ran up and down my covered slit. "These gotta go."

I lifted my hips to allow him to remove my panties, spreading my legs for him as he slid down my body. A part of me felt a little guilty to be here with him while Logan was asleep in her bedroom. Lately I'd just been spending the night at her house to spend more time with Luther, even if it was only for a couple of hours in the middle of the night. I bit my lip as he peppered my pelvic bone with kisses, slowly making his way lower.

He chuckled when I rolled my hips. "Somebody's rather impatient to be so nervous," he murmured.

"That's because I'm ready for the first part of this," I said breathlessly. "What part? You mean…this?"

I moaned when he took my clit into his mouth, shivering when he stopped again. He looked up at me and put a finger to his lips, gesturing toward the door with a nod of his head. Right; Logan. I nodded to let him know I understood him and grabbed one of his pillows, holding it over my mouth firmly enough to muffle any sounds of pleasure I made. He took my clit into his mouth again, squeezing my thighs as he released a deep growl of satisfaction. My entire body tingled all over. While I was nervous about doing anal, I was excited to try new things with him. Though he wasn't the first guy I'd had sex with, he was the first guy I allowed myself to get attached to. I'd known him so long that I couldn't fathom letting anyone else possess my mind, body, and soul the way I'd allowed him to.

A small sliver of dread clouded the lust I felt though. I knew at some point, I'd have to tell him I was pregnant. With him going back to college in fall and me starting my senior year, I wasn't sure how he'd react to a potential baby. I looked down at him between my legs, his rapid tongue flickering against my clit as his beautiful brown eyes looked at me. I ran my hands through his soft, dark hair and wondered whether or not our baby would have the same hair. The same eyes. Everything that made up Luther Evans. Or if it would be more like me. The thought brought tears to my eyes. I forced myself to close my eyes and tilt my head up toward the ceiling. Now wasn't the time to get lost in thoughts that could be dealt with tomorrow.

"Oh fuck," I whispered as I moved my hips faster against his speedy tongue. "Fuck…fuck…Luther, I'm coming!"

He squeezed my thighs as I muffled my orgasmic moan with a pillow, riding out the pleasurable wave until Luther finally unlatched from my clit and kissed my inner thighs. My legs trembled as he moved away from me, his weight disappearing from the bed. I removed the pillow from my face and looked up to see him standing at the foot of the bed, now completely naked and stroking his hard cock in his hand and covering it in what I assumed to be lube.

"Ready for this, pretty girl?" he murmured. His eyes danced over my face, trying to map any sign of hesitation. I trusted him though. He hadn't given me any reason to believe he'd hurt me. I gave him a soft smile and nodded, rolling over to get on my hands and knees. He got back onto the bed and settled behind me, his warm hand in the center of my back. He gently pressed until my chest was on the bed and my ass was in the air for him, spread for his pleasure. "You can always tell me to stop if it hurts you."

"I know," I whispered as I braced myself for the intrusion. "I trust you."

"I'll take good care of you, pretty girl. I promise."

"Fuck, I'm coming," Luther groaned, tightly squeezing my hips as he dumped his hot seed deep in my ass. I blankly stared at the empty wall across the room, feeling nothing but pain in the lower half of my body. My throat and eyes felt raw from screaming and crying, my energy was low from the lack of food, and my will to live was nonexistent. I said nothing as he finally pulled out of me, wincing as he did. He panted behind me, flipping me back over onto my back but I couldn't bear to look at him. He was no longer the gentle, caring soul he was back then. He wasn't the person I remembered anymore. The old version took his time, making sure that it felt as good for me as it did for him. This version didn't care. All he wanted was to cause me as much pain as he could before he disposed of me. He was nothing but an angry, former shell of himself with a laser focus agenda of destroying as many lives as possible.

Luther moved back from me, his angry eyes never leaving me as he slowly got to his feet. After he fixed his jeans, he finally turned his attention to Rebecca, who sobbed on the floor in both pain and anguish a few feet from me. Her blood slowly leaked out onto the concrete floor, her face a bit paler than it usually was. Luther stalked over to her and grabbed her by the hair, dragging her to the foot of the mattress.

"Go ahead," he said to her, nodding to me. "Do what I know you've always wanted to do."

She looked between me and him with wet, confused eyes. "What the hell are you talking about?" she wailed.

He pointed to my spread legs. "Don't you remember everything I said? Everything I told you I knew you wanted to do?" he said with a smirk.

"I can't handle anymore," I sobbed. Rebecca looked back at Luther.

"You can't be serious," she protested between tears before looking back between my legs. "She's…bleeding."

"And?" he asked, pointing the gun at her, the barrel of it streaked with my blood that I didn't get off. When Rebecca didn't move, Luther reached down pressed his palm against my pussy, his hand covered in patches of blood when he pulled it away. Rebecca screamed as he wiped the blood on her face. "Now you're both bloody. You wanna make her feel better? Eat her out."

"I—"

"NOW!" he shouted, pointing the gun at her head. "I swear to fucking god, if you don't—"

"Okay!" she exclaimed, holding up her free hand that wasn't clutching her injured thigh. She looked to me with tears in her eyes. "I'm sorry, Sevyn."

But I didn't answer. At this point, I was already checking out. I didn't care what happened from this point on. I just wanted all of this to be over. At the beginning of this, a small part of me wanted to believe that I could possibly reason with this man and show him that I wasn't the villain he thought I still was. I wanted him to know that I'd felt guilty all these years, not gloating and living life unaffected as he thought I did. But none of that mattered in the grand scheme of things. Luther was deaf to reasoning and forgiveness. The only thing he'd entertain was new ways to hurt me.

As he forced my best friend to lick my battered, bleeding pussy, I just stared up at the ceiling. I always thought I'd been in my own personal hell as I dealt with my depression, drug use, and self harm tendencies to deal with the emotions I'd felt. But this was nothing compared to what I'd done to myself. Unlike the things I used to do on my own, I had no control over this situation. I couldn't stop when I got too scared at the thought of dying. I couldn't do anything but take whatever he dished out until he finally decided to get rid of me.

I just prayed to god that it would be sooner rather than later.

I winced as Rebecca ran her tongue up and down my slit. I knew she was trying to be gentle, but it all hurt. I just wanted them both to leave me alone. I wanted to sleep. I wanted to die. I wanted to go home. I wanted someone to save me. But I knew none of those things would come anytime soon. Luther's chuckle broke through my mental self loathing.

"You waited all these years and she doesn't even enjoy it," he said to Rebecca.

"Because you hurt her, you asshole. Look at what you did! You practically tore her open!"

"No shit, Sherlock. That's the point of a punishment," Luther said and walked over to the door. When he was occupied with calling someone from down the hall, Rebecca slowly dragged herself up to the foot of the bed.

"Sevyn, I'm so sorry," she whispered, her hand reaching out to touch me, but she stopped mid reach. "I swear I didn't want to do that. I know it probably hurts and—"

"Just get away from me," I croaked, leveling my gaze with her worried one. Her mouth opened and closed a few times, her lips and chin tinted red with my blood.

"W-what? I didn't mean to hurt you, I swear! I'm sorry," she said. "Please don't be mad at me."

"Just get away from me, Bec," I said again and looked away. I could see her shoulders sag in defeat in my peripheral and could feel her eyes still on me. I just wanted to be left alone. I didn't want to be touched anymore. My entire body thrummed with pain that I was scared to move any part of it. I didn't bother to look when someone else came into the room and snatched up Rebecca.

"Sevyn, please! I'm sorry!" she exclaimed over and over as she was taken out of the room, her voice even echoing in the hall. I only stared at the ceiling without a word, silence tears rolling down the sides of my head. Luther's boots sounded across the floor as he walked back over to the bed, his head cocked to the side as he looked down at me.

"Looks like I won that challenge," he said with a devilish smirk before he walked away, leaving me alone in the dark room.

When the heavy door closed and locked, I forced myself to close my legs, biting my lip to keep from crying out as I tried to shift myself over onto my side to curl up in the fetal position. I knew I'd eventually have to pay for what I'd done seven years ago. I just wasn't prepared to pay like this. Being raped two days in a row. Watching my friends be murdered and maimed in gruesome ways. And definitely didn't think it would be at the hand of the only man who'd ever held my heart. It was like I never mattered to him, as if we didn't create something special. A part of me still wanted to blame Logan for putting me in my current position, but it was my own wrongdoings that got me here. And I knew Luther would make me pay for it every single second I was still alive.

I closed my eyes and tried to get myself to fall asleep, unable to as a painful throb settled between my legs and my ass. I had to end this. If Luther asked me to choose who dies tomorrow, I'd pick myself just to finally escape this hell. I couldn't imagine going through this for another second, let alone for days until I was the last living woman of the original seven.

"I'm so tired," I whispered to myself and to whatever God that may be out there. "Please just end my misery. Please."

But I knew it was fruitless. Knowing Luther, he was just getting started and it wouldn't end until he was ready for it to. Death wouldn't be easy to come by when the devil himself was orchestrating the manner in which you'd die. At this point, I prayed for anything to happen. Perhaps a freak accident where I managed to strangle myself with these chains. Maybe the injuries I sustained from my rape would give me a bad infection. Maybe he'd run out of ways to torture me and would just take me out into the backyard and gun me down. Whatever the case, I hope it was swift.

I wasn't sure how much I could take anymore.

CHAPTER 12

LUTHER

" **I** *was the one that told Josh, Hunter, and Tyler that Logan was looking for a good time and was 'that kind of girl.'*"

Rebecca's admission was all that played in my head as I stood under the hot shower spray. The more layers I peeled back from this fucked up onion of events, the more I learned that the situation was so much bigger than Sevyn. I'd believed she'd masterminded this whole intricate scheme that pushed my sister to suicide for years, but other people's involvement was almost more than hers. My sister's screams echoed in the corners of my mind, that hollow feeling settling in my chest as I remembered how it echoed in the practically silent courtroom when the tape was played for evidence. My jaw ached with how hard I clenched my teeth in anger. The nonchalant look on Rebecca's face after she admitted what she did pissed me off to no end. I could at least see why Sevyn was friends with this bitch, as she did the same thing yesterday when we were talking about Logan.

I released a deep breath and scrubbed shampoo through my hair. Exhaustion settled its way deep into my bones, but now wasn't the time to be tired. I was nowhere near done unleashing my hell on the women locked in the basement. I wanted every single one of them to feel every ounce of pain my family and I had to carry for the last few years because of all of them. I'd wanted their screams, their begging, and their tears. I wanted that when I'd raped Sevyn a second time, but she robbed me of that. Her body had gone limp and she no longer made a sound or fought against me. Rebecca pleaded with me to stop, trying to comfort Sevyn through her assault, but she was already too far gone. Even when I flipped her over and looked down at her, the life was gone from her eyes and her voice. And seeing her destroyed like that?

It finally brought me the satisfaction I'd craved, but it still didn't last long.

I'd wanted to end Rebecca after her admission, as there was no way I could wait until the end of the week to kill her, whether Sevyn chose her to die or not. My original plan for her was to leave her last so that Sevyn would suffer as she watched her best friend die, but I wouldn't wait that long now. While they bullied her, that rape practically destroyed my sister's life. She'd been humiliated online when the video was uploaded to the school's forum site. She was expelled from the very expensive private school she attended, had colleges withdraw their acceptance decisions once they'd heard about the scandal, and lost an internship she'd worked hard to get. My sister lost everything she'd worked her ass off for and was shamed for it despite it being one of the most traumatic things she'd ever gone through, and there was no way in fucking hell that I'd let Rebecca stay alive past tomorrow. Everything in me wanted to finish her off tonight, but I knew I needed to pace myself not only to keep myself off the radar, but also my guys.

Patience, Luther, I thought to myself as I ground my teeth. I exhaled deeply. I didn't do all this planning for the last few years just to go and fuck it up with irrational thinking. I'd stick to the plan for now, but I'd definitely rearrange the order in which these bitches would die, and tomorrow would be Rebecca's turn.

A solid knock sounded on the doorframe of the open bathroom door, jerking me out of my musings.

"Yeah?" I called out, pulling my face from beneath the spray.

"We gotta talk, man," Ryan's voice said.

I cracked the glass shower door and stuck my head out. "What?" I asked, wiping water from my face.

"We gotta talk. My dad just called," he said. The tightened look on Ryan's face made me a little nervous. With his father being a retired police officer, there was no telling what he told Ryan. I was sure Carrie's head had been discovered at some point, so I wouldn't be surprised if that was what the call was about.

"Give me a few," I finally said, watching as he nodded and

walked away. I grabbed my body wash and lathered up, washing away Sevyn's blood and my sweat from my body, watching as the filth swirled down the drain. Once I was clean enough, I made sure to rinse out any residual shampoo before finally turning the shower off. I quickly grabbed a towel and dried off, rushing into my bedroom to get dressed. So many different scenarios ran through my mind as I pulled on a fresh pair of boxers, jeans, and a fitting grey t-shirt before walking out of my bedroom to meet with the guys.

"What's going on?" I asked, still towel drying my hair as I approached them all sitting in the dining room with multiple boxes of pizzas opened on dining table. Paul nodded toward the tv playing in the background, a sitting news reporter blabbing on the screen.

"We have breaking news. Affluent family Jessica and Gordon Tate received a gruesome package that marks murder number three in the last four weeks. We have Nick on the scene; over to you, Nick."

"Thanks Michelle. I'm outside the home of Senator Gordon and Jessica Tate, who've just received a gruesome package in the mail. The family says a package was delivered to their front porch as usual, but with no identifying information on the outside. They'd called the police thinking it was a homemade bomb considering the death threats Senator Gordon had received. Instead of a bomb, the family discovered the severed head of their youngest daughter, Carrie Tate, who'd been reported missing after not returning home from a party the night before."

The camera cut to her distraught family inside the house, her mother practically inconsolable. Her father looked up at the camera with teary eyes as he held his wife and I couldn't help but to smirk.

How does it feel to mourn the loss of a child, you fucker? I mused as I tossed the towel over my shoulder.

"I can't believe my little girl is gone," he started, his voice shaking as his wife sobbed next to him. "The only thing the box contained was my poor girl's head and a note that said 'Pay for your sins' from someone named The Collective. I want whoever is responsible for this to be arrested immediately!"

The camera cut again to the mailman Ryan had interacted with earlier. "This old man comes up to me on my regular route and tells me that his daughter lived in that house or something. I felt bad for him, you know? He was going on and on about them not having a good relationship and that he was dying and wanted to give her her mother's ashes. I didn't know it was a freaking head in the box, man! The man was so old that I didn't think he was even capable of something like that!"

Jake looked to Ryan. "That was a hell of a disguise, man," he said as he grabbed a slice of pizza.

"What can I say? I'm a pro at it," Ryan said with a shrug, a cocky grin on his lips as he also reached for a slice of pizza.

"Shh," I said, my eyes still trained on the tv as the reporter outside the house returned back on the screen. "Police are looking into leads to help solve this murder. As of today, this marks the fourth murder in Miami in the last month."

"It'll soon be a total of ten," Tony mused before biting in a slice of pizza loaded with all kinds of toppings.

Paul frowned at him. "That's fucking gross, dude. Anchovies, pineapples, mushrooms, and every meat imaginable?" he asked.

Tony shrugged. "Good to me. Besides, it's the only way I can guarantee that none of you fucks will eat my leftovers," he said and grinned.

"Trust me, you don't have to worry about me eating a single slice of that G.I. tract destroyer that you call a pizza," Curtis said with a shake of his head.

I moved over to an empty seat and grabbed my box of pizza, opening it to reveal my Italian sausage and green bell pepper pizza. Grabbing a slice from the box, I turned my attention to Ryan.

"So, what's up with your dad?" I asked, trying to keep my tone nonchalant.

He swallowed the food in his mouth and nodded. "Right. He called me as soon as he'd heard the head had been found."

"But why'd he call you though?" Victor asked with a raised brow. While it would've put me on edge to know why Ryan's ex-police father would be calling him about a head he'd delivered, I already knew it was all a part of the plan. There was no way I could've gotten away with everything I'd done if I didn't have the very help of someone who knew the police department inside and out.

"He's aware of a little of what's happening," I answered. "Ryan's dad is a part of The Collective."

"What the fuck is The Collective?" Jake asked.

"It's basically like us but made of men set on making people pay who slipped through the cracks of the justice system," Ryan answered.

"Wait, so your dad is like Dexter or some shit?" Paul asked.

Ryan raised a brow at him before cutting his eyes to me, but I only shrugged in response. "Dexter? Like…cartoon Dexter's Laboratory Dexter?"

"No, jackass," Paul said and rolled his eyes. "It was a show. The dude was like a blood spatter analyst or some shit and by day, he'd work in a crime lab and by night, he'd kill criminals that got away. Kinda like a vigilante, I guess."

"Then I guess so. It's made up by ex-police and military chiefs."

"Well, it's good that you used The Collective to keep the heat off of us then," Curtis said with a nod.

"It's still bizarre to know your father's a killer," Paul said.

Ryan smirked. "Why'd you think I started The Brothers of Vengeance?" he asked. "Just following in my father's footsteps."

"Can we get back to the actual conversation you had with him?" I asked impatiently.

"Right, right." Ryan cleared his throat. "He basically said that they're trying to link the murders of those other guys to this one, except the other murders didn't have notes. He said that the police planned to get surveillance footage from cameras on nearby properties though."

"Shit," Victor said, shaking his head. "Think any cameras picked you up?"

Ryan shrugged. "Whether or not they did, they'd only either get the back of me or the mail truck. I purposely stood where I was so

THE DESTRUCTION OF SEVYN

that cameras across the street couldn't get a full-on view of me and made sure to keep my head down and my back to the cameras on my side of the street. Plus, if that mail guy couldn't identify me, then I doubt they'd be able to get it from grainy security camera footage. Besides, I caught him on a street not too close to the house. So, unless they get feed from every single house in the surrounding area, I don't have much to worry about," he answered.

"Has he said anything about the other murders?" I asked. While his father had an idea of what was happening now, I never told him about the three I did on my own. Those were my own personal projects that I'd wanted to do alone. Ryan shook his head.

"Not really. The last thing he'd said was that there was no evidence or DNA to place anyone at the scene. He did say that he'd wanted to shake the guy's hand because that was the cleanest crime scene he'd ever heard about. In his words, 'how in the hell could someone leave a crime scene that brutal without a single fingerprint or hair?'"

I chuckled and bit into my pizza, satisfaction coursing through my veins. "I'll take that as a compliment coming from the top dog of his own underground organization," I mused. "Speaking of killing, I'm taking Rebecca out tomorrow."

Paul turned his gaze to me just as he'd taken another bite of pizza. "Tomorrow?" he asked, bits of food coming out of his mouth.

"Really, man?" Curtis protested, frowning at him.

I nodded. "I learned that she was the one who orchestrated my sister's rape. There's no way I can let that bitch live a day past tomorrow," I ground out, anger heating my skin once again.

"Oh shit. Why would she be stupid enough to admit that?" Ryan asked.

"I forced her to." They only continued looking at me, waiting for a further explanation. "I'd read in Logan's diary that Rebecca tried hitting on her. It was one of the reasons why I thought she was into girls. So on top of forcing her to basically come out and admit that she was in love with Sevyn, she said that because my sister rejected and 'embarrassed' her, she was the one who put the idea in the heads of the bastards who raped my sister."

"Shit," Jake said, letting out a low whistle. "So, what are you thinking then?"

A slow grin crept across my lips. "How about we do a little reenactment? But this time, with an audience."

"Care to elaborate? My brain's too tired from heatstroke to get the underlying meaning of your statement," Curtis said.

"Same."

"Since she's the cause of my sister's rape, I'm going to be the cause of hers," I stated. "Only this time, I think our buddies over on the dark web would love to see her be ripped apart."

"Fuck yeah! I love dark web cam streams," Victor cheered, but he quickly paused in his excitement. "Wait, who'll get to do it?"

"I think it should be me since I'm the one who has to guard her," Paul said matter-of-factly.

I shrugged. "Why not all of you? It's not like only one guy raped Logan," I mused.

"But I get to go first!" Paul announced.

"Whatever, man. It's not like she won't have two more holes to fuck," Tony mentioned.

I looked up at the tv as I ate my pizza, watching as the news replayed the same story. The look on Carrie's mother's face gave me a sense of victory. I'd seen that same look on my mother's every time I looked at her, especially when I'd caught her alone. Even years later, she'd go into crying spells, her eyes red and puffy when I'd go to visit her as if she'd just been crying. It was high time that these parents realized the consequences of their actions and feel the same pain we had.

"So, after the rape, how will she actually die?" Victor asked, cutting into my thoughts.

"Is that sex suit thing still here?" I asked.

"We don't have a sex suit. What the hell would we need a sex suit for?" Curtis asked.

I shook my head. "No, that clear thing that you vacuum seal. You said it was for breath play or some shit."

"Oh yeah, it's a vacuum bed, not a sex suit. And yeah, we have it."

"Well, I'll need that, a Culligan jug of water, and some tubing."

"How poetic to give her a watery death as your sister," Ryan mused as he plucked a pepperoni from his pizza and popped it into his mouth.

I shrugged. "I wouldn't say it's poetic. It's just long overdue."

"You guys ready?" I asked when I finished setting up the camera. I didn't bother bringing the other guys in the room because I didn't want their screams to distract the paying customers who only wanted to hear screaming from Rebecca. The guys all secured their masks, all of them wearing long sleeved black sweatshirts to hide any identifying tattoos.

"Ready," Paul stated, giving me a thumbs up. The others repeated the same, giving me a thumbs up to confirm. Victor re-entered the living room with a limping, naked Rebecca, who cursed and tried to pull her arm out of Victor's grip. The moment he let her go near the bench she'd be strapped to, she crumbled to the floor, unable to bear the weight on her injured leg. She slowly looked up at the exposed hard cocks of Ryan, Curtis, Tony, Paul, Jake, and now Victor, her eyes growing wide.

"No!" she screamed and tried to pull herself across the floor away from them.

"Oh no you don't, bitch," Jake growled, grabbing her by the hair. She screamed as he dragged her across the floor and roughly pulled her to her feet, nearly body slamming her onto the bench. She gasped, the movement knocking the wind out of her as the other men rushed to restrain her arms and legs to the elbow and knee paddings of the bench. I walked over to her and secured the leather strap around her throat, a sinister grin on my lips.

"I think it's only fair that you get a dose of your own medicine, right?" I taunted.

"You're fucking sick! You'll never get away with this!" she screamed as she jerked against the tight Velcro straps securing her to the elbow pads of the bench.

"I am sick," I admitted. "But you and your clique of bitches made me this way. Payback's a mother fucker, isn't it?" She glared at me with red-rimmed eyes, which only turned my grin into a smile as I picked up a camera and pointed it at her face. "Say hello to your awaiting audience."

"Fuck you!" she screamed. I looked up to the guys, who stood still as they awaited for my directions. With a subtle nod for them to begin, they wasted no time claiming parts of her. Curtis wasted no time moving to the front of her, his cock centimeters away from her lips.

"Open wide, slut," he commanded, holding a sharpened straight razor in his hand. "And if you bite me, I promise I'll put this razor to good use."

Rebecca screamed when Paul roughly entered her, violently jerking against her restraints. Curtis took the opportunity to shove his cock into her mouth, groaning as Rebecca gagged around his length.

"For you to be into girls, you have the best throat for my cock," he ground out as he grabbed the back of her head and quickly pumped into her face.

Rebecca's sobs were muffled by Curtis' cock, her hands balled into fists as my guys continued assaulting her. I walked around them to catch different angles on the camera, the laptop in the corner pinging with notifications from the dark web feed.

"Rebecca Colt, the resident whore," I said, speaking through a device that distorted my voice. "Taking two men with three more waiting for their turn."

Curtis pulled back long enough to allow her to catch her breath. A string of saliva dripped from her mouth as she gasped, tears running down her face.

"Please stop!" she screamed. "I'm sorry."

"Just like I told your friend, it's too late to be sorry," I stated and looked to Paul. "Switch."

The look in Paul's eyes told me he wasn't happy about it, but he didn't say anything as he pulled out of Rebecca and switched spots with Curtis. Rebecca turned her head when Paul held his red-tinted cock in front of her face.

"It's your blood, bitch. Get it off me," he ordered, grabbing her hair. Her mouth opened on a scream when Curtis pushed into her, Paul wasting no time forcing himself into her mouth. Tony looked to Jake.

"Wanna play tic tac toe on her back?" he asked. Jake shrugged.

"May as well while we're waiting," he said and took the straight razor from Curtis. The guys walked over to her body, Jake carving a game board onto her back. She sobbed and tried to squirm away, but there was nowhere for her to run. Not this time.

When he was finished, he took a small step back and cocked his head to the side. "How's that?"

Tony shrugged. "It's a little crooked since she moved, but it's usable. You can go first since you're already holding the razor."

I pointed the camera at her back and watched as the guys carved x's and o's in the spaces Jake carved out, Rebecca releasing a muffled scream every time the razor sliced her skin.

"Ha! I fucking win!" Tony exclaimed, slicing a line through his winning line of o's.

"I want a rematch!" Jake exclaimed. I chuckled as the men played multiple games of tic tac toe, finally pausing when Curtis grunted, his hips stuttering against Rebecca.

"Fuck," he panted before he slowly pulled himself out of her, Rebecca's blood tainting his brown skin. Paul wasn't that far behind him, closing his eyes and moving his hips quicker until he finally released with a deep groan. Rebecca sobbed uncontrollably when Paul finally removed himself from her mouth before spitting his come out onto the floor. I pointed the camera at her face, catching her pathetic tears, running mascara that was a couple days old, and drool running down her chin and dripping to the floor.

"Doesn't feel good to be violated, does it?" I murmured. She only sobbed harder in response as Jake and Tony prepared to take their turns.

"What do you want first?" Tony asked.

Jake shook his head. "I only want her to suck my cock. You know how I am about blood. That's why I asked to fucking go first," he said.

Tony shrugged. "Suit yourself. I was going for her asshole anyway," he said and moved to stand behind Rebecca.

"Please don't," she sobbed, her voice hoarse and cracking.

"You think those assholes listened to my sister when she begged them to stop?" I snapped. "Do you think they cared when they made her bleed?"

Before she could answer, the guys had started round two of their assault. Notifications constantly went off on the computer, so much so that I was curious as to what the audience was saying about the performance. I mounted the camera on the tripod before walking over to the laptop, my eyes scanning the screen with a grin.

Holy shit! Tic tac toe on her skin? Fucking sick! Best live stream on the entire dark web!

I'd love to be a part of that gang bang. What an innocent face she has. I'd love to break her in.

I ground my teeth. That bitch was far from innocent. If they knew the truth about her, the extent of what she did, they'd do the same thing I had my guys doing.

I swear this is my favorite live stream. I aspire to be like The Brothers of Vengeance one day!

Hell yeah, BoV! Get that bitch!

Get wrecked! Look at that whore taking all those cocks!

I grinned to myself as I read comment after comment, praising my guys and I for what they were doing. And as I watched Rebecca as she suffered, I couldn't help but to feel proud. I couldn't say that Logan would be proud if she were here. She was never into violence. In fact, she'd said that she'd forgiven them all in her suicide note, saying that she had to do what she did because she had no life left.

Either way, I wouldn't stop until they were all dead and I left a trail of blood behind in my wake.

The assault went on for hours, the order of the guys switching up. After Jake and Tony, Ryan and Victor went before the cycle repeated after he'd finished. Soon, Rebecca stopped screaming, her eyes closed and her body limp before the guys actually stopped.

The guys all plopped down in the chairs that the girls were usually restrained in during the day with content sighs.

"And that's the end of tonight's live stream," I announced, pointing the camera at Rebecca's body. "Brothers of Vengeance are signing off."

I cut the camera off and officially ended the livestream on my laptop before closing it shut.

"That was the best fun I'd had in a long while, eh guys?" Jake finally said, breaking the silence. He looked toward me and nodded toward her battered body. "You're not gonna get any?"

I shook my head. "While it's tempting, I already had my fun with Sevyn. Besides, she's my main focus, so I'm a one-woman kind of man right now," I said.

Victor snorted. "You're usually a man whore. Finally saving yourself for precious Sevyn?" he teased.

"Fuck off," I said with a grin. "Get her back to her room."

"Like this?" Paul asked. Rebecca's back was covered with streaks of blood from Tony and Jake's games, her pussy and asshole both bleeding. I shrugged.

"It won't make much difference. She'll be dead by tomorrow

afternoon anyway. Might want to put her on a sheet of plastic though. I don't want her blood throughout the house," I said.

"Well, since all of you helped me fuck her, you can help me move her," Paul said, glancing over at the rest of the guys.

"Whatever. Let's get this over with so I can get a shower and sleep my life away," Ryan muttered as he pulled himself from the chair.

The other guys grumbled under their breath as they followed suit, Paul leaving long enough to grab a sheet of plastic and spreading it out on the floor. My phone went off in my bedroom, the distinct ringtone already telling me who it is.

"I'll be back," I said to the guys and quickly scrolled across the room, heading down the small hallway and straight to my bed where my phone sat. [Redacted] showed up on my screen, the special name I'd given for this contact.

"Hi," I said upon answering.

"Hi there, my sweet boy. How are you?"

I sighed deeply and sat on the edge of the bed. "I'm good. You?"

"I'm good." Silence filled the line for a moment. "I saw the news."

"Yeah, I watched it earlier myself. Fourth death now," I said.

"Are you safe?"

A soft grin settled on my lips. "I'm fine, Mom. Everything's fine here."

"I just want you to be safe." She was silent for a long moment. "How many left?"

"Five are left right now."

"Five? Then where's the other body?" she asked.

"In the freezer. It'll go out later tonight. It wasn't something we could do in broad daylight."

She released a breath. "Right. I'm sorry. I got a little impatient there."

"It's fine. I know you've been waiting for this just as long as I have," I murmured.

"I'm so proud of you, darling. I want you to always know that," she said.

"I know, Mom."

"And I expect you to come back for dinner soon also," she mused. I chuckled.

"Fine. But if you invite Dad, I'll probably have to kill him," I warned.

"That's if I don't do it first," she joked and let out a light sigh. "He won't be at the next dinner. It'll just be the two of us."

"Good. Once I get everything finished here, I'll be sure to stop by," I promised.

"I'll hold you to that," she said with a giggle. After a moment of silence, she added, "I'd like to request something of you."

"Anything," I said.

"I know you said you were saving Sevyn for last, but...I'd like to be present when you finally...you know," she said, her voice timid. I frowned.

"I don't know if that's a good idea, Mom," I said.

"I just want to know why. I want to hear it with my own ears for my own closure. Can you do that for me?"

"Can't I record it for you? Or have her call you or FaceTime you during?"

"I want to see her face to face, Luther. I want to look her in the eyes when I ask her what made her hate my little girl so much that she pushed her to suicide," she said, her voice trembling as if she were about to cry.

"Okay, okay. Don't cry, Mom. I'll have to ask the guys. Anyone who comes out here never leaves alive. I'd need to make sure they're okay with showing you this place. I won't make any promises, but I'll try."

"I understand. I just want closure."

"I know you do. That's why I'm doing this," I murmured.

She sniffled. "Well, I'll let you go. I'm sure you're busy with everything going on there. Just be sure to check in a little more often, okay? I always get nervous when it's been too long since I last heard from you," she said.

"I know, Mom. I promise I'll call a little more often as long as things aren't too hectic here. I'll talk to you soon though."

Okay, sweet boy. I love you," she said.

I closed my eyes and exhaled deeply. "I love you, too, Mom. Take care of yourself, okay?"

"I will and you do the same."

"I will. Good night."

"Good night, honey," she said and hung up. I tossed my phone on the bed beside me and pressed the heels of my hands to my eyes. I hadn't anticipated my mother wanting to be here. I wasn't too sure how the guys would feel about bringing my mother here, and I knew I couldn't deny her that. I shook the thoughts from my head. I'd deal with it when it came closer to the time to worry about it. For now, I had to prepare for Rebecca's funeral tomorrow.

CHAPTER 13

SEVYN

I could feel his eyes on me as I sat on the side of the pool with Logan, both of us in bikinis as we tanned. He sat on the opposite side of the pool, a couple of his friends already in the water and throwing a ball around.

"I'm so glad school's out," Logan finally said with a soft sigh. "If I had to have another day of Calculus, I would've lost my mind."

I giggled but didn't respond. My eyes were now on her older brother, my lustful gaze hidden behind my dark sunglasses. The sun reflected off the beads of water on his wet skin, his eyes squinting against the sun as he looked at me, a slight smirk on his lips. It was as if he knew I was checking him out as well. One of his friends hit him in the side of the head with the inflatable ball, taking his gaze away from me as he went after the ball to throw back at his friend.

"Any plans for your birthday next week?" Logan asked, grabbing my attention again.

I shrugged. "I don't know. My parents asked if I wanted to take a trip, but I'm not in the mood to travel," I said.

"You're so lucky. If my parents gave me the option, I'd totally go to Bali," she said. I slightly turned in my lounge chair to face her and grinned.

"What if we go?" I asked.

"What? Go where?"

"To Bali, duh. I mean it'll be fun! What's the point of having rich friends if you're not also having fun?"

Logan gave me an unsure look and shrugged. "I don't know if my parents will let me leave town, let alone the country."

"Then tell them that Luther can come, too. You know how protective he is over you," I mused, glancing over at him. He was now back in the water, he and his friends tossing the ball between each other.

"I don't know. I don't know if I want him hovering over me either," Logan finally said.

"Then I'll ask your mom," I stated, hopping up from the lounge chair and heading back into her house.

"Sevyn, wait!" she shrieked. "She's gonna say no!"

"I'd rather hear her say no than to listen to an assumption!" I called out over my shoulder. I opened the glass sliding door and entered the air-conditioned kitchen, where her mother stood at the counter making pepperoni Stromboli's. She looked up at us when we entered and smiled.

"Hi, girls," she said as she continued placing loads of pepperoni and cheese onto rolled out dough. "What are you two up to?"

"Nothing!" Logan immediately exclaimed, cutting her eyes at me and giving me a subtle shake of her head. I only grinned at her before turning my attention to her mother.

"Mrs. Evans, I was actually just talking to Logan about my birthday," I said.

"Oh, that's right! The big 18, huh?"

"Yes."

"Do you have anything special planned?" her mom asked me as she placed the exposed dough over the toppings and pinched the dough halves closed.

"Well, my parents had asked me if I'd wanted to travel abroad somewhere, but I kind of wanted to spend it with my friends, you know?"

"So, you're having a party?"

"Not…a party, per say. I'd chosen to go to Bali but….I kind of wanted Logan to come with me?" I asked with a sheepish shrug.

Her mother finally stopped fiddling with the Stromboli's long enough to look at Logan and I. "Bali. As in out of the country?"

"Yes, but my parents will be there so there won't be any funny business going on," I quickly said.

"I don't know. I mean if there's an emergency—"

"Mom, come on. You know it's one of my dream places to go. Please? It's only for the weekend anyway," Logan pleaded, clasping her hands together. Her mother looked at us for a long while before she sighed softly and smiled.

"Since it's just for the weekend, I'll allow it. Though, I would like to speak with your parents about it first and I'd feel a lot more comfortable if Luther went with you."

"Mom!" Logan protested as I snickered.

"Told you," I said.

"Luther goes or you'll stay home," her mother said, pointing at her before she turned away to put the pan into the oven.

"Ugh! Fine," Logan said before pulling me back out into the backyard. We walked over to the side of the pool occupied by Luther and his friends. He looked up at us from the water as Logan looked down at him, her hands on her hips.

"Take a picture. It'll last longer," he joked, hitting her legs with the ball. She glared at him.

"I have to bring you to Bali with me," she said, knocking the ball back into the water.

He scoffed. "Bali? I'm not going to any fucking Bali," he said.

"Mom said you have to. Trust me, I didn't want you to go but she said you had to."

He grinned. "Wait, so you're dependent on me going in order for you to go? Then I'm definitely not going."

"Luther, please! I'll pay you!" Logan begged.

"Don't be an asshole, Luther. It's just for a weekend," I interjected with a frown. His bright brown eyes met mine with a raised brow.

"What, is this a trip you're planning for the two of you?"

"It's for my eighteenth birthday, yes," I said, putting a hand on my hip. His eyes scanned my form before they moved back to my face.

"What if I don't have enough money for a ticket?" he finally asked.

"I didn't ask whether or not either of you had money for a ticket. I just need to know if you're going," I said.

"Oooh, rich girl is wielding her money around," one of his friends said.

"Shut up, Anthony," Logan snapped before turning her attention to her brother. "Are you coming or not, Luther? She needs an answer ASAP."

He shrugged. "Whatever. But I'm not babysitting you if that's what Mom is wanting me to do."

"Good, because that's the last thing I want you to do," she said and rolled her eyes before pulling me away from the guys. A small smile pulled at my lips as we made our way back to our lounge chairs. While my parents were going on the trip, they always did their own thing whenever we went on vacation, leaving me and my friends to do whatever we wanted. And with Luther coming along, I wasn't sure how much he'd stifle the trip if he was his usual, overprotective self. Either way, I was excited for the trip now and couldn't wait to see what Logan and I got up to in Bali.

I opened my eyes and stared up into the darkness. My entire body hurt, my tongue thick in my mouth, and a disgusting taste in my mouth. I slowly stretched out and pulled myself from the fetal position I'd slept in, every muscle and joint in my body protesting with each movement. My entire lower body throbbed with pain in the rhythm of my heartbeat, forcing me to clench my jaw as I tried to reposition myself. My mind drifted back to my dream as I sighed. Sometimes I wished I could go back in time and right all the wrongs I'd done. Before all this shit with Luther happened, I'd rarely thought about Logan unless it was close to her birthday or the anniversary of her death. I'd been dreaming about her a lot, reminding me of all the amazing times we'd had and how amazing of a friend she'd been. Reminding me that I was a shit friend to her and didn't deserve her friendship. Reminding me that I was a large part of why she was dead.

Wincing against the pain, I finally got myself into a slightly more comfortable position with a huff. I had no idea what time it was. I was hungry, thirsty, and really needed to pee. I wasn't sure what the consequences were for going on the bed, so I forced myself to hold it, even though it hurt to tighten anything down there. To give myself something else to think about other than the bathroom, I thought about the first time Luther and I hooked up near the end of the Bali trip.

"I'm so tired," Logan said with a yawn when she finally got out of the shower. "This has been the best trip ever."

"I agree. Thanks for coming with me," I said as I ran a brush through my hair. She looked at me, still dressed in my bikini.

"You're still going out? It's a bit late, isn't it?" she asked.

"I'm just going down to the beach for a little bit to listen to the ocean. I won't be far," I reassured her.

"I don't know. I don't think it's a good idea to go by yourself," Logan protested. "Luther!"

"Shh! No!" I exclaimed in a whisper.

Luther appeared in the doorway, his gaze lingering on me longer than it should have before he turned his attention to Logan. "What?"

"Could you walk Sevyn to the beach?"

He frowned. "It's literally right outside the house," he said, his tone flat.

"Thank you," I agreed. "It's seriously not a big deal."

Logan narrowed her eyes at him. "Is it a crime to make sure my best friend is safe in a foreign country? If anything, can you sit on the back patio and keep an eye on her?"

"What do you two think I am, a personal bodyguard?" he argued.

"Really, I don't need you to go out there," I said.

Logan rolled her eyes and threw the blankets that she'd just pulled over her body back off. "Fine, then I'll go."

"No!" Luther and I both said in unison.

Luther sighed inwardly. "Fine, I'll go. But just know it's my last time coming on vacation with either one of you twits," he complained before he disappeared.

I shook my head at Logan as I left the room behind him. I stopped by the closet to grab a blanket to lay over the sand before walking out to the patio. Luther already stood outside, looking up at the full moon in the sky. The private beach was dark for the most part aside from the light coming from the patio. He looked over his shoulder at me, his expression indifferent. I swallowed the lump forming in my throat. I'd known him for years, watching him grow and mature over the years. Now he was going into his sophomore year in college, his body a little more muscular than it was when he was in high school. He only wore a pair of swimming trunks despite the fact that he never got in the water today.

"Are you going down to the beach or are you going to keep staring at me?" he teased. I playfully rolled my eyes.

"Don't flatter yourself," I said as I walked past him and headed down the stairs. "You don't have to watch me, you know."

"Logan asked me to, so I'm doing it as a favor to her," he said as he followed me down the stairs.

The sand was cool beneath my feet as I walked across it, settling on a spot that was a few yards from the back patio. I spread out the blanket and plopped down onto it, stretching out and letting the sounds of the waves relax me.

"Where the hell do your parents go when you come here?" Luther asked after a bout of silence.

I shrugged. "As if I know."

"Are your family vacations always like that?"

"Yep. It's why I usually bring a friend or two along so that I'm not completely alone," I murmured.

"Damn. I guess if it's like this in a foreign country, it must be the same at home, too," he said. I nodded but didn't say anything in response. It was always interesting to see other people's reactions when they saw the true dynamic of my fucked up family. Most times, it was pity or surprise. It was as if they couldn't believe that the girl who had it all didn't have a real family. They were just people she shared her DNA with but not people that actually cared about her enough to want to be around her.

"I'm sorry," Luther finally said. "I mean my parents annoy me more than I'd like, but at least they're around to annoy me."

"Yeah. It's why I try to tell people that money doesn't buy happiness when they try to tell me how lucky I am to have the parents I do." I looked over at him, making out his handsome features in the dark night. "All the *money in the world doesn't take away the emptiness of feeling unwanted in your own family."*

"I'm sure," he said. We sat in silence for a while, listening to the ocean waves. He reached into his pocket after a few moments and pulled out a flask. I watched him as he opened it and took a long pull from it before glancing over at me. "Want some?"

"What is it?"

"Just a little gin I swiped from your dad's alcohol bar," he said with a cheeky grin. "He has quite the collection of alcohol."

"He's gonna kill you if he finds out," I said and giggled. "Some of those are special."

"Oh well. He probably won't even notice anyhow," Luther said with a shrug before taking another pull.

"Give me that," I said, snatching it from him and tilting the flask up to my lips. The amber liquid burned as it went down, causing me to cough and sputter the rest that was in my mouth. "Holy fuck, that's gross!"

He took the flask back from me and chuckled. "Even though you're eighteen, your taste buds are still young, grasshopper," he teased. "It's an acquired taste for us adults."

I rolled my eyes. "You must've played a lot of drinking games in college then."

"Eh, maybe. Still doesn't negate the fact that you have fetus taste buds," he retorted. I laughed and playfully pushed him.

"Fuck off," I said before turning my gaze back out to the water.

"Did you enjoy your birthday at least?" he asked.

There wasn't too much to enjoy. My parents had gone off on a yacht for

*the day with another couple they knew, and I'd spent it with Logan and
Luther. We didn't do too much, mostly spending time on the beach, going
to a fancy lunch and dinner that my parents were at least considerate
enough to arrange. And even though Logan did her best to make sure
I had a good time, I was still filled with an overwhelming sadness and
deep-rooted anger. I was upset that my parents thought being on a yacht
with someone else was more important than my birthday, which was the
whole reason we'd come here. Even now, they still weren't back to at least
tell me happy birthday, only texting it to me this morning before they left.*

"Yeah," I finally murmured.

"Bullshit," Luther countered.

I frowned at him. "Why is that bullshit?"

*"You didn't seem like you enjoyed it." He took another pull from the
flask before closing it up and putting it back in his pocket. "You seemed sad."*

"It's whatever. I'm used to it at this point."

"Have you ever talked to them about it?"

*I scoffed. "You mean when they're home long enough to talk? All they
tell me is that it's necessary in order for them to continue making money
and connections for our family and that I'll understand when I'm older."*

*"That fucking sucks," he said, leaning back on his hands. "Well…do
you have a boyfriend you can run to to get away from the madness in your
house?"*

*I scoffed. "I don't have a boyfriend and not interested in getting one.
Everyone just seems to use me to get close to my parents or the money they
give me access to," I muttered.*

"They're stupid then. I'd be more focused on getting more acquainted

with someone as gorgeous as you," he said, his voice dropping a couple of octaves. I looked over at him, my cheeks heating from his words.

"Shut up," I said instead. "You don't have to lie just to make me feel better."

"Is that your way of fishing for compliments?" he mused. I rolled my eyes, though he probably couldn't see that.

"I'm just saying that you don't have to say things like that just to make me feel better," I clarified. He shrugged.

"Just telling the truth. Anyone would be blind to not see that for themselves," he said. I could feel his heated gaze on my skin as I forced myself to look out at the ocean. "You know…if you weren't friends with my sister, I totally would've tried to date you."

His words sent chills running up and down my spine, but I willed myself to keep my budding excitement off my face. "Is that really the truth? Because when I'd drunkenly asked you out, you told me I was too young," I reminded him.

He chuckled, low and deep. "While that was the case then, it's not the case now. You're eighteen now, and no longer jailbait."

"So, what's stopping you?"

He nodded toward the direction of the house. "Logan. I wouldn't want anything to happen to your friendship with her if things didn't work out with us."

"I see," I murmured.

He was silent for a good while, the only sounds around us being the crashing waves. He turned his body toward me. "That is…unless you don't tell her until we actually become serious," he murmured. I only looked at him, no idea what to even say to a proposal like that. It wasn't like I already didn't have fantasies of this guy. I'd had a crush on him ever since Logan and I became friends. In fact, the initial reason I'd became friends with her in the first place was because she was the new girl with the hot brother I'd wanted to get close to. I knew how agitated she would become if I even mentioned making a move on her brother, so I knew doing something like this would be risky. But I wanted to try. I wanted something in my life that I could hold on to, to get love from someone that I didn't get from home, even if it was temporary. I could handle that…right?

"Yeah," I finally replied, a small smile on my lips. "No strings attached right now until we figure it out."

His hand reached out to cup my cheek. "I kind of want to kiss you right now," he whispered.

"I kind of want you to," I said, my voice trembling with excitement. He slowly closed the space between us, my lips tingling in anticipation. He kissed me, his lips soft against mine as his hand moved through my hair to cup the back of my neck. A soft whimper slipped through my lips as he roughly pulled me to him before cradling me in his arms. His warm skin smelled of sandalwood and sand, the strength of his arms around me giving me a sense of security.

I didn't fight him as his hand wandered under my bikini covering, raising goosebumps on my skin as his fingertips caressed my outer thigh. He broke away from the kiss when his hand reached the string on my left hip that kept my bikini bottoms together. "Should I stop?" he asked, his voice thick with lust.

I shook my head. "No," I whispered and connected our lips again. He pulled the string loose and slid his hand along my exposed ass cheek, *squeezing it slightly in his hand.*

"You're not a virgin, are you?" he asked as he kissed along my neck.

"No," I replied as I closed my eyes. "Wait. Do you have protection or anything?"

"I wasn't planning on having sex with my sister's best friend," he said. "I'll pull out in time."

Even though that definitely didn't sound like a safe idea, I was so anxious for whatever he'd had planned for me that I didn't care. I made a mental note to get a Plan B as soon as we touched back down in Miami just to be on the safe side.

"Sevyn?" Luther called out.

"Sorry." I gave him a soft smile. "That should be fine. I'll get a pill when I get back home just in case."

"Good," he murmured. "Let's make this a birthday you'll remember."

He sat me up and pulled the bikini cover up my body and over my head before tossing it aside in the sand. I helped him untie the strings of my bikini until I was naked underneath him. Lust harbored in the depths of his eyes as he looked down at me, his hand resting on my throat.

"You're so fucking sexy," he murmured before devouring my mouth once more. He reached between us, his fingers circling my clit. I fisted the sand above my head as pleasure overwhelmed me, rolling my hips against his hand. I kept my moans low despite the fact that we were outside, the stars and the moon in the sky being the only witnesses of our passion.

"Yes," I moaned when he took my nipple into his mouth, his fingers still working my clit. He wasn't the first guy I'd been with, but he was the first that had an actual clue on how to please a woman. Everything he did

made my body hum in pleasure, a pleasure that I wanted every day of my life. My walls squeezed him when he finally slipped two fingers into my wet pussy, eliciting a sexy chuckle from him.

"Would you look at that? See how wet your pussy is for me?" he murmured before planting a soft kiss on my lips.

"Mmm...so good," I whispered, closing my eyes. His fingers moved quicker as he continued stroking my clit with the thumb of his free hand, watching as I came undone before him. "Oh...oh...right there, right—ah!"

My body shook beneath him, the stars in the sky seeming to quickly multiple as my vision blurred. Luther didn't let up though, only mirroring my movements while continuing his pleasurable assault with his fingers. After a few moments of my squirming and moaning, he finally pulled his fingers from my pussy and put them in his mouth, humming in satisfaction. I looked up at him breathlessly, so turned on by the man before me. I whimpered when he thrust his fingers back into me a couple of times before removing them again, holding them to my mouth.

"Taste yourself," he ordered, though his voice was still soft. I held his gaze as I took his fingers into my mouth, sucking my essence off of them. He removed them and devoured my mouth with so much passion that it nearly took my breath away. His hand lightly squeezed my throat as his other hand worked to free his hard cock from his swim trunks. I moaned when the head of it pressed against my clit, shivering when he slowly rubbed the head up and down my pussy. "So wet for me, pretty girl."

"Luther," I whispered, closing my eyes.

"You can always tell me to stop," he murmured. I shook my head as I ran my hands along his firm shoulders and biceps. I'd thought about this man in this very position every time I masturbated after seeing him at Logan's, never thinking this would ever happen. As he looked down at me, a ball of guilt sat in my gut. A part of me felt as if I was betraying Logan, especially when I'd promised her that I wouldn't go after him.

All thoughts of Logan dissolved when he slowly eased himself into me, robbing me of my voice. Slight pain licked up my spine as he sank into me, his hand between us again as his thumb rubbed circles on my clit.

"You okay?" he asked.

"Yeah," I said breathlessly. "Keep going."

And he did, slowly stroking me and taking his time as he gave me inch after inch of his cock. I wrapped my legs around him as the pain melted into pleasure when my body finally adjusted to his size. He sat up a little and grabbed my throat, slightly squeezing. He growled as my walls contracted around him every time he squeezed my throat.

"Does my pretty girl enjoy being choked?" he murmured, his hips snapping a little harder against me.

"Yes," I moaned. What started off as the worst birthday in history turned out to be the best in my life, spent with the one person that I never thought I'd get alone time with.

"No matter what ever happens between us, you're mine now. Understand?"

"Yes," I answered. I didn't care what he wanted of me. I didn't want anything else but to belong to the very man I'd crushed on for years.

"Everything of you is mine. Your mouth," he kissed me hard, "these tits," he let go of my neck as both of his hands reached up to tweak my nipples, sending another wave of pleasure through me.

"Yes," I agreed.

He let go of my tits and moved his hand back between my legs. "This sweet pussy is mine, too," he murmured against my lips as his fingers quickly circled my clit. I nodded, unable to speak as the pleasure consuming my body nearly strangled me. "And your tight little ass is mine, too."

"It's all yours," I squeaked out, my body tingling all over. "I...I think I'm gonna come again!"

"Come for me, pretty girl. I want you to come all over my aching cock," he groaned, leaning forward to rest on his elbows, which sat on the sides of my head. His hips moved quicker, faster, his breathing quickened he moaned. "Fuck, Sevyn, come with me now."

He didn't have to tell me twice. I tightened my legs around him as he pumped his last few strokes before he quickly pulled out and jerked his cock over my belly, his seed painting my skin as he moaned.

"Oh my god," I panted before I giggled. "I can't believe we just did that."

I prepared for him to fix his swim trunks and to walk off as if nothing happened, but he hovered back over me instead, placing a kiss on my lips.

"I don't know how we're going to keep this from Logan for long when I can't see myself leaving you alone long enough to not be suspicious," he whispered upon my lips.

I smiled. "I think we'll deal with that when the time comes," I replied and kissed him again.

"Happy birthday again," he said with a cheeky grin.

"Thanks. You were right; I'll remember this one forever."

I jumped when the door opened and the light flipped on. Luther stalked toward me holding a tray in his hand. Tears burned my eyes as I looked up at him. It broke my heart that he was no longer the guy I remembered, but I couldn't blame him. Circumstances that I had a hand in made him that way. The person I knew died when Logan did and every time I saw him, I could only associate him with pain. Suffering. A thirst for vengeance and blood. He put the tray next to the bed and released my wrists from the shackles. He'd left the door opened and a part of me wanted to make a run for it, but I knew there was no logical way out. I could barely turn over without pain; I already knew I wouldn't make it far before he caught me and did something else sinister to me.

"I'm sure you're starving by now. Eat," he ordered and sat down in the wooden chair. I winced as I slowly pulled myself up, opting to lean on my hip because sitting upright hurt too much. I could feel his eyes on me as I grabbed the tray holding a peanut butter and jelly sandwich and a cold glass of milk. It was nothing that I'd eat outside of here, but anything was better than nothing.

I didn't say a single word to him, only eating what he provided before curling up in the corner away from him. And even though I'd continue my silent treatment until I finally died, my full bladder wouldn't allow me to wait much longer.

"I have to go to the bathroom," I said, my voice barely above a whisper.

Luther cupped his ear and leaned forward. "What was that?"

I swallowed hard, my throat sore. "May I use the bathroom, please?"

He stared at me for a long moment before he finally stood to his feet. "We have to go upstairs anyway, as it's a new day and time for a new person to die," he said with a chuckle. I ground my teeth. He said it so casually as if he was talking about an everyday activity that normal people did. Maybe this was normal for him and his equally psychotic friends. Perhaps they killed people for sport on a regular basis. I mean how else do you explain them being so comfortable with watching others die?

Luther frowned at me and cocked his head. "Are you going to get up or do I have to drag you up the stairs?" he asked.

I slowly forced myself to my knees, unable to stop myself from crying out in pain. Luther grumbled under his breath before he stalked back over to me. My body froze as he reached for me, squeaking when he picked me up and tossed me over his shoulder like a rag doll. It burned like hell as he held my legs closed. Silent tears rolled down my cheeks as he carried me out the room and down the hall of the basement. I dropped my head as he ascended up the stairs to the main floor and back to his bedroom.

He put me back on my feet when we entered his bathroom. "You had to go to the bathroom, so go. And when you're done, get in the shower. A friend is going to help you get cleaned up. Don't want you getting an infection before I'm ready to kill you," he said, leaning against the bathroom counter.

I dropped my gaze and turned to the toilet, raising my blood-stained nightgown before sitting on the toilet. I tightly gripped the edge of the toilet seat as I emptied my bladder, silent tears of pain pouring from my eyes. It burned so bad, making me wonder just how much damage he'd done. I thought back to my dream of him. I never thought he was capable of something like this. A killer. An abuser of women. He and I had history, but it no longer meant anything to him.

"Hurry up. I don't want to keep my friends waiting," he said. "And while you're in the shower, you should think about who you want to choose to die today."

I gave him a nod, already knowing who I'd choose. I didn't know how much I could deal with being in this hell with him. I couldn't keep watching my friends die one by one every single day and deal with Luther torturing me at night. So, I knew exactly who I'd choose today.

I'd choose myself.

CHAPTER 14

LUTHER

I watched her silhouette as she stood in the shower. From what I could see, she only stood under the spray for ten minutes, unmoving. Just as I was about to give her another reminder to hurry up, her form finally moved. She looked pathetic when I went into the room to get her, her skin pale with dark purple bruises on her thighs from where I'd gripped her to keep her still. My mom's words bounced around in my head, reminding me that I needed to ask the guys about her request.

After a few minutes, the shower finally turned off, the glass door slowly opening soon after. She stepped out and grabbed the towel without a word, patting herself dry. Once upon a time, her body used to turn me on in ways that I couldn't explain. She was addicting back then, which was part of the problem. While I was only looking for a fling before going back to school, there was something about her that beckoned me back to her time and time again. Even after I broke things off with her, it took everything in me to just stay away and not fall back into the that trap with her. She was like a poisonous spider, infecting me with her poison to where I'd always come back to her no matter where I was in life.

But then my hatred of her became my antidote.

Any lustful thoughts and sexy memories I had of her became redundant when I'd learned the full extent of what she'd done to Logan. I beat myself up daily for not taking Logan as seriously as I should have. She never went into details about anything when she'd call me, only saying kids were giving her a hard time. I gave her the pathetic advice of "telling someone or ignoring it," not knowing how bad it truly was. Sevyn's unknown secret came back to the forefront of my mind, even more so now that my mom also wanted to know the truth as well.

She grabbed the clean nightgown I'd put next to the towel on the counter, her baby doll face contorting in pain as she pulled it on. Her eyes scanned the rest of the counter before settling on the floor.

"Are there no panties?" she asked, her voice soft.

"Not yet. Still need to get you patched up," I said and pushed off the counter. "Let's go."

I stepped back into the bedroom and motioned for her to get on the bed, which was covered in a sheet of plastic. She looked at it, hesitating a bit before she slowly limped over to the bed and slowly got on it. I strolled over to the bedroom door, nodding for Richard to come in. He was a retired Sergeant in the army and the second-in-command of The Collective. He was a medic back then, now using his skills whenever they either wanted to play with their toys a little longer after nearly breaking them or when one of the guys got hurt.

"Who do we have here?" he said when he stepped into the room. Sevyn kept her eyes low and didn't say a word.

"Someone I waited seven years to kill," I responded. "I need you to clean her up a bit. I don't want anything to get infected. I want her death to be by my hands, not an illness."

"Ah. Preserving our toys, are we?" he mused as he moved over to the bed and placed his bag down on it.

I shrugged. "Something like that. She'll be dead in a few days anyway, so she doesn't need to be preserved too long," I replied.

He nodded knowingly as he unzipped the bag. He pulled out packs of gauze, a pair of rubber gloves, a cleaning solution, a stitching kit, and creams. I raised a brow when I saw the tube of lidocaine cream.

"Don't use lidocaine," I ordered.

He looked back at me, confusion creasing his already aging skin. "You sure? From what you described, she's gonna need stitches right?"

"I want her to feel every ounce of pain here, including the stitches," I ground out. Sevyn trembled on the bed, fat tears trekking down her cheeks. Ever since sense she claimed that I couldn't hurt her worse than she'd already hurt herself, I was set on proving her wrong. I was always up for reminding people why I was called

Lunatic Luther when I was younger.

"As you wish. It's your toy," he finally said with a grin and looked to Sevyn. "Lay back."

She looked at me with tears in her eyes and shook her head. "Please. Everything hurts so much and—"

"Lay back, Sevyn," I ground back.

"Luther—"

I didn't allow her to finish her sentence, grabbing her tightly by the throat and roughly pushing her onto her back. "When I tell you to do something, you fucking do it. Do you understand?" I growled. She only gagged and clawed at my hand in response, her face turning red as she struggled to breathe. "If I tell you something and you don't listen, I promise you I won't have a problem with ripping every single one of those stitches with my cock. Do you understand?"

I loosened my grip on her throat for her to speak. She greedily sucked in air before the sobs came, her entire body shaking.

"DO YOU UNDERSTAND?" I bellowed.

"Yes!" she croaked and covered her face with her arm as she sobbed.

"I think you might need to secure her. I don't need her moving during the process," Richard said. I nodded and walked over to my closet to retrieve a set of chain restraints and a pair of hand cuffs. I roughly grabbed Sevyn's wrists and slapped the cuffs on them before looping a chain around them and attaching them to the bars of my headboard.

"How far do you need her opened?" I asked. Richard walked to the other side of the bed and grabbed Sevyn's right leg. I mirrored his action on her left side, watching as he leaned over to look between her legs.

"Just a tad bit more," he said, still looking at her pussy as Sevyn screamed in agony. We pulled her legs apart a tiny bit more before he finally nodded. "That's good."

I secured the metal cuff around her ankle and attached the chain to the bed, making sure the chain didn't have any slack so that she couldn't move. Richard repeated the same thing on the other side, giving it a jerk for good measure.

"I think we're good now," he said and took his position at the head of the bed. Sevyn's screams filled the room as Richard cleaned her. He continued working completely unaffected, his brow furrowed as he concentrated on the task at hand. The moment he began stitching her up, I watched her. Her mouth was open and the veins in her neck and across her forehead bulged, but no sound came out. Tears poured from her eyes, the pain rendering her silent. Richard looked up at her from time to time, probably to make sure she hadn't passed out. He finally finished stitching up everything that needed stitching before putting an antibiotic cream on it.

"You'll want to keep an eye on that," Richard said as he stood and took his gloves off and tossed them in the small trash can near the bed. "Since you've done this two days in a row, she could've already been exposed to bacteria that could still cause infection."

"Will do," I said with a nod. "Thanks for coming all the way out here."

He waved me off. "No problem. Ryan's my god son and anything you guys need that I'm able to help with, I'll be here." He looked at Sevyn, who still didn't make a sound despite the fact that she cried so hard that her body shook. "Hmm."

I watched him as he walked over to stand next to the bed, feeling along the sides of her neck. "Looks like she's been doing a good bit of screaming. Her vocal cords are swollen pretty badly."

"So, what does that mean?" I asked.

"It means she won't be screaming anytime soon," he said and stepped away from her. "Or making any kind of sound at all."

I ground my teeth in frustration. How the fuck could I punish her and relish in her suffering if she couldn't even scream? This would do nothing but force me to pace myself. There was no satisfaction to be had if I tortured a silent, limp doll.

"Is there something that can be done for the swelling? Ice or something?" I asked. Richard shook his head as he packed his bag up.

"Not quite. She'd have to rest her voice for a little while."

"What's a little while?" I asked with a frown.

"Could be a few days, could be a few weeks. But in this environment, I doubt it'll be hard for her to do unless you leave her alone for a while," he said with a shrug.

I shook my head. Leaving her alone wasn't an option. I still had more of her friends to kill and more ways to cause her pain. But if she was going to be silent through it all, what was the fucking point of it?

"If that's all, I'll be on my way. I'm going to chat with Ryan for a bit before I mosey on along," Richard stated, breaking into my musings.

I ground my teeth and nodded. "Yeah, that's all for now. Thanks again," I said, shaking his outstretched hand and clapping him on the shoulder. He took one last look at Sevyn before he left the room, leaving me alone with her.

"Still sure I can't hurt you more?" I murmured? She only sobbed in response, her entire body shaking as she refused to look at me. My jaw ticked in annoyance. I'd have no fucking choice but to wait for her to get her voice back. I couldn't get the secret out of her if she couldn't fucking talk. I made another mental note, adding Sevyn's voice issue to the list of things I needed to talk about with my guys.

"Luther, are you nearly ready?" Jake called out from the living room.

"Yeah, give me a second!" I called back. I released Sevyn from her restraints, a light squeak coming from her as she sobbed all over again. She collapsed into me when I pulled her off the bed, her legs weak. I lifted her over my shoulder again and walked out into the living room, putting her in the chair with the rest of the girls and locking her wrists and ankles in place.

"What's the deal with her?" Victor asked as he observed Sevyn.

"I need a meeting. Now," I ground out. They all followed me into the dining room, all eyes on me as they waited for me to speak. Ryan and Richard, who were already talking over a glass of whiskey stopped their conversation and looked to me.

"What's going on?" Ryan asked with a raised brow.

"Her voice is gone," I ground out.

"Who, Rebecca's?" he asked.

"Sevyn's," Curtis said.

"How the fuck am I supposed to get the information I need from her when it's her turn to die if she can't even fucking speak?" I asked as frustration mounted within me.

"The quickest way you can get her voice to heal is letting it rest for a little while. You might have to drug her in the meantime or something."

"Or at the very least, probably manage her pain so that she doesn't have anything to scream about," Tony said with a shrug. My frustration grew as they threw out more and more ideas that involved me leaving her alone or keeping her longer than I'd intended to in the first place.

"Fucking hell, man," I ground out, running my hands through my hair.

"If anything, you can use the time to do a bait and switch like you usually do when you're fishing for info," Paul said. A bait and switch was the last fucking thing I wanted to do with her. She was the last person I wanted to pretend to be nice to. Just the thought of having to show her compassion and appearing apologetic made me want to throw up on the dining table.

"That may be your best bet. If anything, you'd get the information willingly and then you can kill her afterwards anyway," Ryan said.

I scoffed. "Do you know how long it'll take for her to even trust me enough to tell me what it is that I want? Especially after everything I've done to her?"

"I doubt it would take long. You two have some kind of fucked up history. Tap into that. At the end of the day, it's your choice, but it's not the worst that could happen."

"I wanted to stay on schedule," I tried to argue, but it wasn't as if it mattered. I'd stayed off of everyone's radar for years. I changed my appearance with all the tattoos and growing my beard, started my business under a fake name and made sure to work with people I didn't know at all. It wasn't like the police had any idea who to contact or people to question about me other than my parents; it was part of the reason these fucks thought I was dead all these years.

"Gotta have patience, man. Remember Murphy's law: anything that can go wrong will go wrong. You'll planned everything down to the single minute, but you have to account for any hiccups along the way," Tony said as he leaned against the wall, folding his arms across his chest.

I sighed inwardly. "Whatever. Also, my mother wants to come here," I said, changing gears from the frustrating topic.

"The fuck? For what?" Jake asked.

"She wants to ask Sevyn herself why she did what she did. I offered to video call her or have her talk to Sevyn on the phone, but she doesn't want that."

"I don't know, man. Don't you think it's a bit risky to bring your mom out here? If the police start poking around, she's the first person they'd run to," Paul said with a shake of his head.

"How'd she know what you were doing to begin with? Are you crazy?" Ryan snapped.

I narrowed my eyes at him. "Did you fucks think I was doing all of this solely for myself?" I asked. "She knew of my plan before I even told any of you."

My jaw ticked with fresh anger when I thought back to that night. I'd gone to my mother's to check on her one weekend. She hadn't been answering the phone or returning my calls, which put me on edge. Logan's suicide was still fresh on all of our minds, so I expected the worst when I walked into our dark family home. She was on the couch in the living room, surrounded by pictures of my sister as she sobbed. The sound echoed in the dark house, digging a hollow hole in my chest. It broke my heart to hear the pain and grief in her voice as she cried all alone, hugging a picture frame to her chest. It devastated me that there was nothing that I could do to take that pain away.

"Mom?" I called out, standing in the entryway leading to the living room. She looked up at me and trying to contain her hiccups. Moonlight filtered in from the windows, highlight the tear streaks on her soft cheeks. Her hair was wild on her head, a stark contrast from her usual neat appearance. She wore her pajamas and smelled as if she hadn't seen a shower in a few days.

"Luther, honey," she finally said, wiping her tears away. "You're supposed to be at school. I wasn't expecting you to be home until your next break. Is something wrong?"

"I was worried when you weren't answering the phone," I admitted as I slowly crossed the living room. She moved some pictures of Logan to

the other side of her to free space on the couch, patting the empty space.

"Come sit," she said and sniffled.

I closed the distance between us and sat next to her, wrapping my arms around her. "I miss her, too, Mom," I murmured.

"I can't believe they got away with killing my little girl," she sobbed, clutching the sleeve of my shirt tight in her hand.

"What can I do to make it better, Mom?" I asked. She slightly pulled away and met my gaze. A flurry of emotions harbored in her grief-stricken eyes, as if she was fighting with herself about what she was about to say.

"I want them all to pay," she whispered, her voice wavering. "They can't get away with this."

"I will make them all pay, every single last one of them," I promised, a dark edge to my voice.

She stared at me for a long moment and shook her head when my intentions registered in her mind. "Honey...I don't want you getting yourself in trouble. I can't lose you, too. Losing Logan has completely shattered me. I would die if I lost you, too."

I kissed her forehead and hugged her again. "I won't do anything right now. Reacting out of fresh anger would set me up for mistakes of getting caught." I was quiet for a long moment. "I think it's time to remind people why they called me a lunatic."

Back in my youth, I was hell on legs. There was a darkness that was in me that even my parents had a hard time containing. Harming animals, other kids, rebelling against my parents and authorities. Many treatment centers and therapy sessions later, I'd been able to keep that part of me hidden in the dark. But when Logan died, that part of me pounded on the door of my mind, begging to be let out to unleash the hell that people thought they were safe from. "Normal" was what my parents wanted me to be. "Normal" kids didn't hurt animals. "Normal" kids didn't hurt their friends or other random kids. "Normal" kids didn't try to hurt their parents. But I was never meant to be normal, even more so after meeting my friends in college to learn that I wasn't alone. If my mother wanted the heads of all these fucks on a platter, I'd deliver them to her.

"I couldn't tell you to do that, Luther. Murder is a very high crime," she said, flipping back into her motherly role.

"That's the only way they'll pay, Mom. Their money bailed them out of what they deserved, so I think everyone involved should pay. And I want to show that crooked justice system the consequences of letting people pay their way out of trouble."

"I don't know..." she trailed, wiping her eyes.

"You say the word and it'll be done," I said, my voice low. "Logan deserves justice."

Her face contorted as if she was about to start crying again as she nodded. "She does deserve it." She met my eyes with her watery gaze and nodded again. "I want them to pay. All of them."

"And it'll be done," I murmured and hugged her tighter. I'd take my time and plan their demises, research everything I needed to know about disposing of bodies and evidence, and enlist the help of my most trusted guys.

I would get justice for my family, even if it ended in bloodshed.

"Hey, Armstrong, let us know when you're done walking on the moon and ready to come back to our conversation," Victor said, snapping his fingers in front of my face.

I cleared my throat and pushed past memories to the back of my mind. "Either way, I wanted to ask you all. If you don't want me to bring my mother here, then I'll take Sevyn elsewhere so that my mother can still get what she wants," I finally said.

"If you boys are worried about her outing you, I doubt she'd do that," Richard added. "Besides, with Luther being her only living child, she's going to protect him with her life. Having a child lose their freedom can feel like a death also."

"Exactly," I said and looked back to the guys. "So? Yes or no? I need to know ASAP so that I can start planning where I need to take Sevyn."

They all exchanged looks for a few moments before Ryan shrugged. "Whatever. I just hope you know what you're doing, man."

"Don't I always?" I asked with a smirk.

"This talk is nice and all, but can we get on with killing that bitch? I'm kind of curious as to what Luther has planned for the vacuum bed," Jake stated.

"Yeah, let's get this show on the road. I want to get this done so we can still catch the news to see if Jamie's body has been found yet. One of the joggers that go along the trail will have found her soon," I said.

"Welp, I guess that's my cue to hit the road," Richard said as he stood from his seat, throwing back the rest of the whiskey in his glass. "It was good seeing you guys again."

"Thanks for coming," we all told him as Ryan followed him to the door to let him out. We all headed back into the living room with the girls, Sevyn still crying while the others tried to ask her what was going on with her. Their conversations ceased when we entered the room.

"What did you do to Sevyn? And where the fuck is Rebecca?" Crystal snapped when her gaze landed on me.

"None of your fucking business. Unless you want the same thing to happen to you, I'd advise you to sit there and shut the fuck up," I threw back.

"Ready for me to bring her up?" Paul asked.

I nodded. "Yeah, I'm ready for her. Vic and Jake, could you help him with that?"

They both disappeared with Paul while Curtis dropped the vacuum bed and tubing in front of me as Tony struggled with carrying in an unopened Culligan jug, forcing it onto the table I pointed at with a grunt.

"Shit, I need to lift more weights. That was way too heavy," he panted.

"Pathetic," Curtis joked before turning his attention to me. "Anything else?"

"That's it as far as what I need. Now I just need Rebecca," I mused.

After a few moments, the guys came back with Rebecca, who cried out anytime anyone touched her. The girls looked at her with wide eyes when the guys practically dumped her on the floor. The cuts on her back had started to scab over in some spots where the cuts weren't too deep, and some others were still red and fresh. She screamed when the guys pulled the plastic that'd stuck to her skin from the blood drying, and I couldn't help but to grin.

"So, since Sevyn can't speak today, it looks like I'm choosing who dies," I announced but then chuckled. "Who am I kidding? I was going to choose who died whether Sevyn could talk or not. And I choose Rebecca today."

"No," Rebecca said, her voice weak.

I ignored her and continued talking to the others. "I'm sure you all are wondering what happened to your good ol' friend Rebecca," I started.

"I'm not. I hope she got what she deserved," Sarah muttered under her breath.

"Are you fucking serious, Sarah?" Allison exclaimed. "I get that you're upset to find out she was the one your ex cheated on you with, but look at the condition she's in, for fuck's sake!"

"She's no fucking friend of mine to care!" Sarah screamed back at her. "I don't care what happens to her. If that makes me a bad person, so be it."

"Wow, such strong words from women that claimed to be 'besties,'" I taunted.

"You're just making things worst, asshole. You're practically tearing us apart with your bullshit," Crystal argued.

"I'm tearing you apart? That's rich. You sluts weren't really friends in the first place; you were just tolerating and using each other. Real friends wouldn't crack under any circumstances, right? I know my guys and I wouldn't," I countered, folding my arms across my chest.

"That's because you're all a bunch of psychotic fucks!" Crystal screamed. "I bet you all fuck each other when you lock us away, you sick fucks."

"Sorry to burst your weird fantasy bubble, but we definitely don't fuck each other. All of them did, however, fuck the shit out of your friend here on a livestream," I said with a smirk.

Sarah scoffed. "Great. Glad the whole world will get to see how much of a slut she is," she ground out.

"Oh, fuck you, Sarah," Rebecca groaned from the floor.

"And fuck you!" Sarah threw back. "I can't fucking wait until you're dead!"

"I wouldn't be so quick to say that. When she dies, it only winds your time down quicker," I reminded her, grinning when her face paled at my words. She settled back into her chair and clenched her teeth, her eyes blazing with fury. Sevyn wouldn't even look at Rebecca, her head bowed to where most of her hair hid her face. It didn't matter to me whether she watched or not; I didn't need to give her anymore reason to yell at the current moment, so I forced myself to keep her off my radar for now.

"It came to my attention yesterday that Rebecca here was upset that Logan rejected her. Couldn't have everyone know that she was into girls before she was ready to tell them, right?"

"Wait, what?" Allison said and turned her focus to Rebecca. "You're a lesbian?"

"She's also in love with Sevyn. They had a little sexy time yesterday, too," I added.

"Un-fucking-believable," Sarah said, shaking her head.

"It wasn't sexy and you know it," Rebecca argued from the floor. "You forced me to do it."

"Hey, we all have choices," I said with a shrug. "And now my choice is that you die."

I nodded to the guys standing near her, who all fought with her to get her in the clear latex vacuum bed. I'd seen it in plenty of porn videos I'd browsed, always wondering how I could tweak it for what I needed it for. When the idea finally hit me, I couldn't stop the smile that plastered onto my lips.

"Get me out of here!" Rebecca's mumbled voice cried from inside the bag once they finally got her in and zipped the bag up. Curtis hooked up the vacuum hose to the head of the bag.

"I'd advised you to put that straw in your mouth if you want to breathe," he warned. The modified straw on the bed wiggled for a few moments before standing upright, just as Curtis turned on the vacuum. Sarah, Crystal, and Allison all screamed as he sucked all the air out of the bag until you could see every nook and cranny on Rebecca's body. Her screams were muffled as she tried to wiggle, but it was nearly impossible.

"You're going to suffocate her!" Allison protested.

"Don't you see that big straw on the bag? She can breathe perfectly fine," I said. The straw on the bed was a bit bigger than the one that usually came with it, but I needed it big enough for the tubing for the water and the trick I also had up my sleeve. Rebecca's eyes frantically darted around. I wanted her to see everything I was

EMBER MICHAELS

doing to her, which was why I didn't opt for a black bed. I wanted to see the fear in her eyes when she realized she was losing a battle she wasn't meant to win. And I couldn't fucking wait.

"You're killing her because she's gay or something?" Crystal asked.

I shook my head. "No. I'm killing her because she admitted to being the reason my sister was raped," I corrected her. The girls looked at her in confusion.

"You said that Sevyn told you to tell them that," Allison said with a frown.

I shrugged. "Well, she lied. She told them that herself because she was upset about being rejected." I looked down at Rebecca. "You wanted to make my sister pay for embarrassing you, huh?"

She only looked at me with wide, terrified eyes, unable to say anything. Despite it all, Sevyn didn't move from her earlier position. Her head was still bowed, as if she was tuning us all out. I turned my attention back to the task at hand, moving over to the water jug and connecting the tubing to the addition I'd added to the jug before connecting the opposite end to Rebecca's straw. Her chest quickly heaved as the water rushed in, but there was nowhere for the water to go except down her throat. The latex was so tight on her face that she couldn't breathe through her nose, but she also wouldn't be able to breathe with the rush of water constantly flowing into her mouth now. After a few moments, I stopped the water and disconnected the tubing from the straw, watching as she coughed and sucked in as much air as she could.

"Don't do that to her!" Allison cried out, jerking against the cuffs securing her to the chair. I narrowed my gaze at her.

"Would you like to switch places with her?" I asked. She timidly shook her head as fat tears cascaded down her red cheeks. "That's what the fuck I thought. Sit there and shut the fuck up."

I connected the tubing back to Rebecca's straw and started the water back up before turning to Ryan. "Grab the H_2SO_4."

He gave me a sly smirk before he disappeared from the room. *Sulphuric acid.* The women were a bunch of air heads; I didn't want them to know what I was doing before they saw the effects it would have.

"What? What did you just say?" Crystal explained, her head turning from side to side as she tried to see the direction Ryan headed in.

"Sulphuric acid," Sevyn croaked, her voice barely audible. I smirked. What a surprise; she could actually be smart when she wanted to be. I bit my tongue to stop myself from being a smart ass. The last thing I wanted was for her to strain her voice when it was already promising that she'd get her voice back after all.

"She is correct," I said. Ryan returned into the living room with the large beaker of acid and a pair of gloves. I put the acid on top of the jug of water long enough for me to pull the gloves on. The other three girls sobbed as I prepared myself. Rebecca moaned and groaned on the floor, the sound seeming distance as it traveled through the straw. Grabbing the 300cc syringe from the table, I retrieved the beaker of acid and drew it into the syringe. I was laser focused as I connected the syringe to the second connection point of the tubing.

"Want the water off for a sec?" Paul asked, moving over to the jug.

"Yeah," I said idly, making sure the syringe was tightly secured. I disconnected the tube from Rebecca's straw as she sputtered water and coughed. Her tears glistened against the latex, which brought a grin to my face. "Ready for this to be over? Because I am."

Her body tried to move against the tight latex and I tsked. You'd think that she'd try to conserve energy as well as her oxygen, but these women weren't the smartest. I reconnected the tubing and started to flush the sulphuric acid through the tube. Rebecca's body jerked, the acid backing up in the line a little, mixed with a bit of blood as she coughed. Just as the last of the acid finally went in, I motioned for Paul to turn the water back on. Rebecca's body jerked violently on the floor, bloody water moving up the tube before her eyes rolled back and she went still. I cocked my head, watching her chest to see if it moved.

Moving to stand next to her head, I lifted my heavy boot and stomped down on her throat, crushing her trachea. Sarah, Crystal, and Allison all screamed in shock and horror, blood oozing from the corners of Rebecca's mouth as her lifeless eyes stared at nothing.

"Can't spread lies now, can you?" I murmured to her lifeless form as I took my foot from her neck. Sevyn only stared at her without a word, a single tear leaving her eyes. She didn't scream. She didn't sob. She only sat there and stared. Maybe it was shock and she simply hadn't processed it or maybe she wasn't completely present to register that her best friend was dead. I ground my teeth as I remembered that I now had to pretend to be nice to her in order to get what I wanted. A part of me would rather punch myself in the groin before I did it, but I needed to get it out of her. I needed it for my own peace of mind. My mother needed it for closure. With my history with Sevyn, it wouldn't be difficult in the grand scheme of things. But I was a little nervous what this interaction would unearth. One wrong decision with her due to old emotions coming to the surface and I'd ruin this whole plan.

And I wasn't sure if that was a risk I was willing to take.

CHAPTER 15
SEVYN

"**W**hat do you want to do with her?" one of the guys asked Luther.

"Gators. I don't want her found," he answered. "With the sulphuric acid, her body wouldn't last long enough for transport anyway."

I didn't raise my head to look as they carried Rebecca's body away. My throat hurt like hell every time I swallowed, and I barely had a voice. Not being able to talk seemed to anger Luther more than anything, which was the last thing I wanted to do. My pussy throbbed with pain as I sat. All I wanted was to be taken back to my room so that I could lay down instead of sit. I was a bit upset that he'd chosen Rebecca, not because I didn't want her to die bu because I'd wanted it to be me. I was ready to sacrifice myself, no longer wanting to continue going through his torture. I had no idea what he had planned for me in the coming days, but I did know that if I had the opportunity, I'd end up taking my own life.

Now I wished I'd been able to follow through with my attempts had I known this fate awaited me at the end of the tunnel.

Three of the guys left with Rebecca while three others removed the restraints from Allison, Sarah, and Crystal and led them back down to the basement. Luther slowly walked over to me and stopped in front of me. He didn't say anything as he did the same as the other guys and pulled me to my feet briefly. I winced as he picked me up and tossed me over his shoulder again, though I was surprised when we head back to his bedroom. I didn't dare look as I heard the crinkling of plastic, wondering if he just brought me back here to torture me. But instead, the plastic fell to the floor as he continued fiddling with the bed. He carelessly tossed me onto the soft mattress. I braced myself for pain, but the softness of the bed cradled me as if I'd fallen on a cloud. Every tense muscle in my body relaxed as I released a light sigh. I looked up at him to see if he was about to do anything else, but he didn't, only standing there with his hands in his pockets.

"Let me set a few ground rules," he finally said, his voice deep and slightly menacing. "The only thing you should be doing is staying in bed and maybe watching tv or going to the bathroom if you need to. If you try to escape through the window, an alarm will go off and my guys and I will hunt you down and make you wish you stayed in this bedroom. Are we clear?" I nodded, my throat tightening when I tried to speak. "Good. I'll be back."

I watched him walk out of the bedroom, releasing a breath I hadn't realized I'd been holding when I heard the lock click in place. I was curious as to what they did when they'd go outside, but I was in too much pain to get back up to go over to the window. Being in this bed made me realize just how exhausted I was. Everything still hurt and I prayed that Luther didn't have anything else planned. My eyes were too sore to cry, I couldn't scream, and I hardly had the energy to stand on my two feet, let alone face him again. I rolled over onto my side, grabbing one of the pillows and putting it between my knees for a little bit of relief. My mind drifted to Rebecca. I couldn't say I was completely upset about her death; we all had to pay for what we'd done. But I was angry to find out why she'd lied to the boys about Logan. Even when I asked everyone about it after the tape had been leaked, no one claimed they knew anything. Luther blamed me for that. I may have been a bitch to her in her last months, but I would've never done anything like that to her. It made me angry that Rebecca went behind my back and did it anyway while making me take the fall for it, simply because she knew my parents could pay my way out of trouble.

What kind of friend was I to even turn on Logan to begin with? I thought as I stared at the wall in front of me. Logan had been there during my darkest moments when I felt I had no one else. A small sigh left my lips as I thought about when she'd been with me the day I found out I was pregnant and learned that I'd been seeing her brother.

"What's the urgency?" she asked when I let her into the front door of my house. I grabbed her arm and pulled her through my home, not stopping until we reached my personal bathroom.

"I needed to do this with the support of my best friend and before my parents get back home," I said and reached in the cabinet under my bathroom sink. Logan's eyes widened when I pulled out a pregnancy test.

"What the heck, Sevyn?" she hissed, looking over her shoulder before taking the box from me. "Do you think you're...."

"I don't know." I bit the inside of my cheek. "I just know that I haven't been feeling well and my period is a few days late. I think it's best for me to check to see, you know?"

"Oh my god. But what about senior year? College? I mean do you really think now is a good time to have a baby?" she whispered.

I put my hands on her shoulders and gave her a small smile. "First, let's not get ahead of ourselves. I don't even know if I'm actually pregnant. I think I should take the test first and figure out what to do from there once I know."

She blew out a long breath and nodded. "You're right. Um, okay, so how does this work?" She opened the box and shook the contents out on my counter. She opened the instructions leaflet and scanned over it. "So, you just pee on the stick and wait five minutes. Sounds easy enough."

I picked up the stick and Logan stepped out of the bathroom, closing the door behind herself. So many nerves ran though me as I slowly made my way over to the toilet. I knew one thing was for sure; my parents would probably kill me if I were pregnant. The last thing they'd want was for their daughter to be a teen mom, which would ruin their perfect image. They'd probably send me away, that was if they didn't force me to get an abortion first.

My hands were so shaky that I nearly dropped the stick in the toilet. "It'll be fine," I whispered to myself as I peed on the stick. At least, I prayed it would be okay and that the test would come out negative.

"You okay in there?" Logan called out on the other side of the door, knocking lightly.

"Yeah, I'm good. I'm almost done!" I tossed back and quickly finished up. Once I flushed the toilet and put the test on the countertop, I turned on the faucet to wash my hands. "You can come in now!"

Logan opened the door and came to stand beside me. "Should I set a timer on my phone?" she asked.

I nodded. "And close the door, please. I don't want anyone walking in on us," I said.

She set the timer on her phone and closed the door while I dried my hands. The time seemed to drag on forever. I paced back and forth, unable to sit still. There was so much riding on this. What the hell was I going to do if the test turned out to be positive? I bit my nails, something I rarely did unless I was incredibly nervous. Logan picked up the leaflet and squinted at something.

"So… two lines is a positive test and one line is a negative," she read, just as her timer went off. "Let's see what you have!"

I covered my eyes. "I can't bear to look. Just tell me what it says. I might faint if it's positive," I groaned. Logan was silent for a few moments. When I uncovered my eyes, she was staring at me with a strange look on her face. "What? What does it say?"

"I think you might want to find a comfortable place to faint," she murmured. *"It's positive."*

"Shit," I whispered, lowering myself down to sit on the side of my large soaking tub. *"Like...it's two lines?"*

"Yep. Clear as day, too," she said, turning the test to face me. *Those blaring pink lines just put me in for a world of drama if I didn't figure out how to handle this.*

"I'm so fucked," I mumbled, running my nervous hands through my hair.

"Do you know who the dad is?"

Her question stopped me in my tracks. Though she looked at me thoughtfully, I didn't even want to think about how she'd react when she learned that she just may be an aunt soon.

"Yeah..." I said.

"Are you going to tell him?"

"Should I?"

She shrugged. "I think that's the right thing to do. Maybe they'll be really supportive about it. I think support from the dad is the most important thing, especially in the beginning or something."

I swallowed the bile trying to rise in my throat at the thought of telling her the truth. "About that...there's something I should tell you."

She cocked her head to the side. "What's up?"

"Swear you won't get upset?" I asked, my eyes trying to search her face for any kind of negative emotion. She grinned at me.

"I rarely get upset, Sevyn. You should know that," she said.

I took a deep breath, nerves causing me to tremble. "I um...I've been seeing Luther this summer," I admitted sheepishly.

Confusion pinched her features as she shook her head. "What do you mean?"

"Like…dating," I admitted.

"Sevyn, what the heck?" she exclaimed. "My brother?!"

"I know, I know! But one thing led to another and I really like him, Logan. He's so sweet and I like being around him."

"Wait a minute…." She looked down at the pregnancy test and then back at me. "Is Luther the father?"

After a few moments of hesitation, I nodded. Logan sighed deeply and pinched the bridge of her nose. "Luther can barely care for himself most of the time, let alone a baby. I mean what were you thinking? What happens if things take a crappy turn between you two? I don't want to lose my best friend in a bitter breakup."

"I swear you won't," I promised. "And I'll also keep you out of our relationship problems so that you're not stuck in the middle."

She shook her head. "I don't feel right about this, Sevyn," she said on a sigh. "Are you going to tell him? He's about to return to college; I don't know how well he's going to take news like this."

"I'll just ease it into our conversation, but I think we'll be fine. I mean he tells me he loves me, so that has to mean something, right? Maybe this baby will bring us closer together."

"I don't know about that Sevyn," she said and put the test back on the counter. "I should probably go."

"Please don't tell Luther anything," I pleaded. "I want him to hear it from me instead of someone else."

"I promise I won't say anything. If anything happens, just call me or

shoot me a text. Everything will be fine," she promised with a small smile and walked off.

I looked at myself in the mirror with a sigh. What the hell was I going to do with a baby right now? I turned sideways and studied my flat stomach, wondering what it'd look like as it grew bigger. The thought of having a baby with Luther brought a soft smile to my face. He was the only thing in my life that felt right. I could be myself around him and he didn't care about what my parents had or what my family could do for him. He made me laugh, he made me feel special, and now he was about to make me a mother.

I just had to figure out the best way to tell him.

But I never got to tell him.

I closed my eyes as tears threatened to form. I'd been so excited to tell him only to be dumped. I'd been so naive back then, hanging onto his every word like the pathetic, love-craving teen I was. I was so desperate to feel love from someone that I missed all the signs that should've told me he wasn't that into me. At the end of the day, he'd want the truth. He'd punished me again yesterday because I hadn't told him what he'd wanted to know, which was my secret. I needed to be able to explain myself, but it was hard to do that when I hardly had a voice.

Slowly sitting up, I looked around the room. The lock clicked on the door and I froze. Luther stepped back into the room and gave me a weird look before he moved over to the closet to grab a bag. When he glanced my way again, I made a writing gesture with my hands to ask him for something to write with. He raised an eyebrow at me and frowned.

"Is there something you want to say?" he asked.

"Pen and paper," I croaked, my throat hurting.

"Hmph," he grunted. He went back to the closet and reached onto the top shelf, pulling out a notepad before grabbing a pen from the top of the nearby dresser. "I hope you're planning to write a confession."

I didn't say anything as he grabbed the bag and walked back out of the room, locking the door behind him again. I looked down at the blank paper. There was so much that I wanted to say that I wasn't even sure where to start. A part of me wanted to remind him what we used to be, but that no longer mattered to him anymore. That showed in his actions, the way he treated me and my friends, the way he got off on the fact that he'd destroyed me. But I had to include it. He had to know how he hurt me, how his role in this entire thing made his hands just as dirty as mine and my friends. He walked around as if he was some kind of avenger that was doing the right thing for his sister, but he was just as guilty as I was.

He needed to understand that he wasn't as innocent as he thought he was.

I scribbled my thoughts onto the notepad, pouring out everything I'd kept sacred to me. Everything that Logan took to her grave. It was hard not to feel warm all over as I wrote about the memories I had of the old him. When he was kind. Considerate. Caring. I wondered if the man I remembered was tucked away underneath all the rage he now displayed. I wondered if he was lost forever, or if he'd come back after he'd tied up all the loose ends still walking around after his sisters death. I couldn't be sure considering the man he was today, and considering his plans for me, I doubt I'd ever find out.

My hand mindlessly followed my mind, writing down everything I could think of before pausing as I prepared to finally reveal my secret to him. *He probably won't even believe me after all these years*, I thought to myself. There was a high chance that he'd think I was lying just to try to save my life. One weakness that Luther had were children. He'd once said that because he used to do bad things to kids when he was a kid, he felt like he'd been burdened with caring too much for them as he grew up. Before I knew I was pregnant, I'd asked him if he'd wanted kids and the way his face lit up at the question, it nearly made my heart explode. A soft smile touched my lips as I thought of the conversation.

"So, since you like kids, does that mean you'll want some of your own?" I'd asked him as I laid my head in his lap. We were stretched out across my couch, my parents gone for the week until who-knew-when. He grinned down at me.

"Hell yeah. Could you imagine the army of hellions I could create? I'd groom my kids to raise pure hell everywhere they went," he said and chuckled. I sat up and slid closer to him, smirking.

"Don't be ridiculous," I said. *"I wouldn't allow my kids to act that way."*

"Are you saying you're having kids with me or something?" he asked with a raised eyebrow.

I rolled my eyes. He always acted weird if I said anything that meant there'd be a future between us. After being with him for about a month, I was tired of sneaking around. I wasn't one that liked to be hidden when I was exclusive to someone, and Luther had been seeming a bit off lately.

"I'm just saying in general, Luther. I wouldn't allow any kids I have to act that way."

"I don't think you have a choice," he said with a smirk.

Now I raised my eyebrow. "And why the hell not?"

"Because if I said that my kids would, that means yours would, too. Have you already forgotten?" He pulled me onto his lap and slid his hands between my legs, cupping my covered pussy. "This is mine and only my babies will come from here."

"You're awfully possessive for someone who doesn't want to be exclusive," I reminded him.

"Exclusive or not, it doesn't dictate whether or not you're mine. I'm sure you're very aware of who you belong to," he murmured and distracted me with a kiss.

I almost wanted to laugh. I wished that my only problems right now were whether or not we were exclusive instead of waiting in agony to see how he'd eventually end my life. Tears splashed onto the paper as I continued writing. I'd tried blocking all of this from my mind the moment Luther broke up with me, cursing his name every chance I got as my anger built. I thought he was just like the others, using me for free trips or just a warm body to sleep with whenever they felt like it and never when I needed them. I'd made so many mistakes back then and took my anger out on the wrong people. In the end, none of it matter. It didn't change the emptiness I felt. It didn't make me feel better. All it did was give me a load of guilt that I couldn't resolve and a death sentence from someone who wanted rightful justice for his sister.

Life was funny sometimes. I'd spent multiple times trying to take my own life over the past seven years, thinking the depression was too much. The anxiety and paranoia was crippling. It wasn't until you knew were you going to die before you realized how much you wanted to live. While I knew what I was doing to Logan was wrong, I didn't think of the consequences of it until I'd gotten my last picture from her. It was the last message she'd ever sent, a picture of her slit wrists in a bathtub full of bloody water. *I hope you're happy now.*

That was the last thing she'd said to anyone. That image and message stayed with me for years. Even though I immediately called her parents when I got it, it wasn't enough to save her. I always told myself that I would've gotten over it a little better had I not seen the picture, but maybe that was my punishment for helping to destroy the most innocent girl I'd ever known. I continued writing the letter until it was complete, looking over it with a sigh. I wasn't sure what this letter would do. I didn't know if it would make him angry, whether or not he'd care about my personal, raw feelings I included, or if he'd just use it as another reason to hurt me somehow. I'd prepare myself for whatever happened. I wouldn't beg him not to kill me; it wasn't like he was doing something I didn't already deserve. Now that I'd gotten out everything I'd wanted to say, I could at least die knowing that my truth was told.

I folded the letter and placed it on top of the pad at the foot of the bed. I'd just gotten comfortable when the lock clicked in the door. My heart pounded in my chest as I squeezed my eyes shut, trying to appear as if I were sleeping. Even though I'd made the leap and written the letter, I couldn't bear to watch him read it. The suspense killed me as I heard him moving around the bedroom. The silence deafening when he finally stopped moving, the sound of manipulating paper making my heart beat so fast that I swore he'd be able to hear it.

I listened hard as a chair in the corner adjacent from me creaked under his weight. *Oh my god, he's reading it,* I thought.

"I'm sure you know that I know you aren't asleep," his voice suddenly said, startling me. I still didn't move, just in case he was testing me. "Get up, Sevyn."

The warning in his tone didn't go unnoticed and I definitely didn't want to agitate him again. I forced myself to sit up, resting against the railing of the headboard. I couldn't bring myself to watch him, but he did have the letter opened in his lap.

"And drink that," he added. I looked up at him to see him pointing at the nightstand next to me. A steaming mug sat there with what I assumed to be tea. I wasted no time retrieving the mug, glad to have something to occupy me while I waited for him to finish. The room was silent aside from my occasional blowing of my drink before taking a sip. My heart wanted to flutter that he'd been thoughtful enough to get me something to soothe my throat, but the logical part of my mind reminded me that he probably only wanted to heal me before destroying me all over again. He seemed to be spurred on by my screams; what good was I if I couldn't scream the way he wanted me to?

"Bull-fucking-shit," he suddenly said, glaring at me.

I swallowed the tea in my mouth as my heart sped up. I watched him shake his head, staring at one sheet of paper with a mixture of emotions on his face. I braced myself for his anger, his rage, whatever negative emotion that my truth had created. I put the mug back on the nightstand with trembling hands. The last thing I wanted was scalding hot liquid to spill on me if he decided to attack me.

"Your secret was that you were pregnant?" he asked, his tone carrying an air of disbelief. I nodded, keeping my gaze to my lap. The chair creaked as he moved and I winced, prepared to feel him grab me, but he didn't. He only walked out of the bedroom, slamming and locking the door behind him. I stared at the door in confusion.

What the hell just happened?

CHAPTER 16

LUTHER

"So, what exactly do you want us to do?" Tony asked once the body was outside.

"The obvious. How are you going to feed the gators if you don't cut up the body?" I asked.

Paul groaned. "Fucking hell. You know, cutting up bodies was all fun and games until this Florida sun decided to come out," he complained. "I'm really not down for all that work again."

"So, what, is someone going to stand on the pier to make sure the body is properly ripped apart then? Because then you'd be standing in the sun waiting on the gators to finally make an appearance."

"Ugh. He has a point," Ryan said with a huff. "I mean do we not still have a chainsaw? I'm not in the mood to fuck around with an axe today."

"There are only three chainsaws," I reminded them.

"Victor shrugged. "Then three of us will do it then."

"Paul, you can choose one or two people to do it with you or you can do it yourself," I said.

"Tony and Jake," he quickly said.

"Fine." I turned to Ryan, Curtis, and Victor. "I guess you guys can run and get food. It's almost that time anyway."

"Sounds like a plan," he said, just as the sky darkened and thunder rumbled in the distance. "Anything in particular?

"Hibachi," Jake said.

"That actually sounds pretty good. Haven't had that in a while," I said, nodding in agreement.

Ryan type everyone's orders into his phone before he and the other guys headed off.

"If we're gonna use chainsaws, then we need to hurry up in case it actually starts storming," Paul said as he looked up at the sky as thunder sounded again. I nodded as the guys headed to the shed to grab the chainsaws as I went back into the house to keep an eye on the girls.

"Oh Luther, can you grab the bag with the protective bio-hazard gear in it? I think I put it in your bedroom closet last time," Paul said. I nodded and continued toward the house, heading straight for the bedroom. Sevyn froze when I entered, her eyes wide as she looked at me. I watched her for a moment. I wasn't sure what the hell she was up to, but she was bound to make me regret my decision to keep her in here instead of taking her into the basement. After I retrieved the bag from the closet, I cut my eyes back to Sevyn to see her gesturing something with her hands.

"Is there something you want to say?" I asked her.

She winced as she swallowed. "Pen and paper," she croaked, her face contorting in pain.

I scoffed. If she was asking for pen and paper, she better be fucking writing down shit I wanted to actually know. "I hope you're planning to write a confession," I said to her as I put a pad and pen on the bed, leaving her in the room again and locking the door behind me.

By the time I'd reached the foyer, Paul was coming into the house. "Oh, I just wanted to make sure you found it. Thanks," he said as he took the bag from me and headed back outside. I strolled into the kitchen and grabbed a beer from the fridge, popping off the top and taking a long pull from it as I leaned against the counter. I had no idea how the fuck I was supposed to "be nice" to a woman that I wanted to strangle every time I laid eyes on her. She hadn't thought to "be nice" to my sister all those years ago. She could've always stopped what they were doing; she just chose not to. Now my guys are saying that I had to calm down with her a little if I wanted to know her reason, but I wasn't completely sure I was patient for that.

Once upon a time, I probably did love her. But we were young back then. The only thing I had on my mind was having sex with as many local girls as I could before going back to school. There was something about Sevyn that was addictive. In all honesty, the sex we had in Bali was supposed to be a one-time thing. But then it turned into another time and another, to the point to where I was sneaking into her home to have her or she convinced Logan to let her spend the night just so she could sneak into my bed when Logan was asleep. I had to admit that it was fun, but her being my actual girlfriend was never on my mind. Maybe that made me an asshole for playing with her emotions, especially since she'd divulged in so many personal things with me. But regardless of what I'd done or what happened between us, it wasn't bad enough for her to be able to justify going after Logan.

I bitterly took another swallow of my beer before I released a deep sigh. I didn't know what would happen when I went into this bedroom, but I knew I wouldn't be any closer to an answer if I avoided her. Finishing the rest of my beer, I tossed the bottle into the trash and quickly prepared her a mug of chamomile tea with honey before stalking back to the bedroom to try this "be nice" bullshit.

When I entered the bedroom, her eyes were squeezed shut a bit too tightly for her to actually be asleep. I rolled my eyes as I continued over to the other side of the bed, putting the mug on the nightstand. My gaze settled on the folded-up papers at the foot of the bed, my name written across a folded edge. I picked it up and slowly unfolding it, seeing pages her of neat handwriting in a letter addressed to me.

I moved over to the chair in the corner and sat down, propping my feet up on the ottoman. "I'm sure you know that I know you aren't asleep," I finally said. But she didn't move. I almost had to fight the urge to laugh if she really thought that I'd believe she was sleeping. "Get up, Sevyn." She slowly sat up and propped herself up against the headboard, though she didn't look at me. "And drink that." I pointed to the tea on the nightstand before focusing my attention to the letter and began reading. Considering how long it was, I was prepared for her nonchalant bullshit to taint every single page before getting to the petty reason for what she did. A smirk pulled at my lips. While I figured this letter would be bullshit that wouldn't tell me anything I didn't already know, I decided to humor myself and read it anyway.

Luther,

I felt it was better to write this instead of trying to tell you so that I'd be able to thoroughly explain why things happened the way they did. I don't blame you for feeling like you needed to avenge your sister, but you need to remember that all pain has an origin and you're in this story, too. This letter isn't to beg you for forgiveness or to try to get you to change your mind about killing me. As I already told you, I won't beg for something I don't think I deserve. If anything, I at least want this off my chest before my time's up, just in case I can't verbally tell you this when the time comes.

You remember how we got into this beautiful mess? You gave me the best birthday to remember and I've cherished that every single day of my life, even now. We were both young. I should've been careful with you, especially since we were supposed to be a secret. I'll admit I tried to rush a relationship, which made you become distant and a bit uncomfortable. I could blame it on just wanting to be loved by someone, but that wasn't your responsibility. Maybe I didn't love myself the way I should have. I relied so much on the love from other people that I neglected myself in the process. I put my self worth in others and became devastated when things didn't work out. We'd had so many good memories that I hold dear to my heart, even when the new you threatens to destroy the old Luther I knew. The old Luther I loved. I know we aren't teens anymore and so much has changed. I mean I don't blame you. I understand the loss you feel. I've also experienced loss, but it may not be in the exact way you think.

I want you to know that I'm truly sorry for everything that happened. I always say that Logan didn't deserve any of that, but it's way too late for that now. It doesn't bring her back or take the pain away from you and your family. If you think getting rid of everyone responsible is the only way you'll heal, then do what you must. I've long accepted my fate. I've carried around guilt for the past seven years, attempting suicide and failing all because I didn't think I deserved to be here. Why was I here when the purest girl to ever walk this earth wasn't anymore? How did I deserve to be here when she was gone because of decisions I'd made? The number one question I'm sure you and your family had was why did I do something like that? The question has so many potential answers, but it all stemmed from what had happened with us. It wasn't just the breakup, just in case you're ready to blow a gasket. I'll explain why.

The day we'd met up at the park for the last time, I'd planned to share something that I'd only shared with Logan: my secret. I'd gathered the courage to tell you but before I could even open my mouth, you were breaking up with me. A part of me wanted to scream the news at you, but I didn't want you to think I was just saying anything to keep you. So, the secret you wanted to know so badly?

I was pregnant.

I paused. The smirk that'd been on my lips fell as the words I'd just read registered. *Pregnant?* While I expected her to tell me bullshit, I didn't expect to get a solid punch to the gut.

Now I understood what she meant when she said I was the reason for everything. I'd waited seven years to hear her reasoning, wanting to find more reasons to make her into the villain I'd thought she was.

What I didn't expect was to learn that the only villain in this story was me, and I wasn't too sure how I felt about it.

"Bull-fucking-shit," I said, glaring up at her. She didn't say anything. I looked at the letter and read the line again. I had so many fucking questions. This whole thing could've been avoidable had she just opened her fucking mouth and said something. Where was the baby now? Why didn't she tell me anyway? Frustration burned through me as I ground my teeth, jumping up to my feet. I still had pages of the letter to read, but everything in me wanted to strangle her. But to be angry with her would mean to be angry with myself. How the fuck did this get so complicated so fast?

I gripped the letter tightly and stormed out of the room, locking the door before heading back to the dining room. Chainsaws ran in the yard outside, but I couldn't even concentrate on what they were doing outside. Everything in my mind wanted to think she was lying just to save her own ass at this point. If she were pregnant, she would've been pregnant at the trial, but she wasn't. *She could've also got an abortion once you broke up with her,* I reminded myself. I sat at the dining table and continued reading, raking my hand through my hair.

Logan was with me when I found out. I'd also told her that we'd been seeing each other. I'd made her promise not to tell you because I'd wanted to tell you myself. But when you broke up with me out of what felt like nowhere, I felt that you knew and just didn't want anything to do with me anymore. I was so angry and confused. I mean how'd we go from having sex the night before and you telling me you loved me to you no longer wanting to be with me? I'll admit I should've just asked Logan or just told you the next day to confirm whether or not she told you, but I was so caught up in my own emotions that I didn't make the best decisions.

Before you wonder what happened to the baby, there's nothing to worry about since there's no baby anymore. My mom found out about my pregnancy test from the maid. I tried to say it was Logan's not knowing that she'd call your mom to tell her that Logan had taken a pregnancy test at my house. I felt terrible for throwing Logan under the bus, but I didn't know what else to do. Even then, all my mother went on about was how much of an embarrassment Logan would be to her family and how she'd never stand for me embarrassing the family like that. What the hell was I supposed to say to that? Once she realized it was actually my test, I knew I'd never hear the end of it.

As soon as I read that passage, I knew I couldn't deny it anymore. I actually remembered this day. I'd come home at the tail end of an argument my mom and Logan were having about a pregnancy test and my mom made her take another one. Even though Logan had written about it in her diary, she never confirmed that it was Sevyn's test either. When I'd asked her about it, all she said was that Sevyn's mom found a pregnancy test at her home and she said that Sevyn told her mom it wasn't hers and that it belonged to a friend. I never once wondered if Sevyn was pregnant. She and I weren't together anymore so that was the least of my concern. *How could I have been so fucking stupid,* I thought to myself as I continued through the letter.

Everything in me wanted to keep it. Even if we never got back together, I wanted to keep it because it was the last piece of you that I had left, the last sliver to remind me of the happiness I'd experienced for the time I'd been with you. I can't begin to explain how much that summer meant to me, to finally feel like I mattered to someone after spending majority of my life being ignored by the people who made me. But my mom took the decision away from me. She'd laced a drink she'd made for me with an abortion pill and I miscarried hours later in the middle of the night. I was alone. I was scared because I didn't understand what was happening with my body. I felt betrayed that my mom would do something like that to me. Even while I lay on my bathroom floor bleeding and screaming, she didn't comfort me. She just watched as I bled out on my bathroom floor. She only told me she was doing what she thought was best for my future and that maybe that would teach me to keep my legs closed. I'd lost so much blood that night because my mother had given me more medicine than she was supposed to. Instead of taking me to the hospital, she simply called our family doctor over to the house to "save our reputation." I lost our baby and I was alone, hurt, angry, and devastated and there was no one there. All the emotions just bubbled to the surface and I woke up from that painful night feeling like someone else. I didn't feel like myself anymore. I wanted everyone around me to hurt as much as I was hurting, and I didn't care about the consequences.

I had to admit that a small ball of guilt sat in the middle of my throat. I knew her parents were cold, but I didn't think they'd put her in danger like that just to save face. I almost felt bad for her. She'd trusted me and I ditched her, leaving her to deal with the aftermath alone while I continued the rest of my summer unaffected. I had no idea what my actions would've cost her or my sister. I'd been a selfish asshole back then, and the realization that this whole situation had just come back full circle didn't go unnoticed. It all started with me inflicting pain, then she inflicted pain, and here I was again, starting the cycle back over. For years, I'd painted Sevyn as this monster, this evil bitch who got away with destroying the lives of my family when in reality, it was Karma that served that dish back to me. I couldn't call her a monster if I refused to look at my own reflection and acknowledge that I was no better than her at this point.

I practically helped her kill my sister as well.

I don't know what I would've done had my mom gave me the actual decision. I know if I would've kept it, they probably would've disowned me. I wouldn't have been able to go off to college and since we weren't together or talking, I wouldn't have wanted to bother you with that either. It was probably for the best anyway. I don't think I would've made a great mom. It wasn't like I had much of an example to learn from. But with the betrayal from my mother, the loss of the last piece of the one man that'd meant the most to me, and my broken heart was too much to bear. I'd stayed in bed for days after that. I didn't talk to anyone, I didn't go anywhere, I didn't eat anything. All I could think about was how I had no one. How I couldn't trust anyone. How I thought none of this wouldn't have happened had Logan not told you my secret. I just...I hit rock bottom. I was empty and so devastated. I felt as if I had no one in my corner. I was so angry at Logan because I thought she was the reason I lost you. I wanted her to hurt as much as I did. I acted on my emotions because I was hurting and had no one I thought I could count on anymore. I'm not trying to justify anything, but this is the truth of why things happened how it did.

I may never fully understand why we broke up. Maybe I don't deserve to know. But I wanted you to know the truth. I hope this brings your family some kind of closure, to at least be able to understand how all of this happened. But I do know one thing: hurting her didn't fix any of the hurt within me. All it did was make me lose my best friend and the love of my life forever. I'm truly sorry for the pain I've caused your family and I hope that one day, when all of this is over, you can find it in your heart to forgive me.

I'm sorry.

-Sevyn

I sat there staring at the letter for so long that I didn't realize the guys had come back into the house.

"What's up with you?" Paul asked, breaking my concentration. He nodded toward the letter. "What's that?"

"Sevyn's reason," I murmured idly, leaning back into my seat.

"Is it bad or something?" Jake asked. I pushed the letter across the table and he picked it up, his eyes scanning the page as he read. Curtis and Paul huddled on the sides of him, reading the letter with him as I just sat there silently. When they finally reached the last page, Jake pushed the letter back over the table. "Wow."

"Yeah," I said. I was still at a loss for words for what the fuck I was supposed to do. It was so easy to point the blame at others when you were trapped in your own rage. Now it made sense. While I was angry with her, there was something in the back of my mind that told me this situation was bigger than her. It was probably why I couldn't feel the satisfaction I'd wanted while hurting her. It didn't matter what I did, I didn't get the same euphoric feeling I'd gotten after I'd killed the other women.

"So, what are you going to do? I think this kind of changes the gears of things, doesn't it?" Curtis asked. I honestly didn't know the answer to his question. I still couldn't even believe some of the shit I'd read. Her mother spiking her drink with an abortion pill to miscarry the baby? *My* baby? I took a mental step back. The fucking Langdons. The city of Miami held them to this ridiculous standard to where they'd do anything to maintain a fucking image. They'd pay off judges, jurors, practically poison their own daughter just to make sure that nothing negatively affected them.

They shouldn't get away with murder either.

But now I had a dilemma. There was no way I was letting Sevyn go. Anyone who came to this house didn't leave alive and if they left alive, they couldn't leave without killing someone. Those were always the rules. I couldn't see Sevyn taking someone else's life, but I was hesitating on killing her just yet. My freedom relied on which decision I ended up making and if I chose wrong, I'd be the downfall of everyone. The last thing I wanted was for my brothers to pay for sins I'd committed, but this single letter fucked with my head.

Shit had gotten a lot more complicated and I needed to figure it out.

Fast.

FOLLOW ME ON SOCIAL MEDIA!

FACEBOOK: www.facebook.com/EmberMichaelsAuthor

GOODREADS: www.goodreads.com/author/show/19229054.Ember_Michaels

AMAZON: www.amazon.com/Ember-Michaels/e/B07SNGX7KL

INSTAGRAM & TWITTER: @embermichaels

Made in the USA
Columbia, SC
13 August 2022

64521563R00198